WINGS IN THE WIND

The Reign of the Mawh'eyri

BY

ARTHUR D. BARDSWELL

Wings in the Wind: The Reign of the *Mawh'eyri*
Arthur D. Bardswell

Bard's Well Creations
Melbourne, Victoria, Australia
Library of Congress Control Number: 2016910891

To my wonderful wife, Anne

My chosen "Nest-mate" and "Wing-fellow"

ACKNOWLEDGMENTS

My fellow-writers at FaithWriters.com who have encouraged and mentored me through this and many other stories. Special thanks go to Deborah Porter, who awarded an "Editor's Choice" to the shortened version of this story.

Family and friends who gave me valuable feedback and encouragement.

Great writers of the past, mainly J R R Tolkien and C S Lewis, who inspired me to write in this style.

James Kochenburger for his excellent edits, mentoring and publishing services.

Cover Design by Bard's Well Creations and Matthew Crosby.

CONTENTS

PROLOGUE

The earth had become habitable once more. The days of its long and merciless imprisonment in ice were now an almost-forgotten memory. Spring and summer must follow winter. New life and fruitfulness had become the normal rhythm, and winter was now a short sleep, ushering in the renewal of life. Seeds, which had lain dormant under the terrors of the days of desolation, had long sprouted, clothing the clear streams, hills and lower mountains with many hues.

In the Northern Lands, paradise after paradise blossomed in quick succession. But the greatest and most glorious paradise of them all was what men called the Land of the Lost Eagles.

Raised on an tall plateau, it was an exceedingly rich and varied landscape of mighty, snow-clad mountains and lush green valleys. The lower hills and valleys were bursting with life and colour, stocked with many herds of fallow deer and many other wild creatures. Drifts of ever-blooming wildflowers and herbs, their kinds beyond counting, adorned the banks of crystal clear rivers and streams which meandered through the rich grass and rushes. The many and varied rocks in the lower hills glistened with all manner of crystals and semiprecious stones. The air was alive with large, brilliantly-coloured insects and a numerous and diverse population of birds by day, and fireflies by night. Wonderful fragrances filled the air, day and night, even when the blossoms slept under winter's snow.

The sounds of that land were not the least part of its beauty, yet they were also the most mysterious. The songs of the birds were mesmerizing even when they sang alone, and somehow they were always in harmony when they sang together, like a well-trained choir. One could almost hear human speech at times, as though singing tales of long ago. Then the winds would rise, whispering, whistling, roaring around the rocks or sweeping through the valley trees, dancing around the peaks, laughing at the moan and wail of the caves as they passed. When the winds spoke, the birds would fall silent as though listening respectfully to the voices in the winds. As the winds dropped, the birds often took up the songs of the winds.

The mountains themselves provided an awesome and austere contrast to the rich, vibrant valleys. They were monstrous, sheer sentinels that guarded the valleys. Some seemed to erupt from the gently-sloping valley floor as though a mighty subterranean monster had thrust a jagged-edged bone through the surface of the earth. But most mountain ranges rose like many-turreted and buttressed castles, their towers thrust through the clouds, crowned with rocky battlements draped in everlasting snow. The sheer and glistening white walls were softened occasionally by mountain trees, shrubs or flowering herbs which clung stubbornly to any nook or crevice they could find. Occasionally, white-haired waterfalls of various sizes seemed to drape themselves down the sides of the mountain walls, like silken sheets.

The whole land was a magnificent garden with a far-flung series of fortresses surrounding it; with the greatest keep of all founded among the central mountains.

The central range of mountains dominated part of the horizon wherever one stood in that land, especially the highest peak of all—the Monarch of Mountains, as men called it. Its head was seldom seen except on the clearest days, for it towered above an everlasting veil of clouds.

The boundaries of the Land of the Lost Eagles were quite clear—almost abrupt—ending with sheer cliff faces or fortified hills that stood watch over the grassy plains and marshes of the surrounding lands. It was no wonder that the first men thought they had found their way to their heavenly home at last.

But even before men began drifting north again to claim these lands, other strange and wonderful creatures ruled there.

The earliest settlements of men, to their amazement, found traces and relics of a race who were at least as proud and skilled as they, but not bound to the earth as they were. From the scratchings in stone and treasures left behind, the first men managed to piece together the ancient records of an intelligent race—but not in the manner of men. High in the mountains, in caves and on rock faces, they found written characters, markings and beautiful, highly-skilled artistry still well-preserved. Gradually learning the ancient tongue from the writings before them, they found a common strain, like a theme in a song, which spoke of a race of huge birds of prey of a very high order. They were nothing like the common eagles that dwelt in the mountains in the days of men.

Some of the settlers, frightened by the strangeness of the land and the eerie monuments of the previous inhabitants, claimed they were gods or demons and feared to go near the ancient *eyries*. The whisperings they heard in the rocks at night made them think their ghosts had returned. Some settlers even returned to less favoured, but more familiar lands further south.

Others thought they were blended creatures, half man and half bird, and wove many strange tales around them. As a result, the local eagles, though smaller cousins of the great ones, were treated with respect and even befriended by the tribes of men in the Northern Lands. The ancient *eyries* were mostly set high and rather inaccessible in any case, so all except the most curious and adventurous left them alone.

Still, questions hung in the air: Where had these ancient eagles come from? Where had they gone? They seemed to have suddenly disappeared, perished, or fled.

Whenever the men of the Northern Lands went hunting, gathering, or tended their herds, they often returned with new evidence of these "winged folk" of the past. Skeletal remains from carefully constructed cairns were unearthed, revealing the bones of huge birds of prey, as though they had fallen in battle. People marveled at their size and apparent strength, for they seemed at least as large as the legendary Condor, reported to be dwelling in the Far Southern Lands. Yet these were more beautiful and refined, even in their naked skeletal form, than any other large bird they had ever seen.

Gradually, the lore of the Lost Eagles became part of their tradition. It was a common subject of debate as the folk gathered together around the campfires, or feasted together in the forest glades. They loved to tell tales and sing ancient lays of the mysterious land and the great enigmatic birds that ruled it. Children would climb on their mother's knee and beg her to tell these tales, especially "The Lay of the Greatest King of the Eagles."

So I will now tell you the Tale of the Greatest King of the Eagles as seen through the eyes and told through the mouths of the great eagles themselves.

It is the song of the birds by day and the frogs by night.

It is the song of the everlasting rivers that flow through the valleys, the lament of the falling waters formed from the thaw of the white peaks, a tale told by the writings in the rocks found in the highest mountains.

It is the tale told to any man or woman who would stop to listen to the greatest of all the breaths that blow upon the earth, the great Spirit-Wind.

CHAPTER 1

MAWHARIKHAN

Of all the birds that ever lived, the great eagles were the aristocrats.

They were given many names in the lore of men, but the great eagles called themselves the *Eyri*.

Of all the *Eyri*, none were more superior than the *Mawh'eyri* of the mountains of *Mawha*. Seven times the size of the lesser eagles, twice as beautiful and many times more cultured, they ruled the skies, the mountains and the valleys of the Northern Lands before the coming of men. They had their own code of conduct, language and social structure.

The proudest and noblest of all were the Windlords, a select few eagle-warriors and champions who had learned how to conquer the great summit, *Mawharikhan*, or Monarch of Mountains.

The eagle-warrior that became strong enough and skilled enough to fly over that formidable mountain became the chief of all the *Eyri* of the *Mawh'eyri* for one change of the moon. He was the Reigning Windlord. It gave him the right to choose his own nest-mate, build his own *eyrie-palace*, command all the war-bands and eat the choicest foods. It also meant holding a place on the Windlords' Council for life.

He wore a cunningly-woven collar of vines and branchlets, studded with gemstones. All his subjects bowed down to him wherever he went. The first ancient necklace, the *Khanirhidhi*, or Stones-of-the-Sun, had been worn by the first great king of the *Mawh'eyri*. It was said to have been lost or hidden during the first great wars with the Wild Eagles, who claimed it as their own. So the Windlords fashioned the Reigning

Windlord's crown-necklace, the *Khanir*, a gem-studded collar. It was awaiting its next claimant at the cave of Windlord's Crag.

It was also said that a special breath of favour was given to the conqueror of the mountain by the great Spirit-Wind, whom all tribes of the *Eyri* serve. Some successful claimants had been known to prophesy or speak great words of wisdom in that period of the great Spirit-Wind's favour. It was the dream of every young warrior of the *Mawh'eyri* to become Reigning Windlord, maybe for life, if they could find and retrieve any of the mysterious Stones-of-the-Sun.

The Windlords skilled in ancient lore said that these came with the Fathers of the *Mawh'eyri* when the land of *Mawha* was first settled. But when asked from whence the stones first came, the wisest of the wise fell silent or confessed ignorance.

Sadly, some warriors paid the ultimate price in their attempt upon the great summit. As if the height was not enough with the thinner air and unpredictable winds, an even more terrifying danger lurked in the dark caves near the mountain's summit: *Mawharikhùn,* the Demon-Storm, the scourge of the Central Mountains.

Nonetheless, that did not daunt many of the young warriors.

StrongHand, son of Windlord HighSoarer, was not one of those who aspired to that title. He freely proclaimed himself a hunter, not a warrior. He refused to endure the initiation rites into warrior status that his more intrepid younger brother went through.

StrongHand wiped his beak from his seventh meal for that day and looked up as a young, lean warrior eagle alighted on the main ledge of the *eyrie.*

The two brothers surveyed each other for a moment with affection mixed with a little contempt. They certainly made a striking contrast. The elder was solidly built and immensely strong. The younger, although almost as strong, was more streamlined, well-shaped and swifter in his movements. Both had the same genial and alert comportment that characterized the sons of HighSoarer the Great, but the younger displayed a restlessness and impulsiveness quite foreign to his brother's tranquil nature.

'Hail, brother, elder son of HighSoarer the Great!' the young warrior bowed mockingly. 'I trust you and your band of hunters have supped well?'

'Hail, ThunderWing, youngest son of the great HighSoarer, champion of the games of idle warriors!' his brother retorted in derisive formality, not even bothering to bow. 'Do you wish to join the feast?' He heaved one of the carcasses toward his sibling.

'I have eaten as much as a warrior allows himself,' replied ThunderWing disdainfully, turning his back on the offering at his feet. 'Yet I thank you. I must bear as little weight as I may in my ascent of great *Mawharikhan.*'

StrongHand looked up again at his younger brother, and snorted derisively.

'You are too young to join the ranks of the Windlords, brother! Your success has deceived you. True, you are *Mawharhipi,* Swiftest in the Mountains before your time. But that alone is not enough to win you that greater honour. Many seasons and many hunts will it take for you to rise to our father's place.'

ThunderWing sat at the edge of the *eyrie,* gazing toward the ghostly white mountain that pierced the clouds on the horizon. He turned his head a little.

'Are you jealous, brother? I counsel you to eat less and fly more. Then you will be as strong as I.'

StrongHand's talon squeezed tighter on his meat, his neck feathers ruffling up.

'Were you not too swift for me, I would grasp your tail feathers and tear them out, little eaglet! Well have you been named by WeatherWing the Seer, for you bring more trouble than all the storms of *Mawharikhan's* peak. Stronger in flight you may be, but you are the lesser hunter. Further have I flown than you. I do not waste my time on those tournaments and games of warcraft that you young warriors delight in. I am proud to be chief of the hunters, whatever our traditions may say of us. More hares have I captured than all the *Mawh'eyri* hunters in the mountains! More fruits and herbs have I supplied to the *eyries* than any other. For what else do we live?'

'I allow that you give worthy service to our wingfolk, but I live for the honour of our *eyrie*, brother,' answered ThunderWing, his feathers completely unruffled. 'And to win the favour and the right to nest-mate Silver-Song the Fair. Yet I could worst you in the hunt if I chose to do so. But no! It is my destiny to follow my father's path, to soar over *Mawharikhan*, and to defy the black demon-storm. None shall turn me from it!'

'But your brother speaks truth, my son,' said a gentle voice behind him. 'And a season must pass before your time is come.'

Both male eagles turned in surprise, both a little chagrined that they had been taken by surprise in spite of their keen wits. But their mother, LightWind, had been resting quietly, deep in the *eyrie*'s cave, emerging when the brothers' exchange had become a little heated.

Their devotion to her approached worship, for to them and her wingfolk she was a great source of wisdom and inspiration. She was recognized as a prophetess—one who could hear the voice of the great Spirit-Wind. Forgetting their debate, they touched beak to talon in deep respect and affection.

'Hail, LightWind, lady of Windlord HighSoarer the fallen, mother of our *eyrie*!'

'And do you return from the hunt with more prey?' added Strong-Hand, looking up eagerly. 'Are the fruits of the Northern Mountains ripened?'

She bowed her stately head in acknowledgment of their salutation.

'Hail, my sons. No, I have not hunted nor gathered more than is needful. I have returned, rather, from the gathering of the Windlords, as it is my right also.'

She still retained much of the beauty of her youth, although some of her feathers were roughened from years of hunting and gathering. Her quiet dignity never faltered, even with the fall of her beloved nest-mate, HighSoarer, who had chosen her when he conquered *Mawharikhan*.

ThunderWing lifted his head and flapped his wings in excitement at this news.

'The Windlords are at the crag, mother? Will they foster another attempt upon *Mawharikhan*? Are there any *eyrionis* among them to attempt the peak? Is NightFlyer among them?'

His mother exchanged eloquent glances with his brother, although she did not share StrongHand's scorn for the younger eagle's ambitions.

'No, my son. It was a Council of Windlords only. Although they do not forbid any further trials this season, we sense that the great Spirit-Wind has spoken, saying that the Season of Storms comes early, and soon. Dark *Mawharikhỳn* has come forth from the peak more and more. He brings terror to the *eyri*es of the Central Mountains at night. The great White Warrior-Storms have been abroad, seeking him, even before the traditional season has begun.'

ThunderWing erupted into half-flight and beat his talons and beak against the stone wall above the ledge in frustration and impatience.

'Then I may miss my tail breeze if I do not attempt it now! I must go! NightFlyer, my rival, will attempt it before me. If he succeeds, he will be Reigning Windlord for this moon-tide and choose SilverSong as his nest-mate! I must go, in spite of the rage of this accursed *Mawharikhỳn* and his war with the White Wind Warriors. I must go! '

'Settle, my son!' cried LightWind, losing a fraction of her poise. 'It is a worthy goal, but even your father, proud Windlord HighSoarer awaited his time as the Spirit-Wind called him, and sought counsel...'

'I do not despise your counsel, my mother,' he interposed, flying down and spreading his wings earnestly around her shoulders. 'You raised me to be *Mawharhipi* of all the *eyri*es of *Mawha*. You bore me upon your wing on my first flight. But now I must fly alone and swiftly. I must cast off craven fears if I am to reach my goal. SilverSong the Fair shall be my nest-mate when I return. I must go before the tempests strike. Farewell!'

'Then farewell, my son!' She lowered her head in resignation. 'May the great Wind-Spirit bear you upward.'

'Strong wings need no wind! Farewell!'

With that, he gave his *eyrie*'s war cry, which echoed through the mountains:

"Highest heart! Highest height!"

He leapt from the ledge of the *eyrie*, wings spread wide, the very picture of youth and restless strength, soaring downwards and upwards, wings beating strongly. Soon he was merely a moving speck in the rising sun.

'Folly! His pride shall ruin him!' muttered StrongHand. 'But I would grieve to see him fall, foolish nest-eaglet though he be. The tempest season soon comes upon us, but he thinks of nothing but our father's honour and of SilverSong the Fair.'

'This I know, my son,' sighed his mother. 'But all must rise or fall by their own wing-beat. Pride and love have taken him as their prey. He has his father's sureness and aspirations, but not yet his wisdom. Let us sing to the Wind Spirit that he may preserve him.'

ThunderWing finally reached Testing Peak, within view of Windlord's Crag. There was still a group of Windlords who had not left the Council.

Willful though he was, even ThunderWing did not dare to override tradition. He landed on Testing Peak and looked around him as he waited until the Windlords were ready for him.

There it stood before him, swathed in thick clouds, dominating the landscape, dwarfing all other peaks: *Mawharikhan*, the Great Summit, Monarch of the Mountains.

It was not merely the height that daunted most eagles, but it was spoken in Windlords' lore that the lord of all demon-storms, *Mawharikhin* slept within the mountain peak. Prouder than the proudest eagle, he ruled the lands with fear. He rarely ventured forth in those days, partly for fear of the mighty servant-winds of the Great Spirit Wind, who hunted for him. However, he hated the proud wingfolk of the mountains who would not acknowledge his lordship. It was said that High-Soarer, ThunderWing's father, had fallen to his death after being struck by *Mawharikhin* in one of his rampages. ThunderWing still bore the grief from the day that the Windlord messenger brought the news of his death.

'I defy you, evil *Mawharikhin!*' he called fiercely as he watched a dark cloud sweep across the great peak. 'You shall be humbled, though I fall in the attempt.'

His challenging call, similar to that of eagles about to do battle, echoed across the valley. As if in answer, a distant rumble emanated from within the great peak itself.

This distracted the WindLord Council, and they glanced in his direction. The eldest of them spread his wings and flew across to his perch.

ThunderWing knew the old eagle well. He had a few bald patches and scars. His remaining feathers were rough, but he still flew strongly and held his head proudly. They bowed to each other and ThunderWing's beak touched the rock before his senior in deep respect, for he stood before none other than StrongFeather, Father-of-Many, Lord of the Western Crags. Not the least of his children was SilverSong the Fair.

'Hail, ThunderWing *Mawharhipi*, son of HighSoarer! Your father was my greatest wingfellow, and we grieve at his fall.'

'Hail, WindLord StrongFeather, Father-of-Many! You honour us in that you remember our father in great kindness. Do your *eyries* prosper? Do all your eaglets fly high and strong?'

The elder eagle gave a laughing hiss.

'You are courteous! But in truth you ask only for the health and dwelling place of SilverSong, my daughter—this I know well. She thrives, but she presently sojourns upon the Northern Mountains where the singers-of-the-wind gather until the storm season comes. She teaches my eaglets in the ways of the Great Spirit-Wind's song. But she often remembers you with kindness.'

ThunderWing hung his head in embarrassment for a moment, but then lifted it proudly.

'It is true that I desire SilverSong the Fair as my nest-mate, WindLord StrongFeather. I seek to conquer the peak and so to win the right to choose her.'

StrongFeather shook out his neck feathers and settled back to stare piercingly for a moment at the younger one before him.

'I hope that you have her favour in this, for I see the spirit of your father is in you. I would gladly give my daughter to such a one.'

The young eagle hung his head again, overcome with gratitude and gratification. But was this not his due, as a son of WindLord HighSoarer? He lifted his head proudly, only to hear not so good news.

'NightFlyer, son of SwiftSlayer came yestersun on the same errand,' continued StrongFeather, still watching him closely. 'But he contemned the traditions of the *Mawh'eyri* and spoke his desire before the Council were ready to hear him. He demanded his right for the trial of the peak. He was sent away until the changing of the moon as penalty for his disrespect.'

'Then I have come not a moment too soon, Windlord!'

'Yes, he rivals you in many things, and never forgave you for defeating him at the *Mawharhipi* trials. But still, he is one hunting season your senior. Are you not too young to attempt the Summit? The season of tempests draws near also.'

'I am the Swiftest in the Mountains, Windlord,' answered Thunder-Wing in barely-restrained impatience. 'Does that not show I am ready for the attempts? By the wings of the moon, I swear that I will conquer the peak before the coming of the storms!'

StrongFeather tilted his head a little in doubt, but said, 'Very well. Windlord Council has allowed for one attempt, and you are the last of this season to do so. NightFlyer must await the passing of the tempest season. Do you need guidance?'

'I need no guidance, Windlord.'

ThunderWing was too impatient and too proud to delay the process any longer.

The elder eagle shook all his feathers and sighed.

"All must rise or fall by their own wing-beat..."

'You indeed follow the same flight as your father. All must rise or fall by their own wing-beat, it seems. Go then! I will warn you of this only: Beware of the black cave of the southern face. Do not rest upon the crags thereof, for it is manifest that *Mawharikhὺn* is stirring again, and comes forth at night to terrify the *eyrie*-folk of these mountains at times. Fear and terror is as his meat and drink. Yet he hides again in his caves here for fear of the good White Wind Warriors, Servants of the Great Spirit-Wind. Be vigilant, for that demon-storm may be on the watch for us. You *must* return before sun's rest, or you are easy prey to night-eyes of the evil one. It is not as easy to attempt the peak as it was in the days of my youth. There has not been any Reigning Windlord for many hunting seasons.'

He paused, waiting for a response. But since these warnings also did not seem to daunt the young eagle, the Windlord turned to more everyday practicalities.

'There is fresh-killed prey and a water stream at need within Resting Cave, near the mountain's pass. A Windlord shall watch from afar to judge your progress and witness your success, if indeed you do succeed.'

He lifted up his voice in a Windlord's song to the great Spirit-Wind.

'Go, young warrior! May the great Wind-Spirit bear you upward!'

ThunderWing bowed again and leapt off the ledge, his wings spread wide, his *eyrie's* war-cry on his tongue.

Although he did not lack determination and persistence, Thunder-Wing found it far more difficult than he anticipated. The higher he flew, the thinner the air, and it became an intolerable burden to beat his wings. In spite of the risks of awakening the demon-storm within the mountain, he rested on many crags on the way up. But each time he looked upward, his heart sank, for it seemed as though he was no nearer the summit than when he began.

Day after day, he doggedly strove upward, rested, then pushed upward again. At last, nightfall forced him to return to Resting Cave for the next day's attempt. The designated supply of food was diminishing, but he ate little in any case so that he was not unduly weighed down.

One day he made it to the highest crag yet in all his attempts. He rested a long while. His breath came in desperate gasps in the thinning air.

All of a sudden, he felt strange stirrings in the air. His mother had warned him about unfamiliar winds.

'But I, ThunderWing *Mawharhipi* will outfly all strange winds!' he panted defiantly.

Then he heard the unmistakable warning call of a Windlord from below.

'Danger! Return to Resting Cave! Dark clouds come! Beware the tempests!'

He hesitated, for he could just see his goal, the Great Summit *Mawharikhan*, before it was wreathed in fast-moving clouds. It was so close, he thought, almost within his grasp.

'ThunderWing *Mawharhipi* will outfly any strange clouds!' he declared defiantly. Gathering all his courage, strength and skill, he leapt into the air once again, his eyes fixed on the great peak looming near. The air was so thin, he was breathing hard and fast, but he held on, unwavering. So fixed was his gaze, he did not notice the huge, dark cave he was passing. It was like the menacing mouth of a great beast, with jagged teeth-like rocks at its entrance.

Suddenly, without warning, he was enveloped in howling darkness. *Mawharikhùn* had awakened!

It seemed as if the demon-wind had indeed watched for him, and waited for him within the mouth of his cave, as StrongFeather had warned him. A thick black cloud in the shape of a gloating vulturine face turned towards him, crowned with whirlwind horns and eyes of balled lightning, glowing with hatred of all living things that defied him. His monstrous, bat-like cloudy wings began to wrap around his prey. ThunderWing knew he was doomed, for no eagle had ever out-flown the dreaded demon-lord of the peak and lived.

Huge black misty claws reached out to grasp the little eagle, and he cried out in fear. Then he quickly remembered the maneuver that had saved him from attack by the warriors of the Wild Eagle raiders. (It had also given him the final advantage over NightFlyer in the race through the valley.)

He quickly folded his wings and dropped like a stone, spreading wings again only to change course or add speed to his descent. The demon-wind, screaming in fury as he saw his prey slip through his fingers, turned and soared downward after him.

Desperately hoping to outrun the demon-storm and find shelter, ThunderWing dodged around boulders and crags, toward the mountain pass. He had already expended too much strength that day to use his wings effectively, but he managed to avoid capture purely through his maneuverability, for which he was famed among his fellow-warriors.

Nonetheless, his enemy knew the mountains too well to be outwitted for long. Zooming around the opposite direction of one rocky outcrop, he almost had him as they collided on the other side. A split second swerve only just saved ThunderWing from the enemy's clutches.

But *Mawharikhỳn* was also a master of winds. He blew at his quarry with all his strength, loosening rocks and stirring up the air all around them. A sudden updraft from this made ThunderWing lose balance. A sharp fragment of loosened stone flew at him, glancing him on the shoulder. The pain of it caused him to cry out. But his courage rose whenever an impossibility challenged his resolve. He was, after all, the son of Windlord HighSoarer.

'May the White Warriors take you, accursed demon! Slay me if you can!'

One wing was now almost useless. He dropped again. His enemy pursued, his dark breath preceding him. Another gust struck him like a body blow from a monstrous fist and threw him against the far cliff face of the mountain. Feathers scattered as ThunderWing plummeted toward a familiar valley, dazed, where he saw Resting Cave. He had just enough feathers to break his fall, although the break in his left wing hurt terribly.

He lay in a dazed heap, but his ordeal was not over yet. He heard a rumbling sound above him, so he struggled to his feet, expecting to feel cold, black fingers take him and crush the life out of him.

Although he heard howling and thundering above him, the final blow did not come. Once again, the strange breezes he had ignored before blew around him. Whirling white clouds gathered above.

It grew darker still. Thunder and lightning echoed around the valley and a torrent of rain came down, causing the cave entrance to teem with running water. Screams, howls and roars filled the air. It seemed as if war was unleashed among the mountain peaks. It had often been said among the *Eyri* of the Central Mountains that the Wild Tempests would rage against each other as they fought like wild beats for supremacy in the mountain passes. *Mawharikhỳn* had always prevailed over the rest, being stronger and far too cunning.

ThunderWing had heard of the battles between the Wild Tempests in the mountains, but he had lived too far away to be concerned about them. Perhaps the demon-storm would be too occupied to continue the chase. Perhaps he was safe at last. Then he heard the rumbling again, but not the sound of moving air this time. He looked up to see a large torrent of snow and rocks rapidly descending upon him, down the slope.

As a malicious parting blow, the demon-storm had unleashed an avalanche upon him.

Desperately, ThunderWing half flew and half staggered toward the entrance nearby. He only just made it inside as moments later, the cave filled with white snow-mist before the light faded completely.

He was safe for the moment, but that now meant nothing to him. He gave a cry of despair.

'I have lost all! My honour, my wing, my hope! Oh, if I had only been slain by black *Mawharikhùn*!'

The roar of the tumult outside was now less than the roaring tumult inside his head, his labouring lungs, the hopelessness in his heart and the throbbing pain of his left wing.

He finally lost consciousness.

CHAPTER 2

IN THE CAVES OF HEALING

'I have failed. I should have listened to my brother's counsel, and to yours, mother. I am not worthy to be HighSoarer's son. I have brought dishonor to our *eyrie*.'

He hid his head under his shattered wing. He was slowly regaining strength and plumage in Healing Cave. He was healing in body, but not in soul. His mother and another Windlord, skilled in healing, were in attendance.

'Already NightFlyer taunts me from the cave's mouth,' the broken eagle lamented, 'saying I am fit only as servant-gatherer for the *Mawh'eyri* folk. And he speaks the truth. He shall win SilverSong as his own, and I shall live forever in shame. Why was I not left to die within Resting Cave, or left as prey for black *Mawharikhùn*?'

'You have not forfeited your honour, my son, for you attempted the peak in spite of all,' insisted LightWind reassuringly, smoothing and straightening his remaining feathers. 'There are many young warriors that dared not.'

'They dared not because they were not fools and failures, as I am,' came the bitter reply. 'I no longer have the will, nor strength and skill. Now my last hope to shine is blown away in the storms of despair!'

'Your father also first failed,' his mother calmly replied, 'because he placed his confidence in his strength and skill rather than upon the great Wind-Spirit. Yet he held fast to his hope.'

'He failed?' ThunderWing lifted his head from under his wing in surprise. 'I did not know this. And did not his failure bring him shame?'

'He also was young and eager, and swore that he would win me as his nest-mate. He would not wait for counsel. He attempted times many. *Mawharikhòn* slept, but your father was defeated by the first Wild Storms of the tempest season, those that do not heed the ambitions of our young warriors, nor the war waged by the Great White Winds. When the time of the blossoms came, he returned, but bowed to the counsel of a Wind-lord: WindVoice-of-Good-Counsel it was—and learned the ways of the great Wind-Spirit for many moons. Then he triumphed.'

ThunderWing was silent as he dwelt upon his mother's words. It was the first time in a long while since he had listened to her, and gave thought to her counsel.

The Windlord-healer looked up from his task of applying special earth and herbs to the wounds. He was WeatherWing the Wise, highly respected among the greatest of the *Mawh'eyri,* renowned as much for his skills in healing and gift of prophecy as he was for his skills of war. When he spoke, the *Mawh'eyri* listened.

'Know also, ThunderWing, son of HighSoarer the Great: Your battle with *Mawharikhòn* the Accursed is a lay that is sung in many *eyri*es. For Windlord StrongFeather witnessed it from afar, fearful for your safety, but marveled that you outwitted such a cunning and mighty foe for so long.'

The wise eagle flew over and settled in front of his patient to address him in the manner of a Windlord-messenger with momentous news.

'Hear me now also, ThunderWing *Mawharhipi!* Your seeming rash-ness in your attempts in this last moon of the gathering season has served us all well. We, the Windlords had not foreseen it, but it came to pass that the first storm of the tempest season came earlier than before. This one had been sent by the great Spirit-Wind. It was *Mawharhitan,* the White Whirlwind of the mountains, amongst the greatest of the warrior-winds. He came hunting the Black One on the mountain side, as it has often come to pass. But forever the demon-storm has escaped and hid-den within his mountain. *This* time, you drew him forth away from any chance to escape the wrath of the White Whirlwind. The pride of the black one defeated him, for his hunting skill was as the great black spiders of the rocks. He would leap from his lair, grasp, and retreat to his dark hole again. Even your father, the greatest of all Windlords in flight, came to grief at his hand, although he evaded capture. *Mawharikhỳn* has seldom failed to bring down his prey. Your skill and speed foiled him, and that he could not bear. In the folly of his pride, he followed you long and far, then encountered *Mawharhitan* who overcame him before he could take you. Now he has been overthrown and is banished forever from the mountains of *Mawha!*'

ThunderWing gasped.

'So you see, O my son, that you have brought honour to our *eyrie*, not shame!' sang his mother, relaxing some of her poise to spread her fine wings in exaltation.

'Honour indeed!' continued the Windlord. 'For this was the very matter before Windlords' Council at your arrival. It was in debate amongst us that if a warrior storm was sent, some of us should try to bait *Mawharikhỳn* and draw him forth from his lair. But some of us would have perished in the attempt, perhaps even Windlord StormRider the Bold, who has outwitted many a Wild Storm-Spirit, and who offered to lure the enemy forth. You have saved us in your seeming rashness, and now the mountains shall be free of terror for many moons and many seasons. It was for this reason that we carried you here and tended your wounds. We ask that you come before Windlords' Council when you are whole again, that we may offer you our thanks.'

ThunderWing was overwhelmed. He struggled to his feet and tried to bow before the Windlord, but staggered and fell again. His mother insisted that he stay lying down.

'I am honoured with many honours, Windlord, fallen fool though I am,' said ThunderWing. 'I will come before the Council when I can, if you so bid me.'

Then he sighed and lowered his head to the earth again. 'Yet even these honours are second in my sight to the right of choosing my own nest-mate. That is now denied me.'

'Well, the law of the *Mawh'eyri* is not easily changed,' acknowledged the Windlord regretfully. 'But you have won much honour even without the title of Windlord. I counsel you to be content.'

The Windlord soon departed, and his mother soon left also, but not without leaving a gift of two fat hares.

'…….. Caught for you by your brother, StrongHand, for he also holds you in honour, in brotherhood and in fellowship.'

ThunderWing's sense of exaltation was short-lived.

A few days later, a strong young warrior appeared in the entrance of the cave without giving the customary cry of entry. He was a little larger than ThunderWing, his plumage a rich combination of olive and metallic bronze, with black markings. Perfectly proportioned, he was considered the handsomest of all the warriors of his tribe. He was also the proudest and most arrogant, with the tongue, so it was said, of the serpent.

He stood there for a moment, beak held high, his very stance an insult. ThunderWing glanced at him from his recumbent position and looked away again, not even bothering to greet his unwanted visitor. The *Mawh'eyri* code of civility was seldom practiced between bitter rivals, although the warrior's code of honour was normally strictly adhered to.

'Hail, Winglost ThunderWing, the broken, the fallen, the presumptuous fool!' the visitor cried, mockingly. 'Did you trip and fall upon your beak?'

Stony silence was all the answer he received.

'What is this?' continued the sarcastic voice as he hovered over the wounded eagle. 'Did the dark wind take your tongue also? Very well. If you would attempt the peak before your time, little eaglet, and awaken the evil wind in your blundering, it is little wonder that you lie naked and broken before me. You are a fool to even think of challenging me: NightFlyer, son of SwiftSlayer, lord of hunters, fairest and strongest of the warriors of the mountains!'

There was still no answer or even movement from his rival, so Night-Flyer prepared to leave.

'So! It is fitting to keep respectful silence before me, featherlost little egg-chick, for I am destined to be both *Mawharhipi* and Windlord when the season of the hunt comes again. There shall be none to rival and cheat me of victory in the wing-trials then.'

He spread his wings wide and his voice filled the caves and the valley.

'I shall then conquer *Mawharikhan,* and claim SilverSong the Fair as my own! I shall be the lord of the mountains of *Mawha!*'

This was too much for ThunderWing to take. He roused himself to some semblance of dignity, spreading his ragged wings in challenge.

'Will the fair SilverSong take you for nest-mate? I think not, O NightFlyer Wind-Beak, boaster of great boasts! Your very arrogance shall be as rotting meat in her nostrils.'

'Oh, will you challenge me still, robeless one?' sneered the other, turning back to face him. 'Your loss upon the peak has not given you wisdom? She cannot resist NightFlyer the strong, fairest of warriors, greatest of hunters, Swiftest in the Mountains and Reigning Windlord-to-be. Do not forget that a Windlord who conquers the peak has the right to choose—nor you, nor even she can gainsay it. If she is unwilling, I shall take her by force, and not even StrongFeather, her father, can gainsay our laws, nor the will of Windlord NightFlyer *Mawharhipi.*'

Something exploded inside ThunderWing's breast.

'No!'

He hopped and hobbled over and stood beak to beak with his rival, his remaining feathers fully extended in fury.

'You will have neither title, proud and cruel wind-beak boaster! Am I not ThunderWing *Mawharhipi* by right of victory? Have I not escaped the clutches of the Black Storm? And caused him to be banished from our mountains? And if you take the fair SilverSong by force, I shall call *Mawharagh* upon you!'

Such was NightFlyer's astonishment at this challenge, he sat back upon his tail feathers. He threw his head back and laughed aloud.

'*Mawharagh?? Mawharagh* between us? There are no bounds to your boasting, your folly, little quail! Look upon your image when you drink from the pools, little featherlost fool. Even had you the armor and the strength to do battle, by our laws you cannot challenge a champion warrior.'

It was seldom among the *Mawh'eyri* that such warrior rivalries ever ended in these terrible mountain duels to the death, the *Mawharagh*. The Windlords that presided over these disputes generally did their utmost to settle them peacefully. Occasionally, some warriors would contend by non-combative contest over the choicest *eyrie* or the fairest lady among the eagles.

No one, especially the eldest among them, ever wanted to return to the barbaric days when they first settled in the mountains. *Eyrie* had fought *eyrie* over territorial rights. Many fine eagles fell in battle until wisdom prevailed. Laws were agreed upon and then scratched on the Stones of Judgment upon Windlords' Crag. Spontaneous squabbles that turned to blood-letting were dealt with ruthlessly, both parties summarily expelled from the mountains for a season. If one was determined to be at fault (confirmed by the testimony of witnesses), he or she was sometimes banished forever. If the crime was considered by the Council to be worthy of death, the offender was set upon by designated warriors.

ThunderWing had to acknowledge the truth of NightFlyer's response, and sank down in a despairing heap again.

A champion named Swiftest in the Mountains was held in such high honour—a Windlord even more so—that he was immune from any challenge of that kind by an inferior. It was law. If NightFlyer won the racing trials that season, he would be considered a champion. If ThunderWing had his feathers and strength intact, and he still attacked NightFlyer for fair SilverSong's sake, he would be cast out of the mountains forever, if not executed. What use would he be to the Fair One then?

'Farewell, pathetic little raven-chick,' jeered the serpent's tongue. He swung one of his wings, knocking ThunderWing to the floor, then laughed out loud again.

'Grovel for worms if you must. I go to my destiny as Windlord and to claim SilverSong as my own.'

He filled the cave with his *eyrie*'s war-cry, and swept away into the distance.

The moons passed. ThunderWing wearily and sadly watched from the cave's entrance as the mountainsides slowly shed their white down of winter and clothed themselves with the green feathers of spring, tinged with the colours of the blossoms. He watched the lesser birds come and go in their endless hunting and gathering. He even befriended a pair of doves, sharing scraps of his meat with them. The *Mawh'eyri* normally ignored lesser birds, though they protected them. That is, unless they became a nuisance.

He was healing rapidly, being exceptionally strong amongst the young warrior-eagles. He was gradually shedding or pulling out his older, damaged plumage, and beginning to grow new, stronger feathers. His shoulder was still tender, but it had been well treated by a skilled healer, and he could fly short distances. He had even begun to hunt and gather for himself again, to a limited extent.

He meditated much on the wise counsel his mother gave him on her frequent visits, and felt comforted by the honour in which he was held by the *Mawh'eyri* Windlords and his own *eyrie*. Yet all this honour was nothing to the loss of any chance of winning the *eyreira* who had become an obsession to him ever since she had returned from the Northern Mountains. Without her, he had lost all motivation to strive for greatness. He felt he could do little else than serve the *eyries* as hunter and gatherer like his brother did, removing his warrior's mark. At least that had some true honour in itself, little though it was regarded by tradition.

However, to his surprise, his mother still spoke of a future conquering of the great peak.

He just shook his head.

'I am no longer as high of heart as my father, O my mother. I will join my brother in the hunts to serve the *eyries*, if he will. That is honour enough for one such as I.'

'It is true that before greatness comes lowliness, even as a bird must swoop downward to soar the highest. Remember that the caves of the Great Summit *Mawharikhan* are clear of the great enemy because of your attempt. But also mark this: To soar the highest is indeed your destiny, my son. I have heard it on the voice of the Great Wind.'

He could only shake his head in sad disbelief.

His mother did not press him, but paid a visit to Windlord's Crag and spoke privately to StrongFeather. This resulted in a surprise visitor to Healing Cave.

ThunderWing was dozing, but awoke to the sounds of wings approaching. A vision of beauty, one that constantly haunted his dreams, appeared at the entrance.

She was the loveliest eagle-maiden he had ever seen—a princess among the *Mawh'eyri,* with faultless golden plumage, delicate markings and graceful carriage. Her wingstrokes were like joyous laughter. Her eyes were both as brilliant and liquid as the sun shining through the mountain waterfall, as soft and tender as a dove's. Her voice, upon entering the cave, was a song like the soft sighing of a spring breeze. As she alighted next to him, the fragrance of her feathers, brushed with aromatic herbs, washed over him like warm river-streams in summer.

At one sight of her, ThunderWing gaped and swallowed with deep longing. He raised himself awkwardly to bow in greeting, dismally aware of his unsightly state, and then sank down in shame and hopelessness.

She brushed him with a teasing sweep of a laughing wing to get his attention again. He tried to rise, but she stayed him. Standing before him, she bowed gracefully with wings spread, as an eaglet would do homage to a great Windlord.

'Hail, ThunderWing *Mawharhipi,* mighty warrior who defies the black storm! Hail, he who shall be Windlord hereafter!'

Her very voice sounded to him like the trickling music of a pure mountain rivulet.

'Hail, SilverSong the Fair!' he replied, both gratified and mystified by the tribute. He bestirred himself again and sat up. 'Do you honour a fool with your presence? Why do you bow in homage? I will never be a Windlord as was my father. I am not worthy of you. Surely NightFlyer, my rival, may now claim you.'

SilverSong gave a musical laughing cry and butted ThunderWing playfully with her shining golden head.

'O foolish one. NightFlyer shall never be my nest-mate. Do not demean yourself, for I know you. We have been wingfellows, you and I, since our first flights together. Did you not guide me and protect me when I fell on my first flight? Have you not won great honour amongst the *Mawh'eyri?* Are you not Swiftest in the Mountains? You are destined to soar over the Great Summit, and my song shall soar with you.'

ThunderWing raised his head again in disbelief. He felt as though he had been shot skyward by a powerful updraught, and was floating on the clouds.

'SilverSong! Is this true? You will choose me in despite of my folly? In spite of my shame?'

She nestled her head against his and crooned, 'When I heard of your fall, and your wish to choose me, it was then that I knew you were the only nest-mate for me, Windlord or no. I came wingfleet from the Northern Mountains when my father spoke of your plight.'

She turned away in embarrassment and stared out across the valley towards the distant Northern Mountains.

'Indeed, I have been the fool. Do you remember the time when I came among you all in the Southern Hills during the *Mawh'ree* trials? You saw me little at first, for you had eyes only for your goals in the tri-als—even when I called to you, playfellow!'

'I...I did not recognize you,' he protested feebly. 'It was two long seasons since we parted as playfellows in the Western Mountains. I had not realized how beautifully you had blossomed as the mountain moon-flower. When I realized who you were, it was then I knew that whatever was needed to win your favour, I must do it. It gave strength to my wings and hands, and soon only NightFlyer among them all could match me!'

She smiled, sighed, and regarded him with tender mockery in her brilliant eyes.

'*Eyrionis!* You are all such strange creatures! Well, you seemed to be no longer my playfellow, so I turned my attention to others. There I saw many friends of my youth among the *eyrierë*, strutting and simpering like the Mirror-birds of the valleys, displaying their feather-dyes before me, tittering and chirping at me that I refused such vanities. Yet I became the warriors' favourite at the first trials! Some even laid a tail feather before me. My friends were furiously jealous! I reveled in the adulation of all the warriors, and my vanity grew when NightFlyer turned his proud face toward me. I was flattered and blinded by his attentions, for he is the fairest of warriors—this I will allow. Many *eyrierë* swooned over him and I, SilverSong, had conquered his cold heart, him who despised them all! Truly, it was his overweening pride that caused me to weary of him. Then I saw your valour at the games. I rejoiced at your victory at the *Mawharhipi* trials. All still sing of the final moment when you snatched the twig of victory from before NightFlyer's open beak!'

She turned and faced him again, shaking her lovely head at her own folly.

'I thought it was merely our old friendship that drew me to you, as well as your prowess, which I honour indeed. But I was weary of Night-Flyer and the adulation at the warrior games. I was weary of the jealousies and vanities of my friends. I longed for the soothing Songs of the Wind in the Northern Mountains, not knowing my own heart. But when your mother spoke of your longing for me and of your fall, my heart awoke, seeing you as you truly are....'

She nestled her head next to his again, crooning musically.

'..... My protector, the dear friend of my youth, the mighty warrior destined for great things, the lovesick fool who would risk his life for the sake of one *eyreira*; the poor, broken shell of an eaglet who now needs a lifting wing; an honest heart that has learned from his folly and humbled his pride. *That...*is the nest-mate that I look for, my love.'

ThunderWing felt a warmth in his heart and a lump in his throat. He did not know what to say to such a declaration. It was a love that went beyond mere admiration. This wonderful and beautiful eagle-maid took him for what he really was! It was more than he deserved.

But it was useless. He bowed his head again in sorrow.

'But the laws of the *Mawh'eyri* are not readily changed. I will neither have the armor nor the strength to attempt the mountain in the coming season. If NightFlyer conquers the peak, he will claim you as is his right, and this our blossoming love-flight cannot come to fruition.'

SilverSong stepped back, scorn and resolution in her eye and stance.

'NightFlyer? He is nothing but a boasting fool! Cruel, proud and heartless! He deems me to be his nest-mate already! How I came to think the same in seasons gone by, I know not. This I have considered, my Windlord, my beloved. If that black crow should try to claim me, I shall flee the mountains and forsake the *eyries* of the *Mawh'eyri,* and live in solitude in the forests and hills beyond the Western Marches. You may join me there, if you will. We shall make nest in the highest trees or the darkest caves, far away from the tyranny of our law.'

ThunderWing shook his head in dismay.

'This you must not do, SilverSong, my beloved! It is perilous! Nature has not armed us for such a life. It is the realm of *Hauraugh,* the black beast of the four talons, who has the spirit and voice of *Mawharikhùn* within him. They say there are many sharp stones within his very beak. He has the stealth of the mountain spider and flies without wings upon his prey. And what of the wild eagle's tribes, the *Hrah'eyri?* Their warriors would take you by force!'

'I will abide the peril. Better that than as nest-mate to NightFlyer the Merciless.'

ThunderWing tried a gentler persuasion.

'My fairest, my wing-love, what of your *eyrie?* Of the memory of WindSinger your mother? What of your father, good Windlord Strong-Feather? It would drive him to the Crag of Shame where he would moult to his death! Your singer eaglets of the Northern Mountains? Your wing-fellows and songfellows? Will they not all grieve?'

SilverSong turned away and wept.

'All this I know! But they would be lost to me also if I am Night-Flyer's nest-slave. He is a cruel tyrant, and slew his brother when he was young, deny it if he will! What else do I hope for?'

ThunderWing bowed again. It all seemed hopeless.

Then she shook the tears from her eyes and returned to her defiant stance.

'But you alone are my hope! I will flee these mountains if NightFlyer reigns. But if you conquer the great peak when your robe and armor is restored to you, then *you* shall be Windlord! *You* may choose whom you will. Seek me then, and I will return as your nest-mate!'

ThunderWing took a deep breath at this. He spread his shattered wings, ignoring the pain in his shoulder. Head high, he gave his *eyrie's* war-cry:

"Highest heart! Highest flight!"

He settled again before her and bowed the bow of an eagle's oath-taking.

'SilverSong the Fair, my wing-love, this I swear by the wings of the sun, by the flight of the moon: I will conquer great *Mawharikhan,* though it take many moons, many seasons—or die! If I do not fail, I will come and find you wherever you are and make you Reigning Lady of the *Mawh'eyri,* as you are meet to be. Flee if you must, but let this be a token of our troth.'

He pulled out the last of his old tail-feathers and laid it before her talons. She bowed in return.

'I accept your token, Windlord ThunderWing the Great, and will keep it in great honour in my *eyrie's* nest until the day I must leave. If I flee, look for me in the highest cave of the Wailing Hills above the forest of the West. Even *Hauraugh* himself fears the haunting song of the Raven Winds there.'

She nibbled at his beak as she prepared to leave.

'Farewell my wing-love, for the moment. Do not lose heart. I will make song to the Great Spirit-Wind for you.'

'May the Great Spirit-Wind bear you upward, O SilverSong, fairest, sweetest and bravest of all *eyrierë*! Farewell!'

A graceful sweep of her wings, and she was gone.

This meeting, and subsequent visits sustained him through all the remaining recovery period. These were not many, for the tradition of the *Mawh'eyri* frowned upon overt courtship, and she was in demand in the Northern Mountains.

His spirit certainly needed sustenance.

As the season of the blossoms passed, and stomachs were soon replete again, the call went up from *eyrie* to *eyrie.*

'The trials! The time for the trial-flights of the *Mawharhipi* is come! Where are the Windlords? Where are the warriors?'

'Yes!' the Windlords agreed as they assembled at the Crag of Meeting. 'It is time for the trials to begin.'

Messengers were sent to all champions and Perpetual Champions to make preparations. Warriors began their first trials under the watchful eyes of erstwhile champions. The winners of these progressed to the greater trials, overseen by the Perpetual Champions. These winners were called to the greatest race of them all.

ThunderWing watched from his cave as many young warriors sped by, practicing their wing-strokes, dipping and twisting through practice courses as he had done countless times in the previous season. When he had finally stood upon the Champion's Stone with the Twig-of- Victory in his beak, the winner's wreath around his neck, the crowds cheering hysterically all around him, he thought he was equal to anything.

He sadly looked at himself in the drinking pool. Carefully, he tried flapping his slowly-healing wing and sighed.

The day of the great race finally came, and excitement filled the air. The younger eaglets crowded along the ledges and crags that lined *Mawharhipa* Valley, with the older eagles behind them. The best positions, of course, were soon taken by the officiating Windlords who soon arrived. The eaglets who had previously taken these hastily made way or were hustled away by their parents, but this privilege was not the least begrudged. As the great ones arrived, a chorus of welcoming cries and rustling wings arose.

'Hail, Windlord StrongFeather, beloved Father-of-Many! Hail, Windlord WeatherWing the Wise, healer and prophet! Hail, Windlord FarSight, the Seer! Hail Windlord SwiftSlayer, mightiest of warriors! Hail Windlord BraveWing, Victor in Battle! Hail Windlord StormRider, Conqueror of the Tempest.......' and the list went on.

Finally, when the Windlords had settled in their positions down the length of the course, the remotest Windlord passed his signaling cry on to the next, and so it continued down the course to Windlord Storm-Rider, youngest of all the Windlords, to whom the honour of officiating *Mawharhipi* WingTake was given that season.

StormRider was highly honoured amongst all the *eyries*. Songs of his Windlord Flight over the Great Summit *Mawharikhan* were sung at many feasts. It was said that an early storm had come when he was making his attempt upon the peak. Rather than retreat, he actually rode the upper winds of the storm, fulfilling the prophecy of FarSight the Seer, who named him at birth.

Escaping the storm, StormRider ascended over the peak, escaping the clutches of dark *Mawharikhòn,* who cowered from the threat of the White Warrior-Storm, prowling below. But it had almost cost StormRider his life. Descending through the storm, he had been so badly buffeted and broken, he plummeted into the wooded valley below. He landed among the bushes and it was a full day before his friends, braving the unpredictable storm season, could find him—nearly dead. Succoured by WeatherWing in Healing Cave, he eventually improved enough to fly again, but never fully recovered from his fall. One of his talons no longer functioned properly, and impeded his ability to hunt. Much to his chagrin, he had to be fed by hunters and gatherers like StrongHand, son of HighSoarer. Nevertheless, he was considered a hero by all the young warriors, prompting him to warn them all against trying to emulate his exploit. This, however, did not stop him from relishing the challenge of storm-riding when it was fairly safe to do so.

Remarkably, his exploits never went to his head. He was one of those who often agitated for justice to all the *Mawh'eyri* folk at Windlord council, adding to his popularity.

StormRider now perched a little awkwardly on the crag that overlooked WingTake Mesa, the starting and finishing point for the race. Satisfied that all the Windlords and champions were at their stations, he spread his wings and sang the Song of Summoning, soon taken up by the spectators.

Come, O warrior tried and true!
Honour and glory awaits for you!
Spread now your wings, show forth your great skill,
That you may stand upon Champion's Hill.

The young warriors began to appear from all directions. They were strong, proud, and often seasoned warriors, all hopeful of winning honour for their *eyries*—maybe even bearing the greatest honour of all one day: a Windlord's mark upon his beak.

They alighted upon the mesa, one by one, the youngest to the oldest, loudly proclaiming their lineage, their exploits, and their *eyrie*'s war cry.

Last of all came NightFlyer, son of Windlord SwiftSlayer, contrary to custom, for he was by no means the oldest. He paraded himself around the edge of the mesa with his handsome wings fully stretched, ignoring his lineage, but proclaiming himself "fairest of warriors, greatest of hunters, Swiftest in the Mountains, and Windlord-to-be!"

The other warriors muttered among themselves at these boasts, furious at his presumption. It was recognized among them that StrongHand, son of HighSoarer the Fallen, had become the best, most cunning hunter. Eyes turned toward NightFlyer's father, Windlord SwiftSlayer, but he stood in his position, proud and aloof. There was little love lost between father and son, but the father did not show any emotion at all.

One bold and budding young warrior sang out from among the spectators:

'But where is ThunderWing *Mawharhipi?* Is he not among you all?'

He was hushed by his mother, but much fluttering of wings among the gathering followed, indicating that the question needed an answer.

'ThunderWing, son of HighSoarer, has declined to fly in the trials.' announced StormRider, looking annoyed at the breach of protocol. 'His fall at the Great Mountain has impaired his flight, and he surrenders his title as *Mawharhipi* this season. He wishes all warriors well, that the Great Spirit-Wind may be with your wings.'

Disappointment rippled through the crowd. NightFlyer glowered and muttered to himself.

None had ever forgotten the thrilling finish in the previous season's race, when the young eagle seemed to drop from the sky. He snatched the Twig of Victory from right under NightFlyer's open beak. The lay was sung in every *eyrie* (except SwiftSlayer's) and many feasts for many moons following.

The proceedings continued, and the traditional Singer of Ceremonies was summoned. GoldSinger, daughter of StrongFeather, came forward and alighted next to StormRider. A rustle of astonishment went through the crowd as disapproval arose among the competitors.

'But where is SilverSong the Fair, daughter of Windlord StrongFeather, and greatest of singers?' NightFlyer called out, totally disregarding all etiquette.

'We shall have no more flouting of the traditions, young warrior!' came the stern reply from the crag. StormRider glanced hesitatingly, in near embarrassment, up the valley where he could just make out StrongFeather's outline on one of the furthest crags.

'SilverSong, daughter of Windlord StrongFeather cannot come,' he informed them all, 'for she teaches many eaglets in the ways of the Windsong in the Northern Mountains. GoldSinger, her sister, has consented to take her place at our request.'

A collective sigh of disappointment went up from all the warriors. SilverSong was considered the favourite, partly because of her transcendent beauty, but also due to her lively, laughing style of performance, which was far more appealing to any *eyrion*. However, most of the civilian spectators considered GoldSinger to have the better voice. Nor were they disappointed.

GoldSinger did not envy her sister's beauty and popularity, for the family of that *eyrie* was a close-knit community. She had learned everything SilverSong could teach her of the ways of the Windsong, and had surpassed her in technical quality at least. She was surprised at her sister's reluctance, but considered it an honour to take her place.

Spreading back her wings, she attuned her voice to the breeze and began to sing. She sang the traditional ballad sung at the beginning of every formal gathering of the *Mawh'eyri*.

It was the tale of the coming of their tribe to the mountains at the bidding of the Great Spirit-Wind. She sang of their third lord-chieftain, WideWing the Wanderer, wearer of the glowing *Khanirhidhi* and his nest-mate MotherWind the Wise. They tamed the feuding of the *Mawh'eyri* warriors, bringing the *eyries* together under a common code of law. She sang of the rise of the proud Windlords, who took over responsibilities from the traditional chieftains, reformed and enforced the laws, and scratched them on the Stones of Judgment. She sang of the rise of the warrior class, and the united battles against the invasions of the Wild Eagles, the *Hrah'eyri* , who outnumbered them and demanded the return of the *Khanirhidhi*. However, they were defeated by the *Mawh'eyri* under Windlord BrightWing the Brave. The enemy had seldom returned in great force since, except on raids on the outlying *eyries*. The local Watchers of the Walls were vigilant, nonetheless.

GoldSinger also sang of the terrible Storm Season, of the coming of the dark one, the Great Black Storm and his minions, most of whom were slain by the pursuing White Warrior Winds. All the folk of the *Mawh'eyri* hid in their *eyries* in fear as the war raged all around them, and even in those later days, they shudder at its memory. The Great Black Storm finally found refuge within the Great Mountain, even though he was constantly under siege by the mighty servants of the Great Spirit-Wind, especially at the waning of the year. The dark one was renamed *Mawharikhvn*, dark prisoner of the mountain, even though he himself considered it his domain when the White Warrior Winds were far away.

But the darkest times passed, and the *Mawh'eyri* came to accept the dangers of their perilous neighbour. It was even considered a greater honour for a champion *eyrion* to conquer the Great Mountain and outwit its terrifying resident as well. For many seasons it seemed as if he slept, leaving them all in peace.

On that note, GoldSinger ended her song.

A hushed and reverent silence followed.

GoldSinger then lifted her head, and struck up the "Anthem of the *Mawh'eyri*."

Soon they all joined in, with harmonies flowing all the way down the valley and echoing throughout the mountains.

None of them noticed the lonely, ragged young eagle behind the crowds as he quietly took wing, and wearily, awkwardly, and sadly laboured his way toward Healing Cave.

CHAPTER 3

AMONG THE *MAWHARÙN*

StrongHand looked up from his meal as he heard a flurry of wings.

'Hail, ThunderWing my brother,' he said, bowing as to a great warrior. 'Welcome home to our *eyrie* once more. You bring both shame and fame to yourself, but honour to our *eyrie*. Who but you would be both valiant and fool enough to challenge the realm of the Black Storm and draw him out to his doom.'

ThunderWing glanced at his brother as he landed. There appeared to be both mockery and admiration in his brother's greeting. He, however, was not in the mood for the amiable squabbling that they used to indulge in, so he settled in his old corner and lay down.

'Come now, little brother,' pursued his elder, teasingly. 'Are you still so shattered that you cannot play *Mawharagh* with fat brother StrongHand?'

But ThunderWing would not be drawn, so StrongHand, after looking for any signs of permanent damage to his sibling, shook his head and resumed his favourite pastime.

'You have heard, no doubt, that NightFlyer is now.....?'

'Yes!' was the curt reply. 'Indeed, all the *eyries* of the mountains know of his victory. I stayed only to see and hear SilverSong the Fair. But she came not, so I would not wait for the race.'

StrongHand grunted sardonically, but kept his peace and laid down. Silence reigned for a while and ThunderWing watched the sun slowly setting behind the Western Mountains. He nibbled on some meat his brother threw to him. He saw the last of the hunters and gatherers flying home to their own *eyries*. A few of the solitary lesser eagles also returned to their *eyries* in the cliffs, tiny dots in comparison.

After a while, ThunderWing lifted his head.

'It is said that you are the greatest of the hunters and gatherers, brother.'

StrongHand grunted, still absorbed in digesting his large meal.

'It is of little moment to me. Perhaps it is because I feed many that it has been noticed. Had I my own war-cry, it would be: "Feed your stomach, feed the *eyries*." It goes well. I build my hunger in the service of the *eyries* and therefore eat more. So I am content.'

A hissing laugh escaped his brother's throat.

'I now envy your lack of ambition, brother. Yet you are honourable in your service, little though you relish the honour.'

StrongHand looked up, surprised.

'You are courteous! If your pride and presumption has been shattered in your fall, as it now seems, then maybe it has not been loss, but gain. Have you surrendered your dream to be Windlord of the *Mawh'eyri?*

'Perhaps,' his brother replied evasively. His vow to his love was a private matter now. 'But for now I seek a lesser, but maybe better honour.'

StrongHand just blinked at him in bafflement.

'I know not your meaning. What is this honour you speak of?'

'To aid the hunters and gatherers to feed the *eyries*.'

This surprised the elder brother so much, he took wing and almost flipped over. The sudden movement swept the last scraps of his meal off the ledge, but he made no effort to retrieve them.

'You, my brother! A hunter and gatherer? But...do not all warriors despise us?'

'Not this warrior! Nor have I ever done so, save in our banter and word-battles. But is there need for other wings? Can you use my hands in your task?'

For once, StrongHand's enthusiasm showed, despite his outward profession of self-interest. His eyes brightened. This was his passion. He became even rhetorical.

'More and more *eyries* are birthed in the mountains, and more and more eaglets are born to the wingfolk of the *Mawh'eyri*. The mothers are hard pressed to feed them at times, and there is sometimes great dearth in the season of storms, when the mountains wear the Cold White Down. The Watchers of the Marches guard the outer hills, so they cannot hunt, but must also be fed as do those in the Windlords in Council. It is hard labour and long, at times. Yet we are a merry band, we of the *Mawharùn*. We sing as we gather, and sing when we catch our prey. We dispatch the fruits of our labours quickly and quietly, and are fully content when we see that hungry mouths are fed. When times allow it, we feast all together and share our tales of the hunt.'

His face darkened.

'But many more strong young *eyrion* think less of the *eyries* and more of their own glory. They choose to be warriors, and play eaglets' games of war, feeding only their own bellies! Do we have need of more hunters? I tell you, many would starve if we, the despised *Mawharùn* become weary of our task!'

ThunderWing now looked at his brother with new eyes.

'Truly, I have not given you the honour that is due. Let me come with you, then, at sun-arise next. You, elder brother, must show me the ways of the *Mawharùn*.'

'Done!'

So it was that ThunderWing joined the hunter-gatherers for the rest of the season.

He learned to respect the skill of his pragmatic but great-hearted brother. StrongHand knew the best areas for hunting and where the best berries and herbs could be found. He had developed a system of herding and culling their prey without exhausting their resources. He directed the hunters to find food in areas of plenty.

ThunderWing soon learned that speed and strength were not always helpful when hunting. He was surprised at the patience and skill StrongHand showed while stalking his prey. He watched and sensed the changing of the winds so he was rarely detected until the final moment, and it was too late. His speed at the final swoop could rival that of the fastest warrior. He was not named StrongHand the Master Hunter for nothing.

He found his fellow hunter-gatherers to be good-hearted folk. A few were surprised to find a warrior among them, and astounded when they were told it was none other than ThunderWing, formerly Swiftest in the Mountains—he who defied the Black Storm. He showed no sign of superiority, however, so they soon accepted him into the fraternity. Indeed, the goodwill and brotherhood of all members were something of which ThunderWing took note.

There was nothing glamorous or elegant about them. Few took the trouble to groom themselves beyond basic hygiene. They came from many *eyrie*s, often as the weaker siblings, the more fearful, the less attractive members of the family. Many of the eagle maids among them, the *eyreira,* were either too old, too disfigured, or just too plain to be considered as nest-mates by the warriors. Yet they were content to be among the fraternity. There were no pretensions or airs about them. They took pride in their work, and carried the fruits of their labours to the farthermost mountains, without complaint.

StrongHand had a very egalitarian policy when it came to delivering their catch.

'While I am Master of the *Mawharùn*,' he said belligerently to his hunters, 'We shall deliver our first catch to those who are in greatest need, first of all. If warriors, or even Windlords call for prey for their feasting, they must await those that are hungry and destitute—or catch their own prey. I have spoken!'

He would sometimes mutter the occasional remark about certain injustices that occurred among the *Mawh'eyri.*

'Open your eyes wherever you are sent, my brother,' he advised in an undervoice. 'For not all is well in the mountains of *Mawha.*'

ThunderWing thought his brother took too pessimistic a view of the state of affairs, a reaction to the low esteem in which the *Mawharùn* were regarded. Nonetheless, he watched and wondered at some situations in some of the poorer *eyrie*s he visited. He experienced the satisfaction of seeing hungry beaks fed, and the gratitude of many harassed mothers, whose nest-mate had gone to the *Mawh'ree,* the tournaments of the warriors in the Southern Hills, or had fallen through their attempts at the peak, or died fighting the *Hrah'eyri* raiders. He had even heard of cases of domestic violence and forced marriages, where the *eyreira* had fled into the wild. It was a very patriarchal society. ThunderWing began to feel a little ashamed that he had spent so much of his youth at the *Mawh'ree*, forsaking his mother in her loneliness.

Sometimes it was a thankless task, being a hunter.

A hunter arrived at one *eyrie*, hardly recognizable, covered in dust and splashed with a little blood, bearing two hares and a branch of mountain berries. The *eyrie*-mother was rather stressed and a little cross. She had three small wailing chicks and an aspiring young warrior-to-be to feed. There was no sign of the father (presumably, he was at the *Mawh'ree* in the Southern Hills).

'You are late, hunter!' she snapped. 'I cannot leave the nest and my lord is delayed. My chicks are starving!'

The hunter cast his catch before the hungry chicks and waved genially at the eldest of them, who was staring hard at him.

'I cry pardon, *eyrie*-mother.' replied the hunter, patiently. 'There have been so many demands upon us, now the *Mawh'ree* trials are at their height. Prey is becoming scarce in the southern central valleys, so we have to venture beyond the outer borders. It is a long flight.'

The *eyrie*-mother merely grunted, tearing at the meal and carefully depositing morsels into wailing mouths.

The eldest youngster stared intently at the hunter, while munching on berry and flesh, so the hunter kindly asked him questions about his aspirations.

'I know not if I be a hunter or a warrior, master hunter,' the youth replied. 'I like to be both, but cannot.'

'Why will you not be both…?'

'Because his father will not let him so demean himself!' interjected the mother, irritated by the question. 'If you have no more food to offer, pray go and leave us in peace. Do not be late next time!'

The hunter effaced himself hastily, winking at the young aspirant as he went.

'Why you talk to him so, mother? I like him. I see him before at the *Mawharhipi* trials.'

'If you are to be a warrior like your father, youngling, you do not befriend mere hunters.'

The young eagle gasped. He remembered who the hunter was.

'Mother! It was ThunderWing, son of Windlord HighSoarer!'

The mother closed her eyes in exasperation.

'Do not be so foolish, youngling! A champion of his stature would never join the *Mawharùn!* Eat your meat and berries and go to your nest!'

ThunderWing also met some of the older warriors, the Watchers and Guards of the Marches, as he brought meat and fruits to their posts on the outer crags of the outer mountains. Some had known his father, so his sons were held in high honour.

'Hail, son of HighSoarer the great!' said StrongEye, a battered and tattered old watcher, as ThunderWing bowed and laid his meal before him. 'You have my thanks. Your *eyrie* has served me well. Your father saved me in times past in battle with the raiders. Your brother keeps me from starvation so I may keep my post. Because of you, the Black Storm is banished from the mountains, and we may live with less fear.'

He cocked his head sideways at his young visitor, who laid the meat out for him.

'Yet this is a thing unheard of. Have you so demeaned yourself as to have joined the *Mawharùn* fraternity?'

'I am a warrior still, father-warrior,' ThunderWing replied stiffly. 'But I have learned that there is much honour among the *Mawharùn*, little though we warriors could see it. There is much I could learn from them. Proudly do I serve the *eyries* of the *Mawh'eyri*.'

'Very well, son of HighSoarer. But surely warriors are called to a higher calling. It is written upon the Stones of Judgment.'

The old warrior was still too set in the caste system of the mountain eagles to fully see ThunderWing's viewpoint. Then he changed the subject.

'Have you heard what has happened at the Great Peak? The news is spreading from *eyrie* to *eyrie*.'

ThunderWing's heart sank.

'Has NightFlyer, son of Windlord SwiftSlayer, has he attempted the Great Summit of *Mawharikhan?*'

The old warrior snorted. 'He has done so, and failed. But that is not the sole news.'

'NightFlyer has failed??'

ThunderWing's heart soared again.

'Yes, he has failed, the arrogant young fool,' the watcher replied with a scornful laugh. 'And his pride will not let him forbear. But now there is a new enemy upon *Mawharikhan* for a warrior to conquer before he gains the summit itself.'

'Surely it cannot be that *Mawharikhùn* has returned! The rumour of his coming would have left a swathe of destruction in his wake! And he greatly fears the wrath of the Great Spirit-Wind!'

'No, son of HighSoarer. Rather it is many enemies, but not so black, nor so evil, or so it seems. They are the *Khriki* winds of the Wailing Hills who, it is said, have heard of the banishment of the Black Storm, and have come to take residence in his place within the high black caves of *Mawharikhan.*'

'The *Khriki?* The Raven-Winds? Do they do harm to the warriors that attempt the peak?'

'Well…. they have less hatred in their hearts as had *Mawharikhùn,* but they are proud. They harass you like the crows of the valleys, but are far stronger. Our folk are as playthings to them, if we wander onto their territory—or so they call it. They will not slay you, but they will buffet you with breath and wing. They will cause you to be consumed with fear so you lose heart. So it came to pass upon NightFlyer, son of Windlord SwiftSlayer, when he made his attempt, and upon LongFeather, son of StoneWing also. Their thought was that they would have an easy victory over the Great Peak, and great is their consternation.'

Both laughed aloud.

The garrulous old warrior would have chatted for quite a while, having had a long and lonely vigil, but ThunderWing had much to do and to think about. He politely extricated himself from the conversation, bidding farewell, and then facing his beak into the wind and driving rain.

'SilverSong, my wing-love, you are safe for the moment!' he sang to the air as he winged his way back to the hunting fields. 'But Oh! That I may look upon you again, to hear your voice and to speak of this news! Where have they hidden you?'

He continued his work, but his head was full of these new developments at the peak, and their implications. If there was call for meat at Windlord's Crag or at StrongFeather's *eyrie*, he begged to be the one to take it. StrongHand good-naturedly allowed it a few times, but as Hunter-Master, he had to send the strongest flyers to the furthest reaches. ThunderWing was the strongest flyer, and could carry just as much meat as StrongHand, so he was often chosen for the remotest marches.

On the occasions when he was allowed to visit StrongFeather's *eyrie*, there was no sign of his beloved. On casual inquiry, he was told by a young family member that she was still in the Northern Mountains. When he finally arrived in the Northern Mountains, bearing food, it was reported that she had flown back to her *eyrie*. He fretted, wondering if she had grown cold toward him.

He humbly approached her father when he visited Windlord's Crag. Windlord StrongFeather looked a little grim, but he took him aside and spoke to him.

'Son of HighSoarer, my daughter is in hiding. It seems that Night-Flyer, *Mawharhipi* as he now is, already considers her his property. She is safe at my *eyrie* while I remain, but my duties often call me forth. He has been hovering, my son. Hovering as though she were his prey! I have spoken to his father, Windlord SwiftSlayer, but he is proud and will do nothing to restrain his son. They do not speak to one another, father and son, these sunflights. But I have warned his father that if NightFlyer should touch my daughter unlawfully, I will call *Mawharagh* upon him, as is my right. But so says Windlord SwiftSlayer: "Then may the strongest win!"'

ThunderWing was shocked.

'Oh, that I were a champion again, that I may challenge him in your stead, O Father-of-Many!'

'That time may come yet, my son,' said the older eagle, prophetically. 'I am old, and may not prevail as you may. True, you must become a champion again. Perhaps even, as Windlord? I know your mind and that of my daughter.'

He turned away and gazed at the great cloud-covered peak in the distance, disregarding ThunderWing's embarrassment.

'*Mawharikhan* sleeps. But the new enemies sleep not, and they are strong and unpredictable, as dark winds are.'

He turned back and stared at the strong young warrior before him, his stern eyes softening.

'But you are stronger in many ways, I think, my son. But await the right season, for only the Great Wind-Spirit can tell when it is so. The Raven-Winds play havoc with all who come to challenge the peak, even at times with the elders at Windlord's Crag, but they merely play and do not slay. They shall hide in the Black Caves upon the peak during the season of storms, for they fear the Warrior Storms. Go, my son, for so I shall call you. Your time shall come. But wait for it. Your wing-love, my daughter, waits for it also. She is safe for the present. May the Great Wind-Spirit bear you upward!'

There was a lump in the young eagle's throat, so he could not reply. Bowing low, beak to stone, he departed and returned to his own *eyrie*.

He could not see her! But she was safe. That was all that mattered.

He returned to his work, which kept his mind occupied. If he became idle, he felt he would go mad. He sang to the Great Spirit-Wind, beseeching him that his time may be soon.

And there was enough to keep his mind occupied.

It would be unfair to say that he became as skilled as his brother, but his superior flexibility in flight proved to be a bonus at times. His strength and skill developed through this training, and his new feathers grew longer. He was becoming a formidable foe. A few crows, competing for prey, found themselves out-flanked and out-maneuvered. Some paid with their lives if they became too pertinacious, and tried to steal the meat from under ThunderWing's beak. They swore at him in their own uncouth tongue, but left him alone.

Respect for the brothers grew among the fraternity, but when a crisis arose, it developed into full admiration, even deference.

CHAPTER 4

THE BATTLE OF THE WESTERN MARCHES

A day came when all the hunters were meeting near a watcher's post where the western mountains met the forest at a steep cliff. Heather-Wing, a sharp-eyed eagle-maid gasped and pointed with her wing at the top of the cliff.

'The *Hrah'eyri* are come! They lay siege to the watchpost!'

They all crowded around and looked. Sure enough, they could make out a number of black specks circling around the highest point of the cliff, several miles away. They could just hear the screaming war-cries of the Wild Eagles and the answering challenge of the *Mawh'eyri* guards. More watchers and guards came as fast as they could to help them, but it was very evident that they were greatly outnumbered.

'Their numbers are great!' StrongHand said, flying up to an upper bough for a better view. 'They have not dared to attack with such large bands as these since the great war of the Northern Mountains! If they send tidings to the *eyries*, the messengers will be set upon! The Watchers and guards are doomed!'

He flew down to HeatherWing. 'Sister-hunter, you are fleet of wing. Go with wary speed to the Western Crags with the news. Summon the Warband there. May the Great Spirit-Wind give strength to your wings!'

She vanished through the upper branches, flying low to keep out of sight of the Wild Eagle's scouts.

'The Western Crags?' barked ThunderWing as he joined him on the bough. 'That is still many valleys hence. The Warband then must be summoned and made ready. They may come too late!'

'But will not our messenger surely arm the *eyries* for an assault at least?'

'Perhaps, but by stalling the assault, the Warband will come here in force, so there need be no siege of the *eyries*!'

StrongHand had to bow to his brother's knowledge of war.

'But what can we do?' wailed HoneyCatcher. 'We are only hunters and gatherers. We are too few, and not trained for war!'

'Yes we are!' answered ThunderWing, his face set. 'We are all strong and hardened for the hunt. We shall hunt the enemy!'

'But we are too few! And I am fearful, I confess!'

'There is no shame in fearfulness, only if we let it deter us from our duty. Come! I will go alone if need be, for I am warrior trained, but I am not master of the hunters.'

He turned to his brother, who rose to the occasion immediately.

'My brother is right! We may be few, but we can come through the trees and take them by surprise. Perhaps we can stay their attack until the Warband comes. If you fear, it is no shame, but come behind us and aid us when you can.'

He turned back to ThunderWing. 'You, brother, shall be our captain!'

ThunderWing nodded briefly. It was practical wisdom, after all.

He rattled out his instructions: the fastest and strongest hunters were to follow him for the main attack. StrongHand was to take the rest in a flanking maneuver. If the Wild Eagles proved too strong, they were to retreat into the woods at his call and harass them from behind. They knew the woods well and knew how to hide.

As they approached the battle, they could hear the battle-cries of the *Hrah'eyri* getting shriller in frustration. It appeared they expected a quick victory over the guards and watchers and to go on to raid the *eyries* of the Western Mountains, then retreat before the Warband could be assembled and drive them away.

But the *Mawh'eyri* guards and watchers, though past their prime, were well-trained and stubborn in their resistance. They shielded themselves from the first momentum of the swoop of their enemies by dodging behind the rocks, then leapt out upon them and plucked them from the air, talons and beaks rending them to pieces. Dead and dying birds lay around them. They repelled the first assault, but they were greatly outnumbered. Any watchers that tried to escape to get help were singled out and set upon. They were too old to outfly the strong young wild warriors even if they escaped. Weary and wounded, they knew that they could not survive, but they had resolved to stand until the last eagle fell. They would take as many as they could with them before they died, to lessen the impact of the raids upon the *eyries*.

'May the Great Wind-Spirit give strength to our wings and hands to do our duty before we die, brethren!' said the old watcher of the Western Mountains, bleeding from one of his wings. 'We die with great honour! Maybe we shall find the Great *Eyrie* above the skies!'

A huge *Hrahe* warrior appeared in the air above the raiders. He was their captain, a champion of champions among the Wild Eagles. Terrifying to look upon, he was daubed with virulent colours which proclaimed his previous victories. His talons were like great tree roots, tipped with steel. Calling shrilly, he rallied his troops for one final and decisive blow. Time was short and the element of surprise must be maintained upon the Western *Eyries*.

'Death! Death to the mountain vultures!'

With that he soared down with his warriors in a thick phalanx behind him. The rocks would be of little help to the defenders now.

Whooosshhh! Like an arrow, ThunderWing erupted from the trees nearby and flew with all his force, weight, and speed, straight at the huge wild eagle, piercing the heart of the attack. His talons tore, then gripped, then loosed, causing the screaming warrior-captain to spin and fall, spreading feathers and blood as he tumbled down onto the rocks below. Confusion reigned for a moment as ThunderWing disrupted their charge, dodging among them, tearing with beak and talon .

Hardly had the enemy recovered and begun to converge on him than a dozen strong, work-hardened eagles erupted from among the trees and charged from all directions, crying, 'The Warband! The Warband! The *Mawh'eyri* are upon you!'

The enemy went into a panic and scattered in all directions as hunters snapped at their tail-feathers. This freed ThunderWing to execute his next stroke. Noting where the coloured captain fell, he soared after him. He was easy to find among the rocks and bushes where he had fallen—his colouring betrayed him all too easily.

The captain was temporarily dazed, but was recovering fast, roaring with fury at this setback. He gathered his great wings, ready to take flight and deal with the impudent young warrior that dared to outwit him.

'They are too few!' he screamed at his followers. 'They are too few! Turn! Attack them, you cowardly crows!'

Ignoring the blood dripping from his chest and shoulder wound, he spread his wings and prepared to join them.

Too late.

Without checking his speed, ThunderWing dropped like a thunderbolt from the rocks above and dove into the back of the big warrior with all his weight and momentum, smashing his backbone, scattering his feathers. A final tear to his neck finished him. With a choking cry, the great eagle's head fell forward.

Without wasting time on celebrations, ThunderWing took to the air and joined in the attack, shouting 'Your captain is fallen! Your captain is dead! Flee the wrath of the *Mawh'eyri!*'

But some had heard their captain's last command, and realizing that their foes were indeed too few and inexperienced, turned and faced their attackers. These alone outnumbered the hunters, but ThunderWing was ready for this.

'Turn! Turn, hunters of the *Mawh'eyri!*' he called. 'To the woods and to safety!'

Nearly all his own followers obeyed, this time with the enemy on their tail.

They had almost made it to the woods, when once again the trees erupted from both sides of their attackers.

StrongHand appeared from the midst of a large leafy branch, roaring *'Highest heart! Highest height!'* He dropped upon the leading *Hrahe* warrior and brought him down by his sheer weight alone. His prey seemed to disintegrate in midair before he plummeted down to the rocks below, a scattering mess of blood and feathers.

Even the most fearful amongst his followers had swallowed their fear as they saw ThunderWing's bold, frontal attack. Once again, cries of 'The Warband! Warriors of the *Mawh'eyri!*' echoed off the cliff face. Talons tore and beaks slashed as the hidden hunters leapt from hiding upon their enemies.

'These are real warriors!' shrieked many of the *Hrahe*. 'They are too many for us! The day is lost! Flee! Flee!'

Still, some seasoned warriors among the *Hrah'eyri* stayed. These also wore war-paint on their feathers and beaks which proclaimed the many battles they had fought in the past against other tribes. They had a deeply-rooted hatred of the mountain eagles. It wasn't long before the most experienced recognized that they faced only despised hunter-gatherers, unskilled in warfare.

'Turn again! Turn again, *Hrahe* warriors!' shrieked the largest and most decorated warrior. 'Will you retreat before berry-picking woodpeckers?'

But StrongHand kept his head. He could see a large number of the enemy gathering in another phalanx around their new captain. They were ready to descend on the hunters who were heedless in their pursuit of the fleeing foe.

Exhilarating as their success seemed, StrongHand could see that the battle was far from being won. They had merely managed to reduce the numbers of their enemies to match their own. The remaining *Hrahe* warriors were no longer fooled. He knew that his hunters were no match for trained, seasoned fighters when it came to pitched battles. Bluff and open warfare strategy were now useless. The trees and hiding-places were their only hope until the real Warband arrived. In the forest, the hunters had the advantage. At best, they could use guerilla tactics, ambushing and retreating.

'Return, hunters of the *Mawh'eyri!*' he bawled, dodging in and out of the combatants. 'To the woods and to safety! Return, or the hunter will become the prey!'

The more experienced hunters understood his wisdom, saw the gathering of their foes and followed him back to their ambush. A few did not, and were never seen alive again. And where was ThunderWing? Had he gone in pursuit?

The remaining *Hrahe* settled on the lower ledges at the level of the treetops, preparing to attack.

'Yes, flee! Flee to your burrows, little hares!' they mocked. 'We are the hunters now, and you shall pay for your cowardly tricks! We will find you!'

'Stay!!'

The great voice seemed to have been amplified by the cliffs. All the combatants froze, for it sounded as though the mountain winds had come upon them in great wrath.

ThunderWing had come, flanked by the remaining guards and watchers of the Western Mountains who could still fight. He settled on the treetops between the two armies.

'I am ThunderWing, son of Windlord HighSoarer!' he announced to the enemy. 'A warrior and champion among the *Mawh'eyri* am I. Hear me, warriors of the *Hrah'eyri*! I have slain your captain.'

The old watcher near to him spat out a large highly-painted feather onto a ledge for all to see. It was the largest tail-feather of the warrior-captain, specially marked as a badge of authority among the Wild Eagles.

None could dispute ThunderWing's claim now. They hesitated.

The largest painted warrior, now apparently in charge of the raiding host, gasped when he heard ThunderWing's name.

'A son of HighSoarer?'

ThunderWing turned toward him.

'Have you heard of me or my father? A proud *eyrion* was he, and flew only by the code of the warrior. I shall also do so. Why need you to shed the blood of hunters untrained in the ways of war? Is there any honour in this? *I* am a warrior. I call *Mawharagh* upon you in single combat! Was there any one among you who would so challenge your captain? I have slain him. Now you must slay me. If you do so, you shall continue your raid in honour. If I slay your champion, then you must leave and return to your *eyries* in peace, knowing you have not departed in shame. What say you?'

There was a long, tense pause at this bold challenge. StrongHand shook out the feathers of his neck as he watched the drama from behind his ambush.

'I see my father reborn in you, my brother,' he muttered to himself, anxiously changing his grip on his branch. 'You have slain their captain with valour and the skill of the hunter's ambush as I have taught you. But can you fight a wild warrior of greater stature in *Mawharagh,* beak to beak, talon to talon? And have these carrion beasts the same sense of honour?'

Finally, the great *Hrahe* warrior captain spread his wings and landed on a ledge almost beak to beak with ThunderWing and stared at him, more in curiosity than hostility. Even though he had the rough and unkempt appearance typical of the Wild Eagles, and was covered in war-paint, there was something noble in his bearing.

'Hear me, son of HighSoarer, son of StrongWing the Victor. Your father's name is not unknown to me. I am named among my winged people as *Kharòn* the Dispossessed. Yet I am of the wingfolk of *Mawha* by birth.'

This revelation caused a stir among the hunters in hiding.

'He is a traitor then!' whispered HoneyCatcher.

The dispossessed warrior spat in bitterness. He began an oration, pacing the ledge as he spoke.

'Before my banishment, I was a warrior of great worth. I went to the Battle of the Eastern Marches with your father and StrongWing, his father, our captain. I was the youngest of his warriors, and my name was WindChaser, son of SwiftSoarer.'

This declaration startled StrongHand. He burst from his ambush and flew over to perch next to his brother.

'WindChaser, the Wild One! Your name is not unknown to me also. My father spoke of you with great respect and regret. He said you have suffered great injustice.'

The rebel eagle paused in his oration and stared at the two brothers.

'You are his son also? Yours alone of all the *eyri*es of *Mawha* do I spare my hatred. Yours and that of StrongFeather, son of WindRider. For this is my tale: I wished to take WindSinger the Fair, daughter of SwiftHand, as my nest-mate and there was a great love between us. But she was claimed....'

He spat again.

'....She was claimed by SwiftSlayer the proud, the son of Night-Hunter! He would take her from me as his right when he became Wind-lord. I was hot-headed, and I challenged his right as she was unwilling. But to so challenge was a great crime among the high and mighty ones of the *Mawh'eyri*. I was brought before the Stones of Judgment and sentenced to be banished forever from the mountains. I, WindChaser, a champion of war! Banished from the wingfolk I fought for! Wind-lords HighSoarer and StrongFeather alone spoke for my part, but the rest would not change the law and heartless traditions of the *Mawh'eyri*. Then WindSinger fled with me, but we were pursued by SwiftSlayer and his *eyrie*, and they overtook us.'

He beat his wings in a half-flight of fury as he felt again the bitter memory of his troubles. He landed on ThunderWing's branch, looking the brothers in the eyes.

'SwiftSlayer the proud, the cruel, then slew my beloved when she refused to return with him! I flew at him in my fury, but he and his kin were too strong for me. I fell into the forest below, mortally wounded—or so they thought. I lay a day and a night at the door of death until I was found by a kindly mother eagle of the *Hrah'eyri*, not knowing from whence I came. *Kharena*, daughter of *Kharan* was she. She succoured me and took me as her own son, and I will never forget it. I lived among them in peace, taking on their *eyrie*'s name until it was discovered from whence I broke from my eggshell. Three *Hrahe* warriors, one a champion, challenged me because of this, but I defeated them all. Then, as I told my tale, the winged people of the *Hrah'eyri* received me as one of their own.'

He spread his wings and let forth the screaming war-cry of the Wild Eagles.

'What have I to do with the proud and cruel *Mawh'eyri?* Barbarians though we be, by the wings of the moon, I will live and die as a champion warrior of the *Hrah'eyri!*'

His fellow-warriors flapped their wings, stomped with their talons and echoed his war-cry.

'Death! Death to the mountain vultures who stole our *eyries*! Death to the proud ones that cower in their caves!'

The tension was thick in the air, but *Kharòn's* tragic story had a powerful effect upon ThunderWing. It struck a strong chord of sympathy, reminding him of his own hopes and fears for SilverSong. It seemed as though history was repeating itself.

'But wait!' he called, spreading his own wings to get their attention. 'I perceive that you are a people of honour, enemies though you declare yourselves to be. We live but to serve our own *eyries*, even as you do yours. Are you not sons and brothers? Would you not defend your own also? There is injustice here on our part, this I will acknowledge. I have the ear of Windlord StrongFeather, Father-of-Many. Can we not try to right these wrongs? Can we not speak of peace and of treaty amongst all *Eyri* wingfolk?'

There was an astonished silence to this suggestion. But peace was an unfamiliar word to a painted *Hrahe* warrior. They erupted into laughter.

'Peace?' they cried. 'We know not this saying! How can there be peace between our peoples? You, who stole the Tears-of-the Sun from us!'

'A noble but childish wish, son of HighSoarer the just,' said *Kharòn* sardonically. 'How can the prey make peace with the predator?'

It seemed as that the situation was about to deteriorate again, but suddenly StrongEye, the old watcher, looked up and gave a great shout.

'They come! It is the Warband of the West at last!'

The hunters and their enemies all looked up, and sure enough, they could see rank upon rank of warriors encircling the tops of the cliffs. They appeared little more than ordered clouds of wings, for the cliffs were exceedingly high, but it was only a matter of time before they went searching for the remaining foes, once the wounded guards left behind had given their report.

'The *Mawh'eyri* have triumphed!' the hunters sang exultantly. 'They come! They come!'

The Wild Eagles cried out in anger and frustration.

'We are betrayed!'

They prepared to take wing.

'You are cunning hunters, you sons of HighSoarer!' *Kharòn* the Dispossessed commented bitterly, spreading his wings, ready to flee or fight. 'The wisdom of the serpent is upon you. You have delayed us and your trap is sprung upon us! Now we shall be pursued and slain unless we hide in the forest. But then your hunters shall flush us out also, will you not? I have told my tale in vain! Farewell! For I shall not touch any sons of HighSoarer the just.'

StrongEye prepared to take flight also, bowing before ThunderWing.

'Give me leave, my captain, for I and my comrades must give report to the captain of the Warband.'

'No, father-warrior!' cried ThunderWing urgently. 'If you call me captain, await my word, I beg of you.'

Without waiting for a reply, he called to his brother and rose up on wing to confront *Kharòn*, hovering in mid-flight.

'Await, son of SwiftSoarer! You are too great a warrior to be treated thus! Let us help to repair the injustice you have suffered! Come with me through the forest until you are out of sight of our Warband. If I betray you, you may slay me.'

He glanced at StrongHand as he joined him in mid-flight.

'We must give safe passage to these good warriors, foes though they be. Will your hunters allow this, my brother?'

'You are our captain, my brother. Some may say it is treason, but all have heard the story of SwiftSoarer's son. They will obey. I will lead you through the forest.'

'Then let it be so, good brother. Tell them!'

StrongHand bowed his head and banked to the right, soaring down to the treetops where the hunters lay hidden.

'Come then, WindChaser the Wild One, for so I will call you. Gather your warriors, those who will trust us, and follow me through the woods.'

Kharòn was stricken to awed silence at this. He merely nodded and flew off to inform his troops of the new developments.

ThunderWing, meanwhile, swooped down to where StrongEye, the old watcher, stood nervously with his fellow guards.

'Go, father-warrior! Make your report to the captain of the Warband. But say nothing of this treaty with the enemy save that they fled through the woods at the advance of the War band. The hunters stood aside, having suffered many wounded.'

This all was quite true, but some guards looked doubtful.

'Will not the *Hrah'eyri* return again if we let them go?'

'I think not,' ThunderWing answered calmly. 'Barbarians they be, but there is greater honour among them than we have hitherto perceived. These, at least, will remember the mercy of the hunters of the *Mawh'eyri.*'

StrongEye bowed his head before ThunderWing.

'Son of HighSoarer, you speak with wisdom beyond your years. Your valour and your skill in captaincy will also not go unreported. You are my captain, so I will speak as you have bid me. Farewell!'

He spread his ragged wings and flew off and upward, his fellows following suit.

ThunderWing had no time to stop and think. Celebrations of victory and honour among his followers would have to wait. He knew that he took a huge risk. His reputation, maybe his very life hung on this decision he had made. If he was tried for treason before the Stones of Judgment, he would be executed. His own life meant little to him now, but SilverSong would have only her father to protect her, and that would be no more if NightFlyer became Windlord. He would have the right to fight the aging StrongFeather, and would probably prevail, being younger and stronger. She would flee alone into the wild, grieving for her father and her lover.

He waited at the edge of the forest, concealing his nervousness and impatience, with StrongHand on hand. *Kharòn* gathered as many of his band together as he could.

A few proudly refused the offer of clemency, and flew off into the blue toward their *eyri*es. They would be easily spotted and picked off by the *Mawha* Warband from above. But these were old and proud warriors, preferring death over the perceived dishonour of being beholden to the *Mawh'eyri* hunters.

The ranks of the Warband above appeared to be gathering to make their descent upon the forest. After spotting a few of the enemy fleeing above the trees, one rank broke away to pursue them.

'Come, warriors of the wild!' called ThunderWing impatiently. 'Make haste before you are seen.'

They came, many looking bewildered, some wary. *Kharòn* himself flew with the two brothers as they led them through the trees. He was silent for a long time.

It was a long and tortuous journey, but StrongHand knew every tree in the forest like the back of his talons.

The day was beginning to fade when at last the trees began to thin and clearings appeared on the western edge of the forest. StrongHand, the hunter, paused on an uppermost branch, to watch out for his own winged people above. There wasn't a speck in the sky, so he turned and cautioned them all.

'Here is the Western Mark of our hunting grounds, so I must go no further. Go warily when you leave the shelter of the trees. Our watchers and warriors can see from afar. Go from bush to bush and from rock to rock until you reach the hills of your *eyrie*s. Think kindly of us, and leave us in peace. May the Great Spirit-Wind strengthen your wings and hands! Farewell!'

Some of the warriors now fully trusted him and his captain.

'Farewell, and our thanks!' they called as they sped onward. *Kharòn* waited until the last of his warriors disappeared among the bushes, then turned toward the brothers and bowed low.

'There is greater honour among the *Mawh'eyri* than I ever guessed, but it is no surprise to see it in the sons of Windlord HighSoarer the just. This shall not be forgotten. If the friendship of a *Hrahe* warrior and an outcast is of any worth to you, then you have it.'

'It is of great worth, son of SwiftSoarer,' responded ThunderWing, bowing in his turn. 'To us as sons of Windlord HighSoarer you shall never be considered an outcast. Will you not return one day, perhaps when SwiftSlayer, the proud, has fallen his last fall? There would be room next to our *eyrie* for you, and in great honour.'

But the rebel shook his head.

'No, but I thank you. I have changed my allegiance forever, for the Wild Eagle folk took me up where the *Mawh'eyri* cast me out. But perhaps we may meet at a border of the mountains someday?'

'Let it be so, then, my friend and my foe,' bowed ThunderWing. 'But mark this: I have sworn to become a Windlord in the flight path of my father, or die in the attempt. I also have the love of an eagle-maid to give me wings in this resolve, so I have fellow-feeling in your grief. If I do not fail, in my moon-reign, I shall decree that ambassadors shall be sent to try to make peace between our winged peoples. There is room a-plenty and to spare in the mountains for us all.'

But the Dispossessed sadly shook his head.

'Peace will not come between our winged peoples unless the Tears-of-the-Sun are found and returned.'

ThunderWing stared at him with furrowed brow.

'I have heard some wild tales of these Tears of which you speak, but the Windlords frown upon them and insist that the golden *Khanirhidhi* are the only stones of the past, and were owned by none but the *Mawh'eyri.'*

'You have heard the tale only from the lore of the *Mawh'eyri*. But all the winged people of the wild say otherwise, and I believe them.'

The Dispossessed one then told him briefly of the lore of the Tears-of-the-Sun as told him by his adopted tribe.

He spoke of the ancient times when there was constant war between the *Eyri* tribes. The slaughter and cruelty was so great that even the Sun-spirit (whom they also worshipped) was so grieved that he wept golden tears. These tears were like large drops of liquid gold which fell to the earth. Mother Earth, however, was unsympathetic, so the great drops turned to golden glowing stones. The Wild Eagles gathered them together, ashamed for what they had done, and wove them together in a vine to make a royal necklace. They elected a high king among them who would be the head of a great confederation of eagles. He was to wear the necklace for life as a symbol of peace between them all.

The fathers of the *Mawh'eyri* were often elected rulers of them all at the time when they discovered the land of *Mawha*. They became the proudest and most powerful of all the tribes, and would not surrender the Tears when the high king, WideWing the Brave died. The other wild tribes were furious and tried to wage war on them, but were often too divided to be effective, now the symbol of their confederacy had gone.

This anger lasted through generations of war and raids upon the *Mawh'eri*, who fought them off time and again due to their fotress-like land and greater size, numbers and skill. It was said that the necklace was hidden by the *Mawh'eri* when their land was almost overrun, but their king was slain in battle and told noone of its whereabouts.

After many years of war and endless raids, the more peaceable of the *Mawh'eyri* longed for its return which would make peace among all the *Eyri* tribes. The Wild Eagles were even willing to acknowledge the finder as high king if he returned it, but no one could find it, though searches were made by many ambitious warrior, eager to become a high king. The Wild Eagles continued to accuse them of deliberately witholding the necklace, as well as anger over their overweening pride. If real peace was to be achieved among them all, the Tears-of-the-Sun must be found.

ThunderWing sat stunned for a while as he digested the story. There was surely enough truth in it to warrant a renewed search for the Tears— if they had not been lost.

Finally, he flew over to the branch of his new friend and gave the bow of oath-taking.

'By the wings of the sun, I swear to you that it shall be my life's task to find these stones and return them if I can, for the sake of all our winged folk. But go now in peace. May the Great Spirit-Wind bear you upward.'

Kharòn bowed low again.

'I believe that your goodwill is strong, my friend and worthy foe. But it will be a task well beyond your power alone I think. Farewell! May we meet again in friendship only.'

Then, as he spread his wings as he prepared to follow his brethren, he hesitated.

'It is no treachery if I speak of the plans of some other tribes of the Wild Eagles, our foes. The *Hrah'eyri* are of many tribes and often feud with one another, for the Tears no longer unite us. They unite only in their hatred of the *eyries* of *Mawha*, and will then squabble over the spoils. We, the *Harihrahe* of the west, agreed to test the defenses of the mountains. I say to you, son of HighSoarer: Take heed to your marches upon the Eastern Mountains when the hunting season comes again. I will say no more.'

He turned, spread his wings and was gone.

ThunderWing sat for a while in deep thought until his brother (who had gone hunting) called for him.

Members of the Warband of the Western *Eyries* filled the eastern end of the forest as the weary brothers returned.

'Hail, hunter-warriors of the *Mawh'eyri!*' many sang, waving their wings as they passed. 'Great is your victory this day! Hail, sons of High-Soarer! With greater honour again do you adorn your *eyrie!*'

Some of the older warriors looked on with disapproval, however, chagrined that they had little chance to fight.

'By what right have mere hunters to play our part as warriors?' they murmured. 'It is against all the traditions of battle, and they are not trained for warfare, save HighSoarer's son.'

Nevertheless, none could deny the remarkable feat of the hunters, holding tried and seasoned warriors at bay for so long, with such little loss.

The brothers circled and landed on a low ledge where a large, strong eagle with an air of authority, awaited them, surrounded by his four lieutenants. The hunters gathered on branches behind their leaders, wondering what to expect.

The great eagle before them was well known to the sons of High-Soarer, for he was HardyWing, the eldest son of StrongFeather. A warrior of many seasons, and once having born the title of Swiftest in the Mountains, he was held in high honour. He appeared to be stiff and proud, not having the overt kindliness which endeared his father to many, but he was well known for his sense of honour, justice, and great courage. All the *eyries* of the Western Mountains acknowledged that he was the best choice for Wingleader of the Western Warband.

He wore the finely woven collar of his office which featured the blue *gentian* flower of the Western Mountains among strands of willow, representing the valley dominions.

Two of his officers were his brothers, one of whom was WanderWing, a close friend of ThunderWing. He ruffled his feathers and blinked as he caught his friend's eye. But this was not the moment for familiarities between wingfellows.

'Hail, StrongHand, son of Windlord HighSoarer and master of the *Mawharùn*.' said the captain, adhering strictly to formality and courtesy as the occasion demanded. 'Hail, also, ThunderWing, son of the same Windlord, and former champion among warriors. Do you bring news of the raiders of the *Hrah'eyri*?'

The brothers bowed low, but the younger bowed deferentially towards the older as well, making it clear that he considered his temporary captaincy to be over.

'Hail, Wingleader HardyWing, son of Windlord StrongFeather,' said StrongHand, with awkward courtesy. 'All living enemies have retreated through the forest, having seen your Warband approaching. They do not appear to be returning. My brother and I observed their retreat into the Western Hills beyond our realm.'

Amidst the general rejoicing around him, HardyWing was silent and still, deep in thought. Finally, he spoke.

'It is a thing remarkable indeed, that a small band of hunter-gatherers, untrained in the ways of war, should wreak so much havoc upon a large number of seasoned warriors among our foes. I would not have believed it had not StrongEye the Watcher given report. This shall be spoken of before the Windlord's Council. But he spake also of the valour and leadership of your brother. How is this, as you are master of the hunters?'

StrongHand nodded toward his brother.

'I am but a hunter-gatherer, Wingleader. My brother is greatly skilled in warfare, and I have never doubted his valour. The blood of our father flows strongly in his veins. But this also I have seen: he has become a mighty hunter among us, and is held in high honour by all the *Mawharùn*. The plight of the guards of the Western Marches was severe, and they would have been slaughtered to the last had not my brother led us against the enemy. The skills of the hunt he also employed against them which they did not expect. Who better to lead us than my brother who has won much renown in times past?'

ThunderWing exchanged glances with WanderWing, somewhat surprised. The most StrongHand had said of him when they were returning from the forest was: 'You have grown, little brother!'

Then the old watcher stepped forward.

'All this is true, Wingleader. I, myself saw the manner by which he assailed the captain of the *Hrahe* warriors. He alone slew him and led the others into the hunter's trap. If this he had not attempted, all the guards of the march would have soon lain dead, and your *eyries* would have been assailed.'

There was a rustle of wings and murmur of praise from the Warband as they applauded. The captain turned to ThunderWing.

'ThunderWing, son of HighSoarer, you are high in the favour of my father and my sister, therefore you are held in honour also by myself and this Warband. Nonetheless, this challenges the traditions of war in the annals of the *Mawh'eyri*. None of the hunter-gatherer class have ever taken it upon themselves to assail the enemy unless they pass the trials necessary to become warriors. It is not law that they do so, but this sun-flight's work may cause much speech and debate among the Windlords. You have not surrendered your warrior's mark, yet have joined the ranks of the *Mawharùn*—a thing unheard of. Have you anything to say in this, before I go hence to give report?'

ThunderWing bowed, but looked up proudly into the captain's stern eyes.

'Wingleader, I hold it a great honour to be amongst the *Mawharùn*, who serve the *eyries* sunflight by sunflight, feeding those in need. They have become strong and skilled, although not trained in war. Speak to the Council, I pray, for I have news from the very beaks of the enemy when we saw them to the forest's edge. They spake of an attack in the hunting season to follow, by the eastern tribes upon our Eastern Marches! Maybe others also.'

This also caused a stir among the assembled, but ThunderWing was not finished, opening his wings to gain their attention.

'It was not unknown for my father to challenge the traditions in the call of justice and harmony among *eyries*, though his voice was not always heard. I call his shadow forth again and fly under its wings. If I have gained favour in their eyes, then let the Windlords consider this my counsel which I humbly submit to them. It is not the first time that the hunters have been caught in the raids of the *Hrah'eyri*. So let the *Mawharùn* hunters become more skilled in war, and let it be required also of our warriors to be trained in the ways of the *Mawharùn*. Both skills have brought us the victory at this time. The ambushments of the hunters and the hand-strokes of the warrior must be learned by all. Then we *all* shall be the stronger in the storm-cloud times that are to come.'

Gasps came from older and younger eagles alike, but also much nodding of heads as the sound reasoning sank in. Only the oldest and proudest warriors shook their heads in disapproval.

'We shall be warriors, you and I!' said HoneyCatcher excitedly to HeatherWing, who stood nearby.

The captain glanced at the eldest of his officers but said nothing until the hubbub had died down.

'It is not the first time such a thought has been spoken of, son of HighSoarer. Your hunters have proved themselves and have shown the truth of your counsel. But the Council of the Windlords must consider and give final proclamation on the matter. I shall go thence at the first light of sun-arise. Go now, sons of HighSoarer. You shall hear more from me and my father soon.'

He flapped his wings and rose into the air, hovering, facing the trees. His officers joined him.

'To your *eyries* in peace and honour, hunters of the *Mawh'eyri!* We will await the tending of the wounded. Farewell! May the Great Spirit-Wind bear you to your havens!'

With this dismissal, the hunters slowly drifted away, although it was hard to leave, bathing in the new glory with which they had covered themselves.

The brothers flew down to where the healers were attending the wounded. They were joined by WanderWing, who smote his friend genially over the head with his wing. Younger and more lively than his distinguished brother, WanderWing had often engaged in a friendly rivalry with ThunderWing at the warriors' games of war, or accompanied him on some of his hair-brained exploits.

'What is this, wingfellow? Have you become too high-flying and mighty to acknowledge your friends?'

'High and mighty!' returned ThunderWing in the same spirit. '*You* are now an officer in the Warband of the West. *I* am merely a hunter-gatherer of the despised *Mawharùn*. Why should you wish to seek my fellowship?'

'I prophesy that you shall make it a great honour to hunt among the *Mawharùn* before many moons pass. We poor warriors shall lose favour, alas! But I come not to bandy beak-breath with you, my friend.'

He became serious, and leaned his beak against the side of his friend's head, speaking softly.

'I come on an errand from one who wishes to see you, and soon.'

'SilverSong?? How does she fare? O, that I may see her also!'

'Hush! Yes, it is she. She is well, but in some fear. NightFlyer, the cruel, still haunts her, and hovers near the *eyrie* many times, so she is still in hiding. We brothers are her nest-kin and would attack him rather than let him take her, even if we fell in so doing or were brought before the Stone of Judgement. But come to West *Eyrie* Mountain at sunrest on the morrow, and hover over the Valley of the Western Falls. There are caves that few know of there, where she can take refuge. Perform the Dance of the Forsaken in view of all. We shall know it is you and she will see you also.'

A call was heard, summoning the officers of the Warband to their captain. WanderWing prepared to leave.

'I must away. Farewell, my friend. May the Great Spirit-Wind bear you safely. Remember: The Valley of the Western Falls.... the Dance of the Forsaken.'

He was gone, but there was no time for ThunderWing to think or conjecture about the state of his beloved. StrongHand called to him from behind a small pile of granite rocks.

'There is one who wishes to see you, and soon, my brother!'

With a sense of foreboding at his brother's tone, ThunderWing quickly flew over the rocks. He saw his brother hunched in the posture of grief, while watching a mother-eagle, one of the healers assigned to the Warband, putting ointment on the many wounds of a shattered hunter. ThunderWing knew him at once.

'HareChaser! Father-hunter, son of LongTail! What grief is this?'

The old hunter had never had a happy youth. Born with a bad cast in one eye, he was never considered to be warrior material. His more robust brothers, both warriors, had constantly mocked him. Among the *Mawharùn* he had found acceptance, and a new self-respect. He had been the most eager of hunters, and quite skilled — even though his limited eyesight hampered him a little. He had seen three masters of the hunt come and go, but swore that StrongHand was the best of all. All his fellow-hunters loved him for his eagerness, his geniality and his tales of long ago he used to tell over a kill-fest at sunset.

Now he lay with both wings broken from enemy attacks and his resulting fall. There was a large gash at his chest, from which much blood was lost before the healers could staunch it. Nearly all his tail feathers were gone.

ThunderWing looked enquiringly at the mother-eagle, who sadly shook her head.

The old hunter tried hard to raise his head as ThunderWing approached. His voice crackled and hissed in his effort to speak.

'I know my time is short, ThunderWing, son of HighSoarer. Fool that I was….. I stayed not when you called for us to retreat in the battle, though my failing hearing I curse for this. Now I have paid for it. I go now to Mother-*Eyrie* Earth and will be at peace.'

'…And you shall be laid in honour, for you have sacrificed your life that the *eyrie*s might be safe.'

ThunderWing could feel tears coming, and closed his eyes upon them.

HareChaser coughed, and a little blood trickled from his beak. 'You are destined for great things, my captain. With dying eyes…I can see beyond those whose eyes are whole. Do not forget the lessons you have learned among the hunters, for these shall aid you…… in your greatest hunt yet.'

The effort to speak was getting too much, and the breaths came shorter and more rasping.

'I have said…my farewell to the Master Hunter, and he will…speak to my fellows for me….But I could not depart…without…saying…farewell… to my captain.'

With those words, he laid his head down and breathed his last.

ThunderWing covered the face of the old hunter with his broken wings, then took up the posture of grief next to his brother.

There they stayed for a long while until they were roused by the sounds of joyful military departure above the trees. The Warband had finished burying the dead and tending the wounded. Now they were returning to their *eyries*, singing songs of victory, bearing the tail feathers of the fallen foes as trophies of war.

'Is this the joys of war?' ThunderWing cried out in irritation, 'that we lose our friends while you take the spoils? Have you no heart?'

'Hush!' cautioned StrongHand.

Looking up, the brothers noticed a few hunters in the branches above them, those who had not yet departed. They were also hunched in the grieving posture.

Looking in each other's eyes, they could see unashamed tears spilling over their beaks. They found mutual comfort in that moment, united in grief as in victory.

StrongHand finally stirred and directed that a small cairn of stones be erected over their fallen comrade. It would serve as a reminder of the Battle of the Western Marches, a lay that would be sung at many feasts ever after.

CHAPTER 5

THE FEAST AT THE WESTERN EYRIES

The season was changing. The evenings were chilly. The green feather-robes of the valley forests and the mountainsides were losing their freshness. There were tinges of gold, red, and russet appearing everywhere, lending a mellow quality to the Western Mountains of *Mawha*.

But the solitary eagle flying above took no notice of this.

ThunderWing was in a sober mood. He was pondering the final words of the fallen hunter from the day before — words that haunted him and came back to him in his dreams:

'Do not forget the lessons you have learned among the hunters, for these shall aid you in your greatest hunt yet.'

The sun was sinking in the horizon, casting a rose and gold hue upon the peaks, while the valley that opened up below him was cast in varying shades of grey and dark green. Not far ahead of him, he could just see the foaming white mist of the Western Falls.

This reminded him of the reason for his journey toward the Western *Eyries* and he brightened. His wingbeat and heartbeat both quickened. He gained altitude immediately, catching the dying orange rays of the sun so he would be visible for many miles around.

A secret assignation between two young eagle-lovers was normally frowned upon in the traditions of the *Mawh'eyri*, partly because it was a common practice among the freer-living Wild Eagles. Not even a proclaimed champion, as he had once been, was exempt. Nonetheless, it frequently happened.

It was not unusual, however, for *Eyri* who had lost loved ones or dear friends, to publicly demonstrate their grief at eventide, known as the Dance of the Forsaken. Hence there would have been no remark by other passing eagles, returning to their *eyries*, if they saw a solitary warrior slowly circling, soaring, and dipping near the Western *Eyries*.

He had barely begun the slow and melancholy movements of the dance, when he heard in the distance two piercing greeting calls that he immediately recognized. It was the vigilant WanderWing, son of Strong-Feather and SnatchFeather, his brother.

Nearly all the sons of StrongFeather had taken it upon themselves to keep an unobtrusive watch over SilverSong's hiding-place. Thunder-Wing saw them ahead as dark, small silhouettes in the distance, flying around the western face of *Eyrie* Mountain, the tallest of that range. He gave his own greeting call in return and they disappeared behind the mountain. There were no other eagles in sight.

Then he heard a soft, sighing song ascending from below him.
'Although you dance the Dance Forlorn
Your night gives way to a splendid dawn.'
'SilverSong!'

He abandoned the sky-dance and plummeted toward the forest below in the direction of her voice. She, in turn, emerged from the tree tops near the mountain's foot and flew eagerly upward to meet him. Their talons clasped in mid-flight.

Talons locked, head-to-head and wings spread, they began the courtship ritual, spiraling slowly downward. Well-practiced exponents of the dance would have disapproved had they observed it, for the lovers lacked something of the traditional dignity normally demanded, though it certainly did not lack enthusiasm and passion.

ThunderWing guided her to a stone ledge, hiding them from view from above. There she snuggled up under his encircling wings, head upon his shoulder.

Their voices remained silent but much was understood.

The great eagles do not necessarily need audible speech to convey their thoughts and feelings. Sometimes they have to give voice when their passions are aroused, or there is too much distance to read the signs given by wing, feather, talon, beak, or eyes. In this way, ThunderWing was able to determine that she was well, and so very relieved that he was safe and with her again.

She nibbled at his beak.

'Hail, Windlord ThunderWing, champion and victor in battle. My brothers told me all of yester-sun's exploits.'

He snorted.

'I and my comrade-hunters have proved ourselves in battle, yes, but I am not yet proclaimed Champion nor Windlord, my love. Were it not for my vow to claim you, I wish now for neither also.'

She pulled away from under his wing and looked him in the eyes, concerned.

'Have you now so fallen in your own eyes, my Windlord? Why have you forsaken the ranks of the warriors of the Southern Hills? Why did you join the hunters of the *Mawharùn*?'

'Truly, I did so to keep my hands from NightFlyer's throat! But no. I have seen that there is great honour among the *Mawharùn*, but of a different kind than that known amongst our warriors. My brother was right. But for you, I would be content as a hunter-gatherer only.'

'But do you not know that you are destined for greater greatness?'

'The price of greatness is too great. It is an elusive quarry. If it means I may claim you, I will hunt for it. I am torn in twain, for I desire nothing but to serve the *eyrie*s, and maybe establish my own quiet *eyrie* with you at my side and my chicks surrounding me....'

'And so you shall!'

'Yet I can see also a great need for winds of change among the wing-folk of *Mawha*. We must prepare for war with the *Hrah'eyri*, but also...we must prepare for peace with the *Hrah'eyri*—if we are able.'

He went on to tell her of his dealings with *Kharòn* the rebel and his tragic story. SilverSong was deeply moved, but then her mood changed suddenly. She gave a skip and rose up in half-flight.

'But this is true! I have heard it on the wind!'

Her lover blinked at her, confused, amused, and mystified.

'It is true!' she insisted. She came and nestled under his wing again as she explained.

'Before my mother was laid to rest many seasons gone, she said to me these words: "Sing your songs to the Great Spirit-Wind, but learn to hear his songs also." For many passing seasons I sang my songs, but would not listen for the Voice in the wind. I was young and heedless. But when the sun of love arose in my heart for you, I began to hear it. Yet it was not until I hid in fear of our enemy, and my own voice fell silent, that I truly heard it. This you must learn to hear also!'

"Sing your songs to the Great Spirit-Wind, but learn to hear his songs also."

He gave the eagle equivalent of a smile, ruffling up her golden neck feathers.

'My own mother has spoken in like manner, ever since the fall of my father. It gave her comfort and new strength, but I was heedless also, dreaming of war and a warrior's glory, then of you.'

'Yes! In like manner indeed!' she said with enthusiasm, brushing aside the compliment. 'Your mother aided me in the Northern Mountains as we trained the eaglets in the Windsongs. She spoke also of the Voice on the winds, in the rocks, in the song of the trees and herbs and the lesser birds; in the dance of the deer and the skylark. But I also was heedless and vain, looking only to my appearance and listening for the serenades of the warriors rather than the great Voice. But in hiding, alone and afraid, fearful for your safety, I had no more songs to sing to the wind. In my despair, I began to listen. Then I began to hear the Great Spirit-Wind as he spoke. At first, it was as the songs my mother once sang to me in the nest of my infancy, bidding me to be at peace and to rest. Then his voice became clearer, and he bade me look out upon the world from my cave ……..'

The lovers spoke long into the evening as the light faded around them. But ThunderWing needed his sleep for the next day's hunting, so he bade her a reluctant farewell.

The moon was high, so he accompanied her cautiously to her hiding place again, watching for any night marauders. Then with one long and lingering embrace, he tore himself away and flew silently from tree to tree until he was clear of the valley—and any prying eyes. Silently rising from the forest, he followed the shadows out of the moon's revealing light and pointed his head southward toward his *eyrie*.

He had much to think about on his journey.

The *Mawharùn* had gathered early on the open savannah outside the Southern Hills, ready for a hard day's hunting and gathering. Short-handed as they had been previously, they were now even more hard-pressed, for their numbers had decreased.

Two of them were in the Cave of Healing, having been nearly torn apart in the battle. Others were still nursing lesser wounds.

One, of course, would never return.

The glory of their victory in the battle of the West was fading. They were all in a somber mood.

Word had gone out to all the watchposts to double their numbers in case there was a renewed attack—especially on the Eastern boundary. This meant more mouths for the hunters to feed.

HardBiter, now the eldest of them, took off with their first catch. His assignment was the lower end of the string of watchposts in the Eastern Mountains. The rest prepared to scatter in twos and threes.

But no sooner had HardBiter gained altitude than he swung around and swooped down toward StrongHand and ThunderWing again.

'Master! I see the messenger of the Windlord beyond the Southern Peaks. He summons you from afar. There are two warriors with him also.'

StrongHand grumbled at the delay, but responded promptly.

'Take command, my brother!' he called as he took off. 'Let us hope that the Windlords do not command a feast!'

He returned not long afterward, with something less than his habitually dour demeanor—even surprise.

He found his brother by a stream, just having caught a large trout that had arrived late to the breeding streams. ThunderWing looked up.

'Is it a feast we provide for, my brother?'

'Yes, it is a feast. But we are the guests!'

ThunderWing gave a startled laugh and dropped the fish.

'How is this so?'

It seemed that the sons of Windlord StrongFeather, with their father in support, had advocated strongly before the Windlord Council for ThunderWing's suggestion. StrongEye, the old watcher had gone with them, and gave an animated account of the battle, stressing the role of ThunderWing's captaincy and valour. He expressed his amazement and admiration of the hunters' skills and how they proved useful in battle.

There had been some disapproval at first from the Council, especially from Windlord SwiftSlayer. He was a martinet, and a stickler for tradition and keeping the distinctions of rank. Yet even he was forced to applaud the valour of such untrained fighters, and the superb strategy that had surprised and defeated such seasoned warriors as the *Hrah'eyri*.

StrongFeather invited them all, including the hunters, to a feast at the Western Crags that very night. His own *eyrie* would provide for it. There they would further discuss the possibilities of mixed training for warrior and hunter alike. It was a gesture of thanks to the hunters as well.

'Shall *all* the *eyrierë* be at the feast also?' inquired ThunderWing as he looked doubtfully at his slightly ragged image in the stream. It would take a lot of grooming before he considered himself presentable.

'Of the ladies of the *eyrie*s, I do not know,' replied his brother with a knowing chuckle. 'Much preparation there must be for the Windlords' sake. But many champions may also be there as it is their right.'

This meant NightFlyer would likely attend, so SilverSong would stay away. ThunderWing turned away to hide his disappointment. The feast would be a dreary affair after all.

'But there are more tidings that come with the invitation,' Strong-Hand added with a look of satisfaction. 'Windlord StrongFeather will not wait for the deliberations of the Council....'

Two young warriors appeared suddenly from above and landed next to the brothers, and soon provided further explanation. They were the younger sons of StrongFeather—WanderWing and FarFlight. They bowed in respectful greeting.

'Hail, sons of Windlord HighSoarer!' sang FarFlight, the youngest of the two, enjoying his first season as a full-fledged warrior. 'Hail, Master of the *Mawharùn!* Hail, ThunderWing the renowned!'

'We are sent by our father, Windlord StrongFeather, to aid and assist you in the hunt, this moon-tide,' added WanderWing with a meaningful glance at ThunderWing. 'Our brothers are hunting in the western forests to provide for the feast this sunrest. But our father would have us to learn the skills of the *Mawharùn* that may be also used in war.'

FarFlight almost jumped in surprise and turned to his brother.

'But was it not your wish, rather than our father's? You have always flown alongside ThunderWing in his exploits. You begged father....'

'Very well, very well!' said his senior, irritated at his younger brother's embarrassing candour. Turning toward StrongHand, he explained, 'But my father saw great wisdom in my plea, and sent me with his blessing. He was less happy—and so was I—that my brother should also come with me. But it is said that you are in need of aid, and FarFlight begged us ceaselessly, driving us to screeching point, so my father consented.'

The younger opened his beak in indignation, but StrongHand intervened. There was no time to allow for sibling rivalry.

'Then you are both very welcome, sons of Windlord StrongFeather. There is much to be done, so we are grateful for any aid we can find. I will take the younger son with me, if you, brother, take your wingfellow. I ask that you follow our commands with all gravity and attention, for we have little time and many mouths to feed.'

ThunderWing turned away and coughed when he saw the younger warrior looking so crestfallen. Then, with a glance at WanderWing, he seized the fish and the two of them took flight to their first assignment together.

The sun was low in the sky as all the hunters finally arrived at the great plateau, the Table Rock of Honour at the Western *Eyri*es.

Windlord StrongFeather was renowned for his hospitality, although some of his peers thought it excessive for one of his rank. In spite of the fact that he lost his beloved nest-mate many seasons ago, he persevered, and there were plenty of willing hands to help. The Western *Eyries* were a closely knit and supportive community, and the Windlord and his family at the Western Crags were held in great affection as well as high honour.

The folk of the Western *Eyries* waited eagerly, lining all the surrounding stone ledges that looked down on the great Table-Rock of Honour.

Thus, the guests arrived to a thunderous greeting of flapping, foot-stomping and cries of 'Hail, noble hunters!' and many other accolades.

The folk of the Western mountains knew the significance of the hunter's victory. If not for their stand, many of the Western *Eyries* would have been raided and much of their winter storage taken, perhaps some of the eggs, the eaglets and young *eyrierë* captured and carried away as slaves when the Wild Eagles retreated. Many of the young warriors of the Warband were off at the *Mawh'ree* tournaments in the distant Southern Hills at the time, and any that remained would have been taken by surprise, overwhelmed, and killed. The mother eagles would have fought fiercely for their *eyries* as well, but were no match for strong, war-hardened pirates of the skies. Some would have paid the ultimate price.

The hunters, quite overwhelmed, were conducted to a place of high honour upon the great Table-Rock itself. It had been decorated with the last of the autumn flowers, coloured leaves, and aromatic herbs. Flat rocks were arranged upon the Table-Rock with small nests of feathers and aromatic leaves placed by them for each honoured guest to sit upon. Some fireflies had been caught and bound to the ends of branches, set upright around the Table-Rock and on every ledge to provide festive lights. There were signs of festivity everywhere as all the local folk wore flowers and twined leaves around their necks.

StrongHand could detect the smell of food being prepared. He began to salivate, for it had been an exceptionally busy day, with little rest to feed himself. His young protégé had acquitted himself well, although they lost a few field mice due to his youthful impetuosity. He listened more carefully after these mistakes, and his mentor had been remarkably patient.

ThunderWing and his friend fared better in their hunt, and more profitably. WanderWing had a natural aptitude for hunting, and quickly learned many of the tricks of ambush and pounce. On their arrival at the Table-Rock, WanderWing waved farewell to his friend and joined his family upon their own shelf overlooking the guests.

Finally, the Windlords and champions arrived to the usual acclaim. They were given comfortable and well-feathered ledges of their own, overlooking the whole proceedings. These also had a small cave or inset to doze in, if required. One ledge was strangely left vacant, and it was concluded that one guest was absent or very late. Perhaps one of the *eyrie*-chiefs from the other mountains was expected, for all other guests were accounted for—even NightFlyer the Proud.

The latter looked even more morose than usual. The deep humiliation he had suffered at the foot of the great peak had been a great blow to him. He had lost some of the swagger he had displayed after acquiring the title of *Mawharhipi*. He could barely bring himself to look at the guests of honour, seated comfortably upon the great Table-Rock. He was nauseated with all the wonder and acclaim heaped upon the hunters, and had been an outspoken critic of 'mere hunters interfering in warrior's affairs.'

Some of his ambitious peers, feeling threatened by a perceived encroachment by mere hunters on their high calling, joined NightFlyer in his criticism. The large majority disagreed, however. It was whispered that had it not been for SilverSong (assuming that she would be present) NightFlyer would have declined his invitation to the feast.

The last to arrive was the host himself, Windlord StrongFeather, Father-of-Many, the well-beloved. Thunderous applause echoed around the valley as he took his place among his own numerous *eyrie* folk. He looked tired but pleased that all preparations had so far gone well. He looked over to where his daughters stood, ready to serve, and noticed one missing. He bowed his head for a moment and looked darkly across the Table-Rock at NightFlyer. The latter appeared to take no notice. He too was searching among the Windlord's daughters to find the missing one.

The host then arose, stepped to the end of his *eyrie*'s ledge and opened his great wings to catch everyone's attention.

'Hail and welcome, good guests,' his deep, slow voice boomed, echoing down the valley. 'Hail and welcome, all Windlords and Champions of the *Mawh'eyri*. Hail, and welcome all warriors, especially all hunters of the *Mawharùn*. It is for this reason that we call you all together to feast with us: To honour your valour and skill, not only in the Battle of the Western Marches (a lay that shall forever be sung by minstrels of the *Mawh'eyri)* but also for your faithful and humble service to all *eyries* of the *Mawh'eyri*. Hail, welcome, and my thanks I give to my kinsfolk and neighbours who have laboured much to bring this feast to pass.'

StrongHand fidgeted and groaned within himself, feeling his stomach contract and groan as well. It seemed that it would be a long speech, possibly followed by GoldSinger's song and the "Anthem of the Mountains" sung by all, followed by a recital of the history of *Mawha*. The smell of well-prepared food was tormenting him. He would gladly forgo all the acclaim of all the champions that ever lived in the mountains if only he could fill his stomach.

Then the speech took an unexpected turn. The Windlord looked directly at StrongHand and his brother beside him.

'I will now call upon the chief messenger of the Council of Windlords to announce a decree that the Council have decided upon this very sunflight.'

The chief messenger, a very familiar, important, and impressive-looking bird with a penetrating voice, stood forward from his ledge, spreading one wing in the manner of an orator.

'Hear me, wingfolk of the *Mawh'eyri*! The Windlords of the Council …' he announced in measured terms, '….After much deliberation have decided and decreed this decree: That for unusual valour in battle against overwhelming numbers, for cunning and skill in captaincy in outwitting the accursed *Hrah'eyri,* that especial honour and privilege be bestowed upon both captain and master of the *Mawharùn*.'

He paused and folded his wing as the effect of his announcement sank in. Nearly every breath was held. NightFlyer suddenly sprang to his feet, startled, wondering what was coming next.

The orator continued, addressing the guests on the great Table-Rock.

'To the Master of hunter-gatherers, StrongHand, son of HighSoarer the honoured fallen, shall be given command at each change of the moon, of at least two warriors who are willing and able to be trained in the skills of the hunt known only to the hunter-gatherers of the *Mawharùn*. Upon the same son of HighSoarer there shall be bestowed the rank of Warrior-captain, that all warriors may respect his commands and his person. The Council has spoken.'

Stunned and forgetful of his appetite, StrongHand arose and bowed in gratitude toward the assembled Windlords, who gravely nodded in return. A whistling and shuffling of approval arose from the gallery. NightFlyer shook his head in strong disapproval. After a few moments, the messenger silenced the gallery by spreading his wings for attention.

'Now to the captain of the hunters, the warrior-hunter who showed great and exceptional valour alone in battle, and cunning skill in leadership, to surprise and repel the enemy, upon ThunderWing, son of HighSoarer the renowned, shall this be bestowed: As a former champion and tried warrior, he shall be raised once more, and in perpetuity, to the rank of champion, in accordance with the traditions of the *Mawh'eyri* of the past…'

'What is this? It is outrage!' interrupted NightFlyer in an unmannerly outburst. He could not contain himself any longer.

He was quickly silenced as two of the host's sons flew across and stood at each side of him, eyeing him menacingly. The crowd was also on the verge of bursting into loud approval and applause, but the messenger, looking annoyed at being interrupted, silenced them sternly and continued.

'….In accordance with the traditions of the past, where a warrior showing unusual valour in battle was awarded the rank of Champion in Perpetuity. Of such was WarWing, son of WeatherWing the First, who was father and High King of our folk.'

He looked directly, almost paternally at ThunderWing, who was struck dumb with astonishment.

'Son of HighSoarer the renowned, it is not fit for a Champion Perpetual to be absent from his throne. Behold! It awaits you.'

He indicated the vacant ledge.

'It is tradition also that two other champions or former champions accompany you to your throne. Are there two such champions among us?'

Immediately, HardyWing, captain of the Warband of the West, left his place among the folk of the Western Crags, and flew across to stand by ThunderWing, who was trembling by this time.

Then came FastFlyer, son of StrongFoot. He was a perpetual champion for many seasons, and had been a close friend of ThunderWing's father. He bowed before ThunderWing and said, 'Come, son of High-Soarer! Take your place.'

ThunderWing looked helplessly over his shoulder at his comrades, but they waved their wings and stomped their feet, saying 'Go! Go! Good captain, Champion Perpetual, take your place!'

He had no choice, embarrassed as he was. He flew across to the vacant, decorated ledge, with champions at each side. HardyWing picked up the specially-twined crown of leaves that awaited ThunderWing and placed it on the head of the new champion.

The crowd went wild, crying, 'Hail, ThunderWing, Champion Perpetual!'

Windlord StrongFeather then stood forward.

'Hail, captain of the warrior-hunters of the *Mawharùn*. Hail, Champion in Perpetuity! This is our thanks for preserving us from our enemies. Now, let us feast!'

StrongHand let out a long sigh of satisfaction, as the ladies of the Western *Eyries* brought around all manner of foods and delicacies, wrapped in aromatic leaves and bound with twine.

The hum and murmur of mealtime conversation had only just begun when the festive mood was suddenly shattered by a second outburst from NightFlyer.

He had refused all food, sitting and brooding in the back of his alcove ever since the announcement of ThunderWing's elevation. He would have stayed there all evening had not someone from the gallery shouted, 'Hail, ThunderWing, son of HighSoarer, a champion of champions!'

It was the last straw. He exploded with rage.

'I have borne enough!' he shouted.

This time, he could not be silenced by the sons of StrongFeather. He jumped onto the edge of his alcove, preparing to take flight. At most times he was impressive to look at. In his towering anger, wings spread and eyes blazing, he looked magnificent.

'Where are the proud traditions of the *Mawh'eyri?* Why do we elevate mere hunter-gatherers to our proud ranks—*in perpetuity*—and cast the crest and honour of champions into dust? I will not be part of this!'

'Then be silent and be gone! Your rival has truly earned his honours, little chirping eaglet!'

The crowd gasped. It was not the host who had made such a blighting rebuke.

Windlord SwiftSlayer stood forth, his own aging feathers extended in proud wrath. The likeness between father and son was strongly marked.

'*Mawharhipi* you may be,' the father remarked with contempt, 'but this manner and behaviour you display becomes not one of our *eyrie* and blood! You bring us shame! Go forth and earn your own honour for perpetuity, for you have none in my eyes!'

All the guests stared in stunned silence at the father, then at the son. StrongFeather leaned over to his eldest son and murmured:

'Never has Windlord SwiftSlayer given acclaim to his son, greatly though he has striven for it. Theirs is an *eyrie* of many storms.'

NightFlyer, naturally, was beside himself with fury and mortification.

'Very well …. *Father!*' he cried, spitting out the last word. 'If you shame me before all and cast me forth, then my own *eyrie* shall I build in the mountains! Also, I shall win a name and glory that shall last *in perpetuity* when you have long fallen from your perch, a forgotten dotard! Farewell!'

He stormed off into the darkening skies with a furious flurry of wings, scattering a troop of dancing swallows that had been summoned to entertain the guests with their aerial acrobatics. Windlord SwiftSlayer returned to his own feasting, apparently unconcerned.

After a while, the generally festive mood began to return again. The folk of the Western *Eyrie*s were not going to let a family fight spoil their night, although the exchange would be talked of for many moons. They were glad to see the arrogant young *eyrion* go. The clouds cleared, and the moon appeared to add its gracious light to the feast.

GoldSinger, eldest daughter of the host, stepped forward to the edge of her *eyrie*-ledge with a few younger *eyrierë* singers in attendance. She began to sing for the entertainment of her guests, beginning with well-known tunes and ballads. She added a new stanza to a song of past battles, which extolled the skill and valour of the *Mawharùn,* to thunderous applause.

Even StrongHand could appreciate it, now that his stomach was satiated. The fermented mountain-berry was passed around freely and the atmosphere became relaxed and merry again.

ThunderWing began to enjoy himself and his special status. He sighed with relief when he saw his rival depart in disgrace, but he also felt a strange regret.

'The cost of greatness is truly great,' he said softly, shaking his head.

'But you have paid for it, my lord,' said a soft, musical voice behind him.

All thoughts of his rival vanished before the gladness that flooded his soul. He spun around and peered into the shadows of the alcove behind him. A soft, graceful shadow moved toward him.

'SilverSong!' he whispered, both alarmed and delighted. 'Do you find haven under our enemy's very beak?'

'Where could I find a safer haven than this?' she answered, coquetting flirtatiously around him. 'I am in the shadow of my champion.'

She was groomed to look her best, once again. Her feathers were oiled, shining and garnished as one who seeks a mate. She was at her most alluring.

'SilverSong, my love!' he gasped again, as the implication of her last words hit him. 'Will you find haven under my wing, then? Forever?'

'I have waited long to hear those words, my champion.'

She bowed before him, then nestled her head against his pounding breast. Beak touched beak and their talons intertwined.

'I will be your nest-mate forever,' she whispered. 'I now release you from your vow, for you are Champion Perpetual, and need not a Wind-lord's crown. Let us seek my father's blessing this very sunrest.'

Without further ado, the lovers took wing and flew over to the well-feathered shelf of the host of the feast.

It wasn't long before the guests noticed a new presence.

'SilverSong! SilverSong the Fair returns to her *eyrie*!'

ThunderWing was further delighted to see that his mother had journeyed all the way from the Northern Mountains for the occasion, and was talking to their host. She showed no surprise to see SilverSong snuggling close to his side.

'Hail, my son. I see you have swept all before you. Hail also, Silver-Song the Fair. I see you have made your own conquest. You have well heeded my counsel.'

ThunderWing wondered how many more surprises awaited him that night. His beak touched her talon.

'Hail, mother of our *eyrie*, beloved of the fallen. What more could be needed than your presence here at this joyous season? Your coming is timely indeed!'

He turned to his host and bowed deeply again.

'Hail, Windlord StrongFeather, father of my beloved. I thank you greatly for the honours you have bestowed upon me. But there is one greater boon yet that I crave: I come to seek your blessing, that our *eyries* may be joined in joyfulness and that my wings of protection may be spread over your daughter.'

'Hail, son of HighSoarer and Champion Perpetual,' said the Windlord gravely, though exchanging droll glances with LightWind. 'I gladly surrender my daughter to you, for she encumbers my nest grievously. It is a season long overdue for her to build her own.'

'Father!' SilverSong cried reproachfully, with laughter in her fluttering wings. 'But at last I am safe and have no need to hide.'

'Yet we must be wary still, my daughter,' replied her father, soberly. 'For NightFlyer is fey and fell in this mood. He is as the whirlwinds of the plains. Who can tell what he may do? But let us rejoice this sunrest, and forget our fears. Yes, you are under safe wings, now. This is a season of gladness!'

But at that moment, the Windlord's messenger flew in with one of his younger messengers. They both looked sad.

'We may rejoice and forget our fears for a season, Windlord,' said the older messenger. 'But often dark rain follows the sun's shining.'

Seeing the messenger's arrival, Windlords WeatherWing and Storm-Rider flew in to hear the news.

'Hail, WindCrier! Speak! What tidings do you bring?'

WindCrier bowed to his superiors and spoke, a little breathlessly, for he had flown far and fast.

'Hail, Windlords. Hail, folk of the Western *Eyries*. Grievous news I bring from the watchers at Windlords' Crag. This early sunflight...Far-Flyer, son of StrongWing...attempted the Great Summit of *Mawharikhan*. As the sun came close to sunrest, he encountered...the Raven-Winds, who buffeted him furiously. He fell from the sky, down among the Rocks of Death below. We have raised a cairn upon his remains at the mountain's foot.'

'FarFlyer!' cried ThunderWing, distressed. 'I knew him well! He was a mighty warrior and a worthy wingfellow. He would have become Swiftest in the Mountains, had not NightFlyer nosed him out in the race, so it is said.'

Silence reigned for the next few moments. ThunderWing assumed the grieving position.

The host turned to the senior messenger.

'Request the Windlords present that they assemble at my alcove here, for this is a matter for Council.'

The messenger bowed and prepared to take flight, pausing only to say, 'I go, Windlord, but not all the great ones are present at this feast. We cannot make proclamation until all hear and the greater number are of one mind.'

He was always pedantic concerning tradition and protocol.

'Yet all who can be gathered tonight have need of this news, and counsel that LightWind, lady of the eagles brings,' answered Strong-Feather a little impatiently. 'Go!'

There was further solemn silence as they awaited the gathering of the Council.

Three other Windlords soon joined them: SwiftSlayer the Proud, StrongWing the Brave and WindStream the Strong. Others were in the far Eastern Mountains or the Southern Hills and could not come to the feast.

SwiftSlayer looked suspiciously at the great lady standing in their midst.

'Is this right that we suffer the presence of a mere *eyreira* at a counsel of Windlords?'

He had never forgiven her for rejecting his advances in their youth.

StrongFeather answered in stern tones:

'Windlord, you forget our history and the much-needed counsel of the Mother *Eyreira* of the *Mawh'eyri* of old. I have summoned Light-Wind Lady of the Fallen, as guest, and desire her counsel, for she hears the voice of the Great Wind.'

SwiftSlayer bowed stiffly and stood proudly aloof from further discussion.

The Windlords, including LightWind, then gathered in a circle and began to hum a hymn to the Great Wind-Spirit, acknowledging their need for wisdom in counsel. This was followed by a thoughtful silence as a fresh breeze wafted by, ruffling the multicoloured feathers and leaves adorning the ledge. The messengers joined them, taking their traditional stance outside the circle, ready to carry out instructions.

The newly betrothed couple stood back from the circle at first, preparing to leave, but StrongFeather motioned them to join them as invited guests to the Council.

The young messenger was called forth to repeat his news. It was greeted with shocked silence.

'So, the Raven-Winds are upon us!' said StormRider, looking grim. 'They become proud and insolent, thinking that they possess the Central Mountains for themselves. They assailed us at Windlord's Crag only two moons gone, but we fled, for they are too strong for us. Will they fill all the mountains of *Mawha*?'

'Has the White Warrior-Storm banished one enemy only to make way for many worse?' wondered WeatherWing.

'But will not the Great Spirit-Wind send a White Warrior again to cleanse the mountains?'

'At our song, he may do so, but who can tell?'

At that point of the debate, LightWind came forward.

'Windlords, hear me if you will.'

'Speak, lady of HighSoarer' said WeatherWing. 'You have sung many songs in the Northern Mountains to the Great Spirit-Wind. Have you good counsel in this?'

'Windlord WeatherWing, I have sung many. But now I begin to hear his voice in return. When my beloved was taken from me by the Black Storm, I sang dirges and songs of grief. But then I fell silent, wearied in my sorrow, and it was then that I began to hear the Voice—*his* songs. Songs of consolation I could hear in the wind, that echoed within my breast. They gave me strength to live again and raise my sons as my beloved would have them raised. These songs also gave me the wings to teach many young folk the ways of the Windsongs. I have also heard songs of good counsel, of which….' she bowed toward SilverSong before continuing. '….of which I shared with one whom I may now call my daughter. Do you seek counsel of the Great Wind-Spirit himself? He will give it if we will learn to hear him.'

"Do you seek counsel of the Great Wind-Spirit himself? He will give it if we will learn to hear him."

There was silence from the rest as they digested this new information. ThunderWing stared at his betrothed. She had spoken of these things to him before. She nodded in corroboration.

Finally, WeatherWing stirred and spoke his thoughts aloud.

'If there was one who could hear the voice of the Great Spirit-Wind, can this still aid us in our present need? The Raven-Winds have shown themselves to be cunning and wary. They may hide from the face of the Warrior-Storm when they hear the rumour of his coming. Can we not draw them forth far from their lair as we did for the Black Storm?'

He bowed toward ThunderWing as he said this. But Windlord WindStream shook his head.

'It is not possible. Some of our *Eyreirë* have such skill to hear songs of the Great Wind. But it is not right that we endanger them in such a venture.'

'You speak true, Windlord,' replied WeatherWing, becoming almost prophetic, 'but I speak of a tried warrior, skilled in the chase, fleet of wing and high of heart, who is also skilled to hear the songs of the Great Spirit-Wind.'

"I speak of a tried warrior, skilled in the chase, fleet of wing and high of heart, who is also skilled to hear the songs of the Great Spirit-Wind."

SilverSong became alarmed at the direction that WeatherWing's discourse was taking. She flung her wings protectively around her betrothed.

'No! Windlord, say not so, I beg of you! I do not wish to lose my nest-mate only in our first nesting season!'

'Be at peace, my daughter,' said her father, both placating and stern. 'You must not speak so at Council. Nothing is decided in this. Yet there are other warriors who would surely be willing to risk all for the sake of the *eyries* of *Mawha.*'

'Alas, my Windlord!' said LightWind regretfully. 'Most warriors seek only fame and feats of war, and they will not stay to hear the songs of the Great Spirit-Wind.'

"Most warriors seek only fame and feats of war, and they will not stay to hear the songs of the Great Spirit-Wind."

'Well, we must think further on these things, when all the Council is gathered,' answered StrongFeather, preparing to close the discussion. 'The season of storms will be upon us not many moons hence, and the mountains will clothe themselves in the cold, white feather-down. The evil winds will seek their caves and hide from the wrath of the storms until the season of the moulting waters, and the blossoms and green feathers appear. But let us be at peace, forget our fears, and enjoy the feast as we can. Let us conclude our counsels until we all meet at Windlord's Crag at the fullness of the moon.'

They all agreed, and returned to their own feasts. StrongFeather turned to the betrothed couple and visibly brightened.

'And now, my children, I see that your hearts are already entwined as nest-mates. "Even in the midst of grief, joy may blossom still," as the ancient seer once said. Why should you delay? Come! Take the vows before the Great Spirit-Wind and sing for his blessing also. Thus my own joy shall be the greater. There is room and to spare among the Western *Eyries* to begin your own nest if you desire, and my wingfolk will make a warm *eyrie*-bed for you this very sunrest. What say you?'

CHAPTER 6

THE MIDDLE MOUNTAINS REBUILT

The full moon was glowing faintly above once again and the morning was chilly when ThunderWing arose. He stretched, shook the sleep out of his head and surveyed the valley below.

It was a strange feeling, having his own *eyrie* in a different part of the mountains. He looked back at his lady, still sleeping contentedly in a sheltered, well-feathered nook, away from the elements.

His dreams had come true. He had his desire. What more could an *eyrion* ask for?

And yet, he felt a kind of restlessness within him.

Long flights with his lady through the valleys, splashing through the waterfalls, bathing in the mountain pools, and collecting the late herbs and flowers for their nest were all very well for a while. They had been like wingfellows and eaglets again, as in times past.

Then again, they were also lovers.

Those had been memorable moments. What more could an *eyrion* ask for?

Just this: He longed to be productive again. He missed his comrades in the hunt. He could see a few dark specks in the distance and below, darting here and there, disappearing among the colouring trees as they stalked and pounced. By their style and movement, it could very well be RatSnatcher and HoneyCatcher working together, as they often did. Others appeared and disappeared in a similar manner.

He felt a touch on his shoulder and the now familiar warmth of his nest-mate's body upon his back.

'Hail, my champion of the nest. Of what are you thinking, my love?'

'Hail, lady of our *eyrie*. I think....I wish...... No, I am content.'

'Speak! I know you too well to allow you to remain silent.'

He took a breath and looked out over the valley again.

'I am torn in two, SilverSong, my fair. I have all that I desire in you, and yet ..... I wish also to be among the *Mawharùn* once again, serving the *eyrie*s, speaking to our folk, hearing of their ventures, their joys and their sorrows, gathering news.'

He looked her full in the face, smoothing a ruffled feather on her head with his wing.

'But until I know that you are fully safe, I cannot leave you. I have sworn before the Great Spirit-Wind that I would protect you. What else can I do?'

SilverSong's wings of laughter came into play.

'If that is your wish, then let us hunt together. I shall become one of the *Mawharùn* also.'

ThunderWing blinked. The idea had never occurred to him. He had never thought of her as one of the humble hunters.

So it was that StrongHand, busy instructing two young warriors in the skill of stalking, looked up in surprise to see both his brother and his lady approaching.

'Hail, ThunderWing, my brother! Hail, SilverSong, lady of ThunderWing! What brings you here? Do you come to ask for extra provision in the season of the White Down, or do you come as a greeting only?'

The newlyweds first exchanged bows with the two warriors. These suddenly became very shy in the presence of a renowned champion and his lady. ThunderWing then bowed deeply before his amused and bemused brother.

'Hail, son of Windlord HighSoarer!' he sang with all the grand flourish and formality due to a great Windlord. 'Hail, master of the hunt, victor in battle, captain of hunter-warriors, honoured of the Western *Eyrie*s and champion of the feasts of Table-Rock.'

He flew to his brother's perch and landed with a thump, nearly causing his sibling to lose his balance.

'Where are your hunting skills, little brother?' growled the elder, affably. 'Have you not yet learned to perch with care that you do not startle your prey?'

'I have never caught you as my prey as yet, my brother, but tell me: Are you still short of hunters? Here are two that would join you in your tasks, if you will. But we must hunt together.'

The master of the hunt opened his eyes wider yet again, and looked them over.

'What is this? Are you wearied of greatness and glory, O Champion Perpetual? Well, I do not deny that the need for your aid is great, for much store is still needed for the season of the White Down and for the storms. The tree-feathers colour and moult early. But what of your lady?'

He turned and faced SilverSong, cocking his head in mild but polite skepticism.

'Will you endure the toil, the soil, the gore of the hunt and the gather, O Windlord's daughter?'

'Hail, Hunter-Master,' she replied with laughing wings, looking him boldly in the eye. 'All daughters of the Western *Eyries* are called to hunt and gather for themselves when they first gain their flight. But I have my lord to instruct me in the finer arts of the hunt. Do not fear that I shall disgrace you.'

'I shall vouch for her also,' added ThunderWing light-heartedly. 'She is swift of wing and deft of hand and beak. We played together in our childhood, and I taught her the skill of stone-catching. Mark this, brother!'

He flew up and snatched a loose stone from the top of a large boulder nearby. He flung the stone into the air in the direction of his lady. She crouched, watching it's flight, then shot out as quick as a flash and caught it neatly in her beak before it hit the ground.

StrongHand laughed and relaxed his gruff formality.

'Ha! That was well done! You are a seasoned hunter, I see. Times have changed indeed, *eyrie*-sister, for once it was a disgrace for a great *eyreira* to hunt and gather for any but her own *eyrie*. Our comrades will be glad to see you both, and to know that our captain is in our midst once more. Let us begin.'

The *Mawharùn* were delighted at the news. They were buoyed once again by the new status they had gained since the battle, and the folk of the Western *Eyries* especially welcomed them with acclaim when they brought the winter store of food.

StoneBeak was an old former warrior who still bore the scars of both old and recent battles. He was in the forefront of the Battle of the Western Marches, close behind ThunderWing. He lost one eye, but thought it a small price to pay. He landed in front of his fellow-hunters with a thump, crowing like a rooster.

'Our captain returns to the hunt!'

'…. And with his lady!' added HoneyCatcher, clapping her wings in excitement. 'Soon more champions, and even Windlords will join our ranks.'

RatSnatcher, her hunting-partner, was skeptical. He spat out a small bone from his prey.

'It is a one moon's marvel only, say I. When the season of storms passes and we hunt again, the *eyrie*-folk will forget our exploits and disregard us as before. The traditions and stiff-necked prejudice of the *Mawh'eyri* do not change with the winds.'

'But you spake the same doubt when our captain was raised to the ledge of Champion Perpetual,' his hunting partner pointed out scornfully. 'Now he has returned to us in spite of your gain-saying.'

'It is true, but our captain is a rare one among the great,' he mumbled defensively.

'And so too is his lady, it seems,' added StoneBeak, with a hissing laugh. 'I have seen her searching for the great worms among the muddy waters of the *Mawharîsh*, caring nothing for her fair looks.'

HoneyCatcher sighed wistfully.

'I would give a season's mountain-berries to possess her trimness and the gold upon her breast feathers.'

Meanwhile, the celebrities under discussion were washing the soil of the day's toil off their feathers in a mountain stream, preparing to join

StrongHand at his *eyrie*. The older brother complained that his nest was becoming unbearably cold at night since his family had deserted him for other *eyrie*s. His mother had returned to the Northern Mountains to join the Windsong feasts before the season ended.

'Why do you not establish your own *eyrie*, and find your own nest-mate, brother-hunter?' demanded SilverSong with an insouciant brush of her wing.

StrongHand merely grunted and said nothing.

'The captain of the *Mawharùn* has no time for such things,' explained his brother with mock respect. 'But it also means he must share his meat. He would find that hard to bear.'

The ensuing discussion was interrupted by a shrill calling-song of greeting from afar. It was the voice of one of the younger messengers of the Windlords, SwiftWing, son of FarCry, summoning them to an urgent meeting. They took wing immediately.

'Hail, son of FarCry, messenger of the Council! What news do you bring?' inquired ThunderWing, as they all met him in mid-flight.

'Hail, son of HighSoarer the renowned, and Champion Perpetual! Hail *eyrie*-lady and Hunt-Master! Let us alight, for I have journeyed far and must rest.'

Once he gained his breath, the young messenger fixed them with a haunted look, and spoke in tones of urgency.

'I bring grave news and a decree from the great ones: No more attempts are permitted upon the peak of *Mawharikhan,* for the present. So it is decreed by the Council. For two more warriors have tried and fallen by the hands of the terror of the Middle Mountains, the Raven-Winds. One *eyrion* will rise no more, but the other has been carried to the Caves of Healing.'

His hearers were shocked, but wondered if this warranted sending messengers everywhere. SwiftWing took breath and continued.

'And now the evil winds are in very great wrath. They bring terrible vengeance upon those whose lands they invade, perceiving that our wingfolk have sent the hapless warriors to invade their mountain. They have carried their spite into the very *eyrie*s of the Middle Mountains also! Grievous ruin have they brought to the centremost *eyrie*s, and much suffering. The Wild Eagles could scarce have done worse. None but the two warriors have fallen, for the *eyrie*-folk fled at the rumour of the coming of the terror as they did before. But some of our egglings have fallen to their death—broken on the rocks below! That alone is hard to bear, and their mothers are inconsolable. Many nests must be rebuilt before the season of storms comes. My father's *eyrie* is one of them. Some of our folk must seek refuge elsewhere, and some fear to return. All messengers are sent to seek aid of the folk of the outer mountains.'

'There is room in our *eyrie* in the West for your own *eyrie*-kin, SwiftWing,' said ThunderWing promptly. SilverSong nodded. The messenger bowed.

'I am honoured indeed, Champion Perpetual, and I thank you.'

'Have you spoken to my father, the Windlord?' SilverSong asked quickly. 'Many *eyrie*s of the western folk will shelter many.'

'Aye, also in the East,' supplied StrongHand. 'What of the stores of food for the dark season? Are they safe?'

The messenger bent his head and shook it in frustration.

'This is the grief of it. Much had been gathered and spread upon the rocks in preparation for long-keeping with salted rock and herb. All is lost but for the little we could retrieve!'

StrongHand groaned. This meant more work for the hunters.

'We will do what we can, there is no doubt,' said ThunderWing. He then spread his wings and spoke decisively.

'Yet aid we will find in the Southern Hills! We must call upon the warriors to leave their games of war, join in the hunt, and help to rebuild.'

The messenger looked up, blinking with surprise. It had not been thought of before. StrongHand glanced at his brother with renewed respect.

'That would be aid unlooked for and welcome indeed! Warriors whose *eyrie*s are touched by the ruin will surely come, but few others— so I think—unless the Windlord Council command them. But will the Council consent to this?'

The messenger hesitated before he answered.

'Some will do so, for their *eyrie*s have been in the path of the wrath of the Raven-Winds. Windlord StrongFeather has pledged his aid.'

He bowed respectfully toward SilverSong as he said this, but then sighed and looked away.

'I fear to say too much, but I do not think all will give support in united voice. Tradition is still too strong for some to allow warriors to demean themselves as hunters and nest-builders, even in the time of urgent need.'

ThunderWing stamped his feet and ruffled his feathers restlessly.

'The seers speak the truth,' he fumed. 'There is a need for winds of change to blow through the mountains of *Mawha*! Very well! If the Windlord Council will not move, united for the sake of our *eyries*, then maybe willing warriors will do so. Have messengers been sent to the Southern Hills?'

'None as yet, lord champion. I must rest awhile, then go thence. But my heart is with my stricken folk in the Middle Mountains, alas!'

'Then take my counsel: Rest well and return to your *eyrie*! *I* shall bring the tidings in your stead.'

He took wing and landed on a rock nearby. SilverSong immediately joined him. A fresh breeze arose and ruffled their feathers.

'I will take myself to the Southern Hills,' he declared in a voice of thunder, 'where the warriors play their games and heap endless and empty honours upon themselves for the sake of their vanity! Of such, once was I. Maybe they shall listen to the call of ThunderWing, Champion Perpetual, son of HighSoarer the Warrior of Warriors! Are you with me, my love?'

'To the ends of the world!'

'Then there is hope for a good following, if our voice is united. Farewell messenger of the Council, bring your kin to our *eyrie* as soon as you may. May the Great Spirit-Wind give you strength in your mission! I will join your *eyries* this sunrest with whomever I can summon. Brother, I fear you must endure another cold sunrest.'

'No I shall not, for I shall summon the *Mawharùn* to the Middle Mountain *eyries* with whatever we can bring along the way. Go, my brother, with the Great Wind-Spirit under your wings!'

They were about to depart on their respective missions, when ThunderWing checked himself mid-flight and called again to the grateful messenger, preparing to make his return flight.

'Stay, son of FarCry! Tell me! Who were the two warriors that fell at *Mawharikhan?*'

'The fallen one who shall not rise again is FarFlight, son of CloudWing.'

'A mighty warrior, although I knew him but little. I grieve his loss and for that of his *eyrie*. And the other?'

The messenger hesitated again, more for dramatic effect than reluctance.

'It is NightFlyer, son of Windlord SwiftSlayer!'

'NightFlyer??'

'The same!' The messenger almost gloated. 'The Raven-Winds knew him and buffeted him sorely, that he dared to trespass again upon the mountain they claim as their own. He has lost many feathers and much blood, but he will live.'

ThunderWing and his nest-mate stared at each other in astonishment. But only briefly. There was little time for wonder and conjecture in the face of the crisis at the Middle Mountain *eyries*. So bidding farewell, they sped southward.

'The winds of change have already begun to blow,' the young messenger remarked with youthful wisdom to StrongHand before he left. 'They blow southward.'

It all happened a little more quickly than ThunderWing expected.

WideFeather, son of WideWing, was the presiding Windlord over the *Mawh'ree* during that change of the moon. He was gathered together with a group of senior warriors and champions at the Great Cave—something like the administrative centre of the tournaments, where names and events were scratched on the clean, smooth walls. He looked up in surprise when ThunderWing and his lady alighted at the entrance.

Cutting short all ceremony, ThunderWing rapidly gave a brief and forceful report of the emergency in the Middle Mountains. He would have begged permission to address the assembly of warriors below, but there was no need.

'My *eyrie*! My Nest-Mate! My children!' exclaimed WideFeather. Turning to his assistants, he cancelled all the tournament games for the rest of that moontide. He commanded that all the warriors who came from the Middle Mountains should follow him. Leaving the others to dismiss the rest and summon all Middle Mountain warriors, he flew off immediately.

Confusion reigned for a while, and some remaining warriors prepared to leave, a little disgruntled. Others objected and said that they had come to display their prowess and would stay to do so. Others thought it was a good time to practise their skills. Still others merely wanted to stay, watch, and chatter—often merely to avoid the responsibilities of their own home-*eyrie*.

ThunderWing stepped into the breach.

'I will address the throng,' he informed the senior officials, much to their relief.

He flew up to the Rock of Judgment where officials or Windlords often sat to both oversee the proceedings and be heard while passing judgment on the outcome of each game. It was like a natural amphitheatre.

How often in times past had he looked up eagerly at that rock to hear who had won the race, fight, or feat of arms? There were times when he heard his own name reverberating around the valley and felt the intoxicating feeling of standing on Champion's Crag for all to see and honour.

'Warriors of the *Mawh'eyri*, hear me!'

His great voice could be heard from one end of the valley to the other. Many recognized and hailed him, especially when SilverSong joined him at the rock. They hushed their neighbours and gave the great champion their full attention. Soon there was an almost eerie silence, with only the occasional whispering among them.

'The Raven-Winds have come upon our folk in the Middle Mountains, and in very great wrath! They have done great devastation to the *eyries* of the Middle Mountains! Children unhatched have fallen to their deaths! Nests have been swept away! The folk have fled at the coming of the terror, and many fear to return! Their stores of food have been scattered to the four winds and many shall go hungry, perhaps may starve in the season of dearth! It is nearly upon us!'

He painted a bleak picture of the fate of the folk of the Middle Mountains, then made an impassioned appeal for the warriors to come and help rebuild the *eyries* before the season of storms and dearth and the cold White Down came upon them. Food and prey had to be gathered also, assisting the *Mawharùn* in their labours.

To the proudest and more seasoned warriors, this was unheard of.

'Son of HighSoarer, what is this?' called back one hard-faced veteran, sitting on a ledge overlooking the valley. 'We hail you as Champion Perpetual, but to call upon us to demean ourselves to servant's work is beyond our call of duty! We are called to guard and fight, not to carry and fetch food, and nesting!'

'Few folk of the Middle Mountain ever came to our aid in our time of need in the Northern *Eyries*!' called out another. 'Why should we aid them? We uphold a proud tradition here!'

ThunderWing shook his head in frustration, but knew he must persevere. The education of the young eaglets of the *Mawh'eyri* included oratory, and he used all the skills he had learnt to move the hearts of the warriors. But his greatest weapon was his passion—his passion for justice. The ordinary *eyrie*-folk endured not only the normal storms of life, he said, but the towering mountains of heartless tradition. Did they desire the honour of all the common *eyrie*-folk? Then let them follow him to the Middle Mountains to earn it!

Then SilverSong herself stepped forward.

'What of your nest-mates and children? Your fathers? Your mothers?' she cried. 'Would they not go and help to rebuild? For shame! *They* are the ones with true honour!'

This was unanswerable, and the warriors knew it, but they still hesitated.

Then suddenly, a cold gusty north wind swept down the valley, blowing a few of the spectators off their perches. It was the first sign of oncoming winter.

ThunderWing had had enough.

'Now the season of storms is nearly upon us, and the *eyrie* folk of the Middle Mountains shall be caught in it! If none else will come and give aid to his fellows, then we shall go into this battle alone! Farewell, O brave and hearty warriors of *Mawha!*'

Just as he was about to take wing, a champion flew up to the rock. He beat his chest with his talon before them all and announced in a deep and husky baritone:

'I am StormFighter *Mawharhipi,* son of StoneHand the Strong! Am I not Swiftest in the Mountains this season? Yet I am from the Western *Eyries,* whom the captain of the hunters before us saved from destruction at the hands of the *Hrah'eyri!* If ThunderWing, son of HighSoarer, Champion Perpetual and Victor in Battle will humble himself to serve the *eyries,* then so shall I! Who is with me?'

It was like the first pebbles of a landslide. Soon more and more of the younger warriors, especially those from the West, took up the cry: "Then so shall I!" They spread their wings and began circling around the Rock of Judgment, crying 'We are with you, Champion Perpetual, captain of the *Mawharùn!* Lead us! Command us!'

There were at least fifty strong. The champion turned to ThunderWing.

'It seems you have begun a new tradition, my captain. Lead us into battle.'

With a cry of elation, ThunderWing and SilverSong rose up above their circling followers and triumphantly winged their way northward. A few more from the crowd felt ashamed, and followed them.

SilverSong struck up the "Song of the Southern Hills" as they flew. It was a popular ballad which told of ancient times when their forbears first settled in the hills they had just left. They were assailed by the local tribes of Wild Eagles. Then, some warriors of long ago that had been exploring the Middle Mountains to establish new *eyries* heard of their plight. They abandoned their exploration and flew to relieve their fellows in the Southern Hills, even though thunderstorms and contrary winds came against them along the way.

As SilverSong sang the stanzas, the warriors roared out the chorus:

'Take wing, you sons of the Mawh'eyri,
Your distant brethren call!
Though fierce our painted enemy,
Upon them we shall fall.

Though storm may rage and wind make war,
We lack not strength nor speed.
For who can withstand a warrior
If kinsfolk are in need?'

In the Middle Mountains, meanwhile, Windlord WideFeather, together with his older sons, made frantic efforts to retrieve all the scattered foodstuffs they could find. His lady was beside herself. She was struggling to console her traumatized little eaglets; at the same time holding the remnants of their disintegrating nest together against the cold northerly gusts that seemed to hunt and stalk them all around the rocks and crevices.

Similar scenes were unfolding all around them.

In the wake of the rampage of the demon-winds, the terrified *Eyri* furtively returned to find their *eyrie*s swept almost bare, with wisps of nesting material and unprepared food caught in nooks and crannies everywhere. Most of the folk were too stunned to even comprehend what had happened, until one *eyrie*-mother began to wail in grief when she found that nothing remained of her unborn babies but broken egg-shells. Then another began to weep aloud, and then another.

Slowly they all began to collect what they could of their own belongings. Some took to the air and sadly forsook their ancestral *eyrie*s, hoping to find shelter with relatives in the Northern, Eastern, or Western *Eyrie*s. But many had young eaglets that could not fly, so their parents desperately collected what material they could find and began rebuilding as quickly as they could. It was going to be a cold night, the weather prophets said.

Then came the cold north winds—the heralds of winter—and blew some of their makeshift nests away again. The coming of the Windlord and their own warriors brought little comfort, for they naturally went to repair their own *eyrie*s first.

Some families gave up any hope of a warm night, huddling together in any sheltered corner they could find as they watched the sun slowly sink toward the tops of the Western Mountains.

It was then that they heard the rousing chorus in the distance.

'For who can withstand a warrior
If kinsfolk are in need?'
Many *eyrie*-folk paused in their doings to look up into the sky to see what seemed like a small thundercloud, rapidly moving their direction.

'What does it mean? Is it a raid of the Wild Ones? But they are too few!'

'Why, these are our fellows from the Southern Hills!' gasped one of the warriors, staring hard into the blue. 'Has there been a battle?'

Then the coming cloud of warriors broke up into twos and threes at their captain's direction. Each of them carried either food or substantial nesting material. (There had been a rivalry over who could carry the most at the greatest speed.) They descended first on those who had the greatest need and, bowing, offered their gifts.

The *eyrie*-mothers shed grateful tears. The local *eyrionis* found it hard to believe that the proud warriors would stoop to this. Such was the need of the moment, however, no comments were made save words of heart-felt thanks.

Soon, the whole of the mountains echoed with the "Song of the Southern Hills" as the spirits of the locals soared to new heights. There was such a spirit of community that many disheartened families found new strength and threw themselves into the task before them. Nests were soon well inlaid and a small store of provisions was stacked at the back of their caves.

Then ThunderWing commanded the free warriors to fetch loose flat rocks, as large and as many as they could carry. Setting the example, he carried a few to an *eyrie* that looked particularly vulnerable to the winds, and laid them down like a foundation at the entrance. Intrigued, the eaglets watched as he returned with more and more.

He was building a strong, firm wall as a barrier to the winds that swept up and around the mountains. The warriors soon caught on, and many walls soon arose—each *eyrie* beginning to look like a small but formidable fortress.

'Mine shall withstand even the Raven-Winds of *Mawharikhan*,' boasted one of the local warriors, dusting off his wings.

'You are a captain indeed, son of HighSoarer,' remarked the Windlord enthusiastically, watching the construction works going ahead. 'What you have done defies all tradition and usage, but by the wings of the wind, I am glad of it! I name you: Rebuilder of the Middle Mountains.'

'Do I take the glory for the winds of change, Windlord? This has long been needful. Are we not the mighty *Mawh'eyri?*'

Last of all, before the sun went down, StrongHand and his hunters arrived. They bore not only an abundance of food, but also some salt-rock and other preserving materials commonly used to keep produce edible over the winter.

Instead of a sense of desolation, the hunters found a festive atmosphere. They were hailed jubilantly, and offered nests to sleep overnight.

StrongHand inspected all the warriors' labours and the strong walls and grunted with satisfaction. The folk of the Middle Mountains would have a warm winter after all.

WideFeather stood before the Council of Windlords and gave a glowing tribute to the initiative and efforts of the warriors and their captain the day before. He had invited—even begged—ThunderWing and StrongHand to attend.

Nonetheless, although a vote of thanks was given to the sons of High-Soarer, the Windlords were in a sober mood. They had already decided to postpone all attempts on *Mawharikhan* after being driven from Windlord's Crag for the second time. They would only recommence when, and if, the Raven-Winds were driven out.

Windlord StormRider, always conscious of the security of the mountains, stepped forward and spoke.

'Brethren Windlords! We are safe for the moment from the Raven-Winds. Now we must turn our thoughts to the defense of our borders against the raids of the *Hrah'eyri*. ThunderWing, son of HighSoarer, became captain of our warrior-hunters in the Battle of the Western Marches, and though unlooked for, he carried the day. He also, daring great peril, learned of the raids that are planned by the barbarians of the Eastern Hills.'

ThunderWing exchanged glances with his brother. They wondered what the Windlords would have thought if they knew of their dealings with the dispossessed rebel, WindChaser.

'I put it before you, brethren,' StormRider continued, 'that there should be an extra guard and stronger defense on our Eastern Marches. Let there be not one Warband, but two.'

'And why should there be two, Windlord StormRider?' came a languid voice from behind him. 'Are my warriors of the Eastern *Eyries* so weak that they cannot account for a handful of barbarian rabble?'

It was none other than Windlord SwiftSlayer, coming late to the Council. StormRider closed his eyes in pain before he turned and faced his questioner.

'Hail Windlord, and welcome to the Council,' he said with as much grace as he could muster. 'Much has been spoken of already....'

'....But nothing decided without me, I trust!'

StrongFeather intervened, knowing the ongoing tension between both fiery Windlords could easily get out of hand.

'Peace, Windlords! We call Council if all but one is present, although we seek to know the mind of the absent one before we decree. We merely have ceased to countenance more attempts upon the peak until the scourge is gone. This we knew as your wish beforehand also. But now we look to strengthen our eastern borders. We do not doubt the valour of you and your Warband, but the raids upon our borders increase, and become more cunning. We hear intelligence of a massed attack in the East when the seasons turn again. Can you be vigilant from sun-arise to sunrest throughout the seasons? We would not ask it of you. But two captains' eyes can watch in turn.'

Even SwiftSlayer was forced to see the common sense of this, but he eyed StormRider frostily and demanded:

'Who do you propose to be the captain of this second band, Windlord?'

StormRider had ridden storms both real and metaphorical before, and answered quite readily.

'Who better than one who has proven himself as a mighty captain amongst us, even with few warriors and untrained hunters—Thunder-Wing, son of HighSoarer, Champion Perpetual and Victor in Battle?'

Most of the Council were aroused to vocal applause. Even SwiftSlayer himself conceded the value of such an appointment.

'Yes, very well, for his fame will add lustre to our *eyri*es in the East. I would have asked for the honour to be given to my worthless son, had he not made a manifold fool of himself. The Champion Perpetual is worthier by far. But he must be subject to my command!' he added vehemently. 'I will not have mere hunters untrained in my Warbands! We have our proud traditions to consider.'

A number of the older Councilors nodded their heads, so Storm-Rider was forced to acquiesce. At least, as he confided to StrongFeather later, he felt more secure with ThunderWing there under any circumstances, than without him.

The only one unhappy with the appointment was the subject himself.

'My Windlords!' he said, coming forward and bowing low, 'You honour me greatly with this appointment, but I have but just established my *eyri*e in the Western Mountains and .....'

'I know, and greatly shall you be missed in the West, son of High-Soarer' said StrongFeather with a sad smile in his eyes. 'But your talents and your duty call you elsewhere. There is a cost to greatness, alas! Perhaps we can arrange to keep your *eyri*e safe in the event of your return.'

StrongHand then surprised his brother as he stepped forward and bowed.

'My Windlords, I have no attachments, no family, save the lady LightWind, my mother, who is rarely at her own *eyri*e. I shall move to the *eyri*e of the Champion Perpetual and keep it for him, and he shall occupy the proud *Eyri*e HighSoarer of the Eastern Mountains once again, until he needs it no more.'

The sensible suggestion was applauded by all except his brother.

'Then let it be decreed: ThunderWing, son of HighSoarer is captain of the second Warband of the Eastern Mountains, subject to Windlord SwiftSlayer, as it is his right. He may choose and train any willing warrior. Let him so remain until all threat of war is passed at the turn of the season.'

'So be it,' chorused the Windlords. The waiting messenger scratched it upon the sand. Then he brought forth the formal wreath of captaincy and placed it over ThunderWing's head and onto his broad shoulders, to the applause of all present—polite or heartfelt.

When he broke the news to SilverSong, she was at first elated, then downcast.

'O when will they leave you in peace!' she wailed. 'Have you not served the wingfolk of *Mawha* enough? Must they put you in peril's way once again?'

She leaned against his neck, pushing the wreath of office aside, impatiently.

'Your father has said that there is a cost to high office, my love,' he patiently replied. 'I do not wish it, but it is for our wingfolk's sake. I cannot bear to see my father's heritage destroyed. And if my mother and brother were there also…No, we must go. We must move to my mother's *eyrie* in the Eastern Mountains. Are you willing?'

'I go wherever you go, my lord,' she said with a touch of resignation in her voice. 'But it is well. We have friends and kin there, for we lived there in our youth, you and I. It shall be pleasant to look upon the Teardrops of the Eastern Mountains once more. But I hope your brother shall not bring his fleas into our nest here!'

Without further ado, they made the long flight the next day.

Among the few things she brought along with her was a large and slightly disintegrated tail feather.

'Was that mine?' laughed ThunderWing. 'It was token of an oath from which you released me. Let it fall!'

'It is the first precious gift that you gave me, my love. I shall not part with it.'

They settled in quickly and were welcomed with open arms, not only by the Lady LightWind, but by many of their former friends and relatives.

At her mother-in-law's invitation, SilverSong began to rearrange the nest at *Eyrie* HighSoarer. It showed most of the signs of a bachelor's quarters, but at least there were no fleas, much to SilverSong's relief. LightWind and StrongHand flew off later in the day, to set up quarters in *Eyrie* ThunderWing in the West.

'I must go forth and recruit for my Warband, my love. Then we shall hunt for the *eyrie*s again. Shall you come with me?'

She was feeling unusually tired that day, however. So for the first time, she declined to go wherever he called her to go. They had broken their journey a few times from the Western Mountains to the east, and yet she still tired easily.

'Are you well, my fair?' he asked, slightly concerned. He was so used to having her with him, it seemed strange, hunting alone. 'I will return early, then. Will you feel safe if I leave you?'

'Go, if you must, my lord,' she replied with a weary smile in her eyes. 'For reasons unknown, my wings are heavy upon me this sunflight and I will only hinder your going. I am safe enough. Your kin are nearby and will watch over me. Since we were joined as nest-mates, I have felt safe, and now our enemy is fallen and lies shattered within the Caves of Healing.'

On the point of leaving, ThunderWing stopped and stared at her, an arrested look on his face.

'Should we still count him enemy, do you think? We have followed the same flight-path and fallen, he and I, although mine was a kinder father. Perhaps he has learned to forsake the heights and depths of vanity and pride. Perhaps he will leave the Caves of Healing as an *eyrion* reborn, even as I.'

She stared back at him, considering what he said.

'You are gracious and forgiving, my love, but I bear doubts that he will change. And yet….. we have seen how his father, the Windlord, has spurned and rejected him. Surely that would be the deepest wound for any eaglet to bear. His brokenness at the hands of the evil wind-demons would be as feather-strokes in comparison, I think. What should we do?'

He drew close to her and caressed her neck with his beak.

'"SilverSong" you have been named, and yet your heart glows as the golden rocks of the river *Mawharîsh.*'

Then he laughed at the irony of the situation.

'Strange, how the seasons will change the hunter to the prey and the prey to hunter. He *honoured* me with his presence when I lay where he now lies, with half my feathers scattered at the base of the great mountain. Should I visit him in his broken state also?'

'But you are not the hunter here, my love. You are the healer, rather. Yes. It may be that he shall rise again in true greatness, even as the humble hunter before me has done. That would be a victory worthy of the Battle of the Western Marches.'

'You give my wings greater strength in saying so. That is well. I will visit him with a food offering. If he will speak to me and listen to the same wisdom as I did in his place, then maybe we shall gain a friend and lose a foe—like to the dispossessed one of the *Hrah'eyri,* WindChaser.'

'Then fly well, my love, and prosper in your errand. May the Great Spirit-Wind give strength to your wings.'

With high hopes, ThunderWing brought a large hare in his talons to the opening of the Caves of Healing in the Middle Mountains. His heart was beating faster, wondering what awaited him.

All the old enmity strove with sympathy for the way his erstwhile rival had been treated by his father. He barely remembered his own father, except as a kind, magnificent, and lordly being. His mother had greatly extolled his virtues and he strove to emulate him. But it was not so with the one he was about to visit. NightFlyer had no such role-model, even though he had inherited his father's pride, beauty, and skills.

With that in mind, ThunderWing landed on the ledge of the opening and looked cautiously into the cave.

Sure enough, NightFlyer lay at the back of the cave, padded with foliage and spare feathers to keep him warm. The magnificent plumage that many an *eyreira* had swooned over was now only a patchy network of tufted feathers, with many tail feathers—an eagle's pride—now missing. Only three season-turns had passed since ThunderWing lay in exactly the same state.

The shattered warrior, now no longer a champion, lay as if in a deep sleep, his eyes shut tightly. An eagle's facial expression, even that of the sapient and passionate *Eyri* race, appears to be rather austere and arrogant to the inexperienced eye. NightFlyer's expression had an added look of bitter disillusionment, as though the whole world was conspiring against him.

ThunderWing tread silently and lay his offering down near him. He turned to go, thinking that he would return another time and let the broken warrior sleep.

But the eyes snapped open.

'Are you come to triumph over me, son of HighSoarer?'

The voice had lost none of its mockery and biting sarcasm.

ThunderWing turned back to him, feeling the old anger rising again.

'No, son of Windlord SwiftSlayer, I have not! Have I not lain in your place three seasons gone?'

'Do *not* call me by that blackened and dishonoured name!' snarled NightFlyer, struggling to his feet. 'Nor do I need your pity! Any warrior may fall in battle and rise again to triumph in the end. *You* have fallen and rose again to higher heights. But know this, son of High-Soarer, Champion Perpetual and noble nest-mate of SilverSong the Fair: I, NightFlyer, the fatherless; I, NightFlyer the fallen warrior, shall rise to still greater heights than you shall ever dream of!'

He looked so pathetically like the pugnacious little half-grown eaglet that ThunderWing had first met in his youth, that his anger died. The situation they were both in struck him as both ironically sad, yet a little humorous.

'And how shall you do that, O NightFlyer the fatherless?'

'Yes, mock me if you will! That is what you came to do, I know well. But you shall no longer laugh when I return with plumage fairer than before and strength greater than before. I shall outwit the accursed wind-spirits and conquer *Mawharikhan!* I shall be Reigning Windlord!'

Such a boast seemed so fantastic to ThunderWing, he had to struggle not to laugh out loud. He was determined not to repeat his rival's behaviour when their roles had been reversed. NightFlyer was crouched before him in the manner of a cornered snake. The last thing ThunderWing wanted to do was spit the same venom and hate as his opponent did, and to become like him. Instead, he merely shook his head.

'Your dreams of self-glory fly higher than you ever could, my friend,' he said calmly. 'Do you not know that the Council has forbidden any attempts upon the peak until the Raven-Winds are banished?'

'Yes, so your dear mother has informed me. But I have a plan which you would not dare try to emulate: I shall draw them forth just before the season of storms, when the White Warrior Wind comes, even as you did to the Black Storm. But my triumph shall outshine yours, son of High-Soarer! Then all shall bow down to me because I, NightFlyer the valiant, dared to do what you dare not!'

He seemed so lost in his own aggrandize, ThunderWing was lost for words. Finally, he grasped one piece of sense in all the fog of vanity.

'Has my mother spoken to you?'

'Yes, she has done so. She came to triumph over me also, in the guise of pity and friendship, bringing news of your joining with the lady Sil-verSong—*my* lady, the one you stole and deceived into sharing your nest. I kept silent before your mother, but not to you, O great and exalted hunter! If that foolish and fickle jade does not see the coward in you before my triumph is made known, then she shall come flying into my arms when I have won all to my side. You shall lose in the end, O poor deluded hunter!'

The serpent's tongue had finally touched his arch-rival on a raw nerve at the mention of the lady's name. They were beak to beak now, even though his wounds prevented NightFlyer from standing at eye level.

'*I*?? Deluded??' ThunderWing stormed back at him. 'You are raving, son of SwiftSlayer! You are smitten by the sun-demon! A fickle jade you call her? Very well! I shall leave you to dream your dreams of grandeur until you moult into the dust! But do not dare to come near my lady, you featherless crow, or I shall *call Mawharagh upon you!*'

With that parting blessing, he knocked him over with a sweep of his wing as he stormed off into the blue.

After flying at a furious pace and knocking a few sizeable stones off the sides of the mountains he passed, he began to simmer down.

He looked up at the rising full moon and heaved a sigh.

'O moon-spirit, your eye is fully open to see my folly, is it not? That was not worthy of me. How did I let that braying jay-bird arouse my passions so easily? I had thought to outgrow this childish warrior rivalry by now. If I am to captain in battle, surely I must first be captain of my darker passions.'

He recalled a few lines of the calming song of the Great Spirit-Wind that his lady had taught him and turned his head toward the Eastern Mountains.

He arrived home well before dusk, with a catch from the local rapids. His lady was on the lookout rock above and flew out to meet him, without a trace of the weariness she felt that morning. Her eyes sparkled as their talons and beaks met in mid-air.

Her eyes asked a question, but he sadly shook his head. When they had landed and begun their meal, he briefly told her what had transpired in the Caves of Healing. What she thought of her former suitor's insults she kept to herself, but was quite philosophical about the outcome.

'My love, do not look so crest-fallen. You have rebuilt many *eyries* in the Middle Mountains after the Raven-Wind terrors had destroyed them, but there are some *eyries* that can never be rebuilt, I think. My father often said that *Eyrie* SwiftSlayer is fallen already.'

Then she brightened, and the sparkle returned to her eyes as she whispered in his ear.

'Yet there is one *eyrie* that has grown. Come and see!'

She led him to the back of the little cave where they had built their own little nest.

In the corner, half wrapped in feathers and foliage, lay what looked like two perfectly rounded and perfectly matched golden stones.

All sense of failure and sadness was swept away by a flood of joy.

'I am a father!' he gasped.

He spread his wings and soared up into the skies, spinning, twirling, laughing.

'I am a father!' he sang to the surrounding mountains.

Meanwhile, there was still the need to make winter provision for all the remaining *eyries*. So the Champion Perpetual, Victor of the Battle of the Western Marches, Rebuilder of the Middle *Eyries*, Captain-deputy of the Eastern Warband left aside all the glory and honour heaped upon him, and continued hunting and gathering for the *eyries*.

This time, he could not have his lady at his side. She stayed behind to keep the eggs warm.

There was need for haste, for the nights grew colder and coloured leaves were falling.

ThunderWing bothered little about his appearance at these times, but SilverSong insisted on him grooming himself before bringing his produce to the *eyries*. This caused a little friction between them, but she gave in as she realized how late in the season it was.

A few more enlightened warriors joined the band of hunters, even considering it an honour to labour with such distinguished persons as the Master of the Hunters and the great ThunderWing himself. Even those warriors and spectators who stayed at the *Mawh'ree* in the Southern Mountains felt a little ashamed, and enthusiasm for the games began to languish.

Old Windlord WingSmiter, who was presiding over the tournaments during that season, became concerned. He felt it was a matter important enough to raise at the Council, now held in a cave at the southern tip of the Middle Mountains.

'Windlords! It is not fit!' he said, when a comment was made about the help the hunters were receiving from the warriors. 'There are so many warriors who have left the *Mawh'ree* to join the hunters, there are too few to fill the ranks. We cannot continue some events because of this. We need these games to train our warriors for battle.'

SwiftSlayer, one of his contemporaries and an advocate for the traditions of *Mawha*, came to his support.

'The Windlord speaks truth. If the Champion Perpetual wishes to demean himself, so be it, it is his right. But the warriors do not have that choice unless there is the need. It is well that they aided the rebuilding of the Middle Mountain *Eyries*, but they *must* continue their training now that the threat of the Wild Eagles has again arisen.'

He walked to the middle of the circle, holding his head up proudly in an assumption of authority that some of his fellow Windlords found irritating.

'I have called on more warriors, especially those of many seasons, to watch the Eastern Marches. If what the sons of HighSoarer heard the western barbarians say is true, there shall be another raid in the season of the blossoming. That is why I claimed the right as Windlord and eldest of the Eastern *Eyri*es, to lead the Warband should they strike again, and in *my* domain. Let there be no mere hunters to fight for us, valiant though they be. I will *not* suffer it!'

'We do not dispute your right as captain of the Eastern Warband, Windlord SwiftSlayer,' said StormRider, his feathers ruffling a little in annoyance. 'But I have learned to ride with the winds of change rather than against them. The sons of HighSoarer have shown us the value of the hunter's skills that blend with those of the warrior's. I, for one, will continue to press for the training in both, as called for by the Champion Perpetual. Our foes become more cunning and we must outwit them in any way we can. If we cannot always hold the tournament in the South, so be it.'

Windlord WideFeather, a family-minded *eyrion* stepped forward.

'I would also remind you, brethren, that the Middle Mountain *Eyri*es where I dwell are now walled and provisioned for the season of the White Down, and that is full thanks to the sons of HighSoarer and their following, especially ThunderWing, Champion Perpetual. That should never be forgot. If he had not called upon the warriors, defying the traditions, we would not survive by the time the White Down is moulted.'

The debate gained more and more in intensity until StrongFeather stirred and stepped into the circle. He was recognized as the most senior and normally had the last say in all debates of the Council.

'Well, my Windlords, both sides speak truth to some measure. Let us end this debate with agreement. I submit that we only call upon the warriors to aid the hunters where there is the greatest need. If some warriors wish to join them to learn the ways of hunter's war, we shall allow two only in turn, but continue with the *Mawh'ree* for the rest. What say you?'

This was endorsed by WeatherWing the Seer, which culminated in a general agreement, albeit a reluctant one in some quarters.

CHAPTER 7

THE NIGHT VISITATION

'See, my love! The cold white down falls from the dark floating nests above and clothes the mountainsides. Is it not exceeding fair?'

ThunderWing looked up from sorting through the winter storage at the back of their *eyrie* cave. He glanced at the falling snow and merely grunted, turning back to his task.

'But is it not beautiful to look upon?' she insisted.

'It means that this sunflight we cannot hunt. That seems not something beautiful to me.'

SilverSong gave vent to mild exasperation.

'*Eyrionis!* You are all the same! All you ever think of is food, fighting, and females. *Come and watch!*'

'Oh, very well. But I have looked upon the white down many a time. As eaglets, we would play in it, you and I. The wonder of it is lost to me now.'

The wonder of it was not lost to SilverSong. Just watching the child-like expression in her face was captivating enough for him, so he abandoned all his thoughts of food for the moment and joined her at the mouth of the cave.

Her head was cocked a little to one side as though listening to something. The expression of wonder widened to awe.

'Listen, my love,' she breathed excitedly. 'Can you hear it?'

He obediently listened, but could only hear the occasional furtive sighing of fleeting breezes over the rocks. The thick layers of snow seemed to cover everything with a heavy, sleepy silence.

'The rock-sprites are all I hear. Would you have speech with such creatures, my beloved?'

'No, I do not! Can you not hear him? It is the song of the Great Spirit-Wind? He gently calls us.'

Again he strained to listen, but without success. He shook his head, mystified.

SilverSong was about to scold him again, but checked herself.

'But, of course...you listen with your outer ear only. It is a skill I have learned from your mother in the Northern Mountains. You have been trained to think only in the ways of the warrior. But even a good warrior calls upon his instincts. Yes?'

'That is so. It is not the first time you have spoken of these things. Tell me more.'

His attention was fully caught now. Maybe there could be some practical value to the ways of the Windsong after all. Previously, he had thought it was a phenomenon peculiar only to *eyreira*, but on occasion he felt some strange stirrings around him which could not be attributed to natural causes. One such incident happened just before his fall at the ghostly hands of *Mawharikhvn*.

'Teach me then, my fair wise one. Does the Great Wind-Spirit speak in words? In song? In dreams or visions?'

SilverSong raised her head to the skies. A faraway look came into her eyes.

'He speaks in many ways, and none can tell what manner or form he will take. Like the wind that passes, the moment is quickly gone, and it is easily unnoticed or quickly forgotten. Yes, he will give us dreams and visions if we seek to hear his songs, but sometimes he speaks in strange ways. When I was in the Northern Mountains, I once heard him whispering my name as he passed among the rocks. I was in ecstasy that he would call me, but foolishly, I did not stay to hear more.'

She looked back at him with a strange smile upon her face.

'I once looked into a mirror-smooth pond in the Valley of Peace in the Northern Mountains, thinking to see only my own image. But a breeze passed across its surface and it rippled, even though I did not feel it upon my feathers. When it cleared, I saw the face of

ThunderWing, son of HighSoarer. You were wounded and in pain, my love, and you whispered my name. It was then that I knew that I loved you. When my father came and spoke of your plight, I instantly left all to find you.'

He was awestruck.

'Did he speak of our future, my love? The future of the *Mawh'eyri?* My part in all this?'

Her eyes dropped before his and she looked away, changing the subject. She began to busy herself in rearranging some nesting feathers around the eggs.

'Your mother is more greatly skilled in these matters than I, my lord. Speak to her.'

He did not notice the change in her manner, being distracted by his own thoughts as new possibilities opened before him.

'The Great Spirit-Wind can be both terrible and gentle, it is said, and cares for all winged peoples of the *Eyri* race. If I could see what the future held for us all—the raids, the movement of the Raven-Winds— that would aid us mightily!'

'Perhaps LightWind, your mother can teach you these things, but you must first learn to sing to the Great Spirit-Wind and rise up in the Trance of Prophecy. It is a task beyond us.'

'The Trance of Prophecy?'

'Yes, but it is beyond my skill. We who live to extend our *eyri*es have more important matters to attend to. Should we not build a rock wall as you did for the Middle Mountain *Eyri*es, my love?'

He built her rock wall.

Puzzled a little by her own sudden reluctance to speak of the Wind-songs, however, he flew across to the Western Mountains on the first clear day that dawned. The sun glistened on the mountainsides and snow-covered treetops. There was not a breath of wind to help him on his way. It was not the most ideal day to investigate the power of winds, he thought, as he toiled all the way to his western *eyri*.

His mother was waiting for him at the cave's entrance, almost as though she was expecting him. StrongHand had gone off to see if there were any winter berries that could be found among the snow-covered valleys.

After the formal and affectionate greetings and inquiries after each other's health, ThunderWing came to the point.

'Mother, can you teach me the Trance of Prophecy?'

'I knew you would soon ask it of me, my son, for I have seen that you have grown to care for our wingfolk and would look to their future. Few warriors have looked beyond their own beaks! They trust in their own swiftness and strength alone. Some Windlords have attempted the highest peaks of the Windsongs, but only WeatherWing the Seer has succeeded to some measure. Perhaps you may become a seer as he. But the Trance cannot be learnt in one day. You must first learn to sing to the Great Spirit-Wind and learn to hear his voice also.'

'But I have learned the Windsongs in the Northern Mountains when I was an eaglet, mother.'

'You have also learned to be courteous, but with your mother and your nest-mate you go beyond mere courtesy.'

This took a while for his practical mind to assimilate.

'You speak in mysteries. What is your meaning? Do we sing to him as I would to my loved ones? From my heart? How can this be? He can come as a mighty thunderstorm! All should fear him! Yet you speak of him almost as a father.'

'It is true. I have heard him as a gentle breeze, bringing comfort and strength in my time of need.'

It was many days and not a few visits before ThunderWing made any progress at all. He began to hum and sing many of the songs he had been taught in his youth. Some he had forgotten, partly through lack of use, and this was partly due to the heedless seasons he spent amongst the warriors in the Southern Hills, thinking of nothing but his own glorification. His mother patiently taught him the words, but made it clear it was up to him to sing them from his heart.

When he went hunting, he sang them to himself. He sang them even louder when he was on his own. He sang them together with SilverSong in their *eyrie*.

But although he listened carefully, he could hear nothing but the ebb and flow of the common winds of the world as he had always heard them. He despaired, so he asked his mother again what he should do. She was unperturbed.

'You listen with your natural ears, my son. It is the ears within that hear the songs of the Great Wind. He will sense your earnest desire and speak—if you stay vigilant.'

Her son grimaced at that.

'Simple vigilance on the Marches is simple for a simple warrior, mother. But try as I may, this I cannot do. I do not know what even to watch for! Cannot the Great Wind send me a simple vision? Even a night visitation?'

'Just wait and be patient, my son. Be watchful within, knowing that he shall speak if you are at least willing to hear. Do not fail to sing the Windsongs at every instant you may.'

After a while, he began to appreciate the soothing effect of the Windsongs. He was no longer singing to the air, he was singing to the Great Spirit-Wind.

'But I would still crave to see a vision or receive a night visitation—even if it bore evil forebodings,' he said to SilverSong one night before they settled into the nest. 'It is better than bearing the burden of the fate of the *Mawh'eyri* alone.'

'Then lay aside the burden, my love. Come and rest awhile.'

ThunderWing stood perched upon Watcher's Rock on the Eastern Marches, with a warm and fragrant breeze blowing in his face. The Eastern River was bubbling over the edge of the cliff nearby, where it became known as the "Tears of the Eastern Marches," as a memory of the ancient war that devastated the Eastern and Middle Mountain *eyries*.

'....But not in my generation,' he said with confidence.

He looked out over the misty marshes and planes beyond the eastern border toward the distant Wild Eastern Hills. Uneasily, he observed a dark cloud gathering rapidly around them, crowned with flashes of lightning.

The breeze changed suddenly to a cold wind, and the thunderstorm, still building rapidly, began to advance in his direction. He decided to seek shelter. Then he noticed that the dark mass of cloud was, in fact, a huge mass of birds. Looking closer with eagle-sight, he could see that they bore war paint—the mark of the Wild Eagles.

'Where are the guards of the Marches?' he cried. 'Sound the alarm of war!'

He took wing to raise the alarm at the *eyri*es, but the *Hrah'eyri* quickly overtook him in massive numbers. He knew he was about to die. Hate-filled faces of the dark painted warriors circled around him, leering and screaming. He prepared to make a last stand.

Then suddenly, a large painted warrior came in between him and his would-be slayers.

'Peace!' the warrior called, addressing his comrades. 'Do not touch this or any son of HighSoarer the Merciful. Seek rather the cruel ones.'

The dark host turned away obediently, spiraled upwards, and thundered on toward the interior of the mountains of *Mawha,* singing songs of war and destruction.

ThunderWing turned to thank his preserver and beg him to save the *eyri*es, but the words died in his throat.

He was looking into the grim face of *Kharòn* the Dispossessed, as he had seen him in the Battle of the Western Marches.

'You know whom I seek, son of HighSoarer!' he informed him, fiercely. 'But neither you nor your *eyri*e shall I touch. Rather will I defend your *eyri*e! But forget not the Tears-of-the-Sun of which I told at our last meeting!'

Then he was off into the darkening sky in the manner of a hunter seeking its prey.

ThunderWing prepared to fly after him, or summon the Warbands. But then the whole scene became a bizarre nightmare.

A real thunderstorm came in the wake of the invasion.

He cringed as lightning flashed and struck the rocks nearby, which appeared to disintegrate and flow into the river. The river turned red as though it flowed with blood. Yells and screams of fighting and dying warriors came up from the depths below.

Then in the distance, coming from the west, he saw a dark shadow that still haunted his worst nightmares. It was *Mawharhikùn.*

He had never heard the voice of the demon-storm before, but it seemed to roar over the mountains and valleys, loud and clear. 'Tremble, Son of HighSoarer! I am coming to reclaim my mountain and my crown once again! I send my servants and my winged slaves before me to prepare my way. I shall feast on the flesh and drink the blood of the *Mawh'eyri.* I shall destroy you as I destroyed your father!'

ThunderWing awoke with a gasp and a shudder. He was still curled up safely in his own *eyrie.* He breathed a song of thanks.

Looking around, he could see all the signs of a lovely spring morning. The last of the snows were melting away and many blossoms were appearing on the mountainsides, filling the air with wild perfumes. He sighed with relief.

His waking startled his spouse into wakefulness.

'ThunderWing, my lord! What restiveness is this? Have you had night visitations?'

He nodded, then stared intently at her as the implications struck him.

'We must return to our *eyrie* in the West—and soon!'

She became alarmed at the note of urgency in his voice and shook her head.

'Our egg-children may not survive the journey! What is this that alarms you? Are we in peril?'

He tore at the rock-face in frustration, which calmed him a little.

'Yes, I think it is so...but not yet.'

He quickly told her what he had seen in his night visitation, a phenomenon *Eyri* folk would never believe was a meaningless dream.

The blood drained from her face.

'Then...*Kharòn* the Dispossessed spake the truth?'

He paced the ledge, deep in thought.

'I never doubted him somehow, but this is a warning that an attack is looming; I would swear it by the wings of the sun. I must have speech with Windlord Council! But how can I leave you?'

'Go if you must, my lord, but will the Council be in session at the crag?'

'They shall do so with this news.' he replied, grooming himself, ready for a long flight. 'Windlord SwiftSlayer dwells at his mansion-*eyrie* in the Eastern Mountains, and does not know his peril. But will he believe me? He despises the Wild Ones and may mock the warning I bring. Should I expose his crimes he committed against *Kharòn* and his beloved? No! We must be united against the coming storm, and let the Great Spirit-Wind execute vengeance in his own manner and season. I must keep silence, especially to the Windlord.

"We must be united against the coming storm, and let the Great Spirit-Wind execute vengeance in his own manner and season."

Also there is this: Why would the Dispossessed one join the wild eastern tribes when he said that they are at war with each other? They came from the east!'

Shrugging off the mystery, he came to a decision.

'Whatever the truth is, I must speak to the Council, and soon.'

Then he put his head down to touch that of his nest-mate, wrapping his wings around her.

'My dearest, I shall ask my kin to guard you while I am gone. I shall seek your father and speak of my night visitation. He is wise and will not treat this matter with scorn. I may be gone a full moon perhaps. Think of me, and sing your songs to the Great Wind.'

'Go with his wind under your wings, my lord,' she said, anxiously nibbling at his face. 'But hasten back when you can, or perhaps your children shall be hatched before you are present to see it.'

StrongFeather looked confounded when he heard of the night visitation. He never doubted that it was from anywhere else but the Great Spirit-Wind.

'Let us seek the counsel of Windlord WeatherWing the Seer in this.'

When WeatherWing heard the tale, his eyes opened wide.

'This has the touch of the Trance of Prophecy upon it, or I am a crow. Windlord, we must summon the Council!'

Now a frequent guest at the Windlords' Council, ThunderWing urged them to reconsider and send an extra Warband ready for a battle, that was not only imminent, but larger in scale than many realized. He described his dream in detail. He used all the eloquence he could muster, but to little effect. Tradition and prejudice still ruled among most of the older Windlords—especially SwiftSlayer.

'Who is this young warrior to challenge our pride and traditions?' he countered with a touch of angry contempt in his voice. 'Is not one *Mawha* worth two talon-counts of savages?'

StrongFeather was obliged to keep a warning wing on StormRider's head to keep him from bursting into hot speech.

Other traditionalists spoke in support of SwiftSlayer's position, in more measured terms than he did, but clearly implying that Thunder-Wing was either too inexperienced or maybe a little too ambitious to have his recommendations endorsed.

ThunderWing politely excused himself from the Council on family grounds, but he also knew he would speak hastily and out of turn if he stayed any longer. On the way out, StormRider intercepted him, pulling him aside.

'Fear not, son of HighSoarer. We beat our heads and hands against stone cliffs at times. I feel it sorely. I have heeded your counsel, and will hold my own Warband in readiness at need. Send messengers to me at the Caves of *Mawh'ina,* east of the Middle Mountains. I will train my troops there this season.'

ThunderWing thanked him, grateful that there was some support on the Council.

'Now I must go forth and recruit and train my own Warband. We will need all the skill and cunning we can find!'

He chose carefully, for there were many warriors he knew that would be reluctant to learn the new ways of warfare he insisted on.

His first choice was StormFighter *Mawharhipi,* son of StoneHand, the champion who helped him rebuild the Middle Mountain *eyries.*

Ambitious, but faithful, he swore eternal allegiance to his captain, and finding him approachable and reasonable, they became firm friends. He was immediately promoted to captain's lieutenant and became very helpful in finding a good number of strong, willing, skilled, and disciplined warriors. These would be the core of his troops destined to defend the Eastern Marches. They were not too proud to learn from the hunters, for many of them came from the Western *Eyries* or had rebuilt the Middle Mountain *eyries* with their captain. They soon caught the vision ThunderWing had for the future of *Mawha*.

Chatting with StormFighter while hunting one day, the younger champion turned to him.

'My captain, I hope to be a Windlord one day. Is that an unworthy ambition?'

'It is not an unworthy ambition for a worthy heart, *Mawharhipi*. But we must first deal with the enemy that dwells upon *Mawharikhan*. Why do you ask this?'

'Because you yourself have no longer striven for it. To me it is a strange thing that you do not. I would see you as Reigning Windlord before me. I would follow your lead.'

'Have you not heard of my fall, my friend? It is a true saying: Many fallen rise higher than they would had they never fallen, for so I have learned from my mother's counsel. But the Raven-Winds are an insuperable barrier at present. Nor do I have the desire to reign.'

"Many fallen rise higher than they would had they never fallen..."

'Wings of the sun! My captain, why do you not wish for it? What more could a warrior desire?'

ThunderWing's face relaxed to an eagle's smile.

'It is strange to hear myself speak as a grey-feather, but I say that you are still young and do not understand the burden of greatness. Even when fame was thrust upon me, it was like the intoxication of the fermented mountain-berry for a moment—a brief watch of the sun. Then there are demands and burdens placed upon me which I would gladly forgo. I have all I wish for: the fairest *eyreira* under the sun as my nest-mate, my own *eyrie*, and two children close to hatching. But if my call is to be captain of a Warband, I will heed it. It is the duty of any *Mawha* warrior or hunter, be he ambitious or not.'

The younger champion found all this hard to understand, but he persisted.

'But well, my captain, if so be that you are called to be Reigning Windlord, what would you decree?'

ThunderWing had so long abandoned all ambition for this, he had to stop and think.

'Well, *Mawharhipi*, my friend, there are many things in the land of *Mawha* that could be set in order. You have heard me speak to our troops of rebuilding a better land. I would forbid any forced marriage to take place, which may force the poor, unwilling *eyreira* to flee into the wild. I will call on all warriors, willing or unwilling, to learn the ways of the hunters, and learn to serve the *eyries*. It will open many eyes to see the burden that our *eyrie*-mothers must bear. I would command all warriors to spend more time with their spouses and less at the *Mawh'ree*, although that also is needful.'

He remembered another highly ambitious warrior, still recovering in the Caves of Healing.

'This I would decree also: Any further attempt upon the peak shall only be done by those who have proved themselves humble enough to willingly serve the *eyrie*-folk, even helping to rebuild and gather and clean the dirtiest *eyrie* with his own hands. But...if there are those among the Windlords who will change the law again when my reign is complete, then little may be achieved. But who knows? If the *eyrie*-mothers will arise and stand firm, maybe their spouses will be forced to submit to their duties.'

StormFighter laughed.

'The brave warriors of *Mawha* tremble before their fierce nest-mates! I would fight for that just cause myself, my captain, even though a storm of warriors come against me.'

'So are you named, my friend.'

CHAPTER 8

TEARS IN THE EASTERN MOUNTAINS

Spring had well advanced.

ThunderWing made ready for the coming offensive and visited the Eastern Marches.

Any older warriors who were willing and acknowledged his captaincy, he sent to strengthen the watch and guard. Then he thought he should try and liaise with his superior commander, SwiftSlayer, at his *eyrie*.

As he feared, he found the old Windlord in a difficult mood.

'So, Champion Perpetual, the Council insists that you should lead a Warband? You rise through the ranks swiftly, it seems,' he commented with a touch of derision. 'I cannot see that it is needful for a second Warband, save to bolster your own pride perhaps? One Warband under my command shall more than suffice to repel any number of barbarian hordes. In the Battle of the North, many seasons gone, they turned tail at the very sight of us. They are undersized, dirty little eaglet-savages that know not real warfare.'

This did not accord with the account of the battle ThunderWing had heard from his father. SwiftSlayer had figured very little in it, but ThunderWing was too respectful of the Windlord's position to say so. Instead, he reiterated the intelligence he received from following the western Wild-Eagles, and that his night visitation was very clear and vivid. He felt they should have too many troops, rather than too few, for the sake of their *eyries*.

'Oh, very well. But what is this I hear of secret and furtive warfare? This is a *raid* we deal with! It is not a *hunt*, son of HighSoarer.'

ThunderWing tried his best to explain, extolling the success of the *Mawharùn* in the Western Marches, but SwiftSlayer merely laughed out loud.

Patronizingly, he lectured ThunderWing on the ways of war, drawing from the days when he fought alongside ThunderWing's father, using "…brave talon-handstrokes and beak slashes", rather than what he called 'these furtive and cowardly hunter's ambushes.'

'I seek the glory of the *Mawh'eyri* in open battle!' he asserted fiercely. 'Face to face and talon to talon with the foe!'

'I seek also our glory, Windlord, but also to save the needless shedding of blood. I wish for a swift victory. There will be times for open warfare, but if they come in overwhelming numbers, we must use all our skill and cunning, not our valour only.'

SwiftSlayer lectured and ranted in vain. Although ThunderWing acknowledged and bowed to the old Windlord's past glory, he still respectfully held to his intent to adhere to his tactics.

The old eagle flew into a rage.

'Insolence! You take too much upon yourself, young warrior, Champion Perpetual though you be! Very well then. I am in a mind to send you forth from the battlefield altogether. What will you do then?'

ThunderWing bowed, partly to conceal his own impatience with the obstinate old Windlord. Angry words, however, would make the situation worse, so he calmly looked the troublesome old warrior in the eye.

'Windlord, you shall do as you see fit. But if you do so, I must then report your command to the Council, and beg them for another Warband if the number of *Hrahe* warriors are too many.'

Furious though he was, this gave the old eagle pause. The younger eagle was high in the Council's favour, and he himself had given his vote to promote him for the remarkable victory he had achieved in the West. ThunderWing knew that the rest of the Council would have berated, even expelled the old Windlord from the Council if he took such extreme action against the young champion.

'Pray consider, Windlord!' ThunderWing pursued persuasively. 'If we fail, our *eyries* are prey to the barbarians. I would sacrifice a little of our ancient ways if we can but protect our greatest treasures, our loved ones.'

His respectful persuasiveness finally took effect. It was obvious to the elder eagle that his subordinate would not budge from his position.

'Very well!' snapped the old eagle, raising wings in readiness to depart. 'Take your band and train them as lowly hunters if you wish. But I will show you, young one, how a warrior of *Mawha* conducts himself in war. My Warband shall advance upon the enemy when the alarm is raised, in courageous open warfare—beak to beak, hand to hand. *We* will not fail, whatever you choose to do, hiding among the trees. I promise you, by the wings of the moon, that we will finish the task before your bunch of gatherers come within war-cry of the battle. Beware that this shame may not strip you of your new honours. Farewell!'

'Farewell, Windlord. May the Great Spirit-Wind…'

But the cantankerous old captain had already flown off toward his own troops in the valley beyond the hill.

ThunderWing shook off his own annoyance and flew off to strengthen his own band. Somehow, he knew he had little time, and if the attack came earlier than expected, and in greater numbers than theirs, he would be hard-pressed indeed.

It didn't take long to win over more warriors to his Warband. Most of the *Mawh'eyri* already held him in high esteem, and the warriors even more so. There was nothing proud in his manner as he addressed them, and his openness as to the risks was also appreciated. His mere presence inspired even the most timid with confidence, and while he spoke of victory, none could doubt him.

Some of the veteran warriors looked at each other when he spoke of the hunter's warfare tactics. The younger ones, however, embraced them enthusiastically, looking for the same quick victory that was achieved in the Battle of the Western Mountains, and the fame that would come with it. The former victory was still talked of among them, and members of the *Mawharùn* were frequently asked to speak of the battle each time they visited the *eyries*.

It wasn't long before his Warband had perfected the skills of ambush and surprise attack, as demonstrated by RatSnatcher (now an initiated and trained warrior) and HoneyChaser (though tradition forbade her from actual fighting). ThunderWing decided they were ready, and left them all in his lieutenant's capable hands while he flew off to reconnoitre at the Eastern Mountains.

Keeping low and well hidden, he found a Watcher standing alert at his post on Fallen Rock, the site of many battles in previous generations.

The honour of Captain of the Watch in the Eastern Mountains was passed down from father to eldest son over many generations, as far back as any of the mountain eagles could remember. ThunderWing knew the current incumbent from his youth and apprenticeship as a warrior.

'Hail SunChaser, son of MoonWatcher. I grieve at your father's final fall, but rejoice to see you fill his post.'

The Watcher-Captain bowed low.

'Hail ThunderWing, Champion Perpetual, and my thanks. My father would have been proud to have been here, to do battle with the accursed *Hrah'eyri* once again. But his day is passed and he is at peace. Now that we have you among us, we have sure hope of swift victory.'

ThunderWing bowed his head to hide the laughter in his eyes and added:

'There was a time when I was considered to be of little account, son of MoonWatcher.'

The other hunched his shoulders and looked a little embarrassed.

'We were rivals in the *Mawh'ree*, it is true, O Champion Perpetual. But you have proven yourself the better—that I will not deny.'

'Well, we are in true battle now, and we must both prove our valour once again. It is skill, valour and vigilance that will bring victory, not the glories of the past. But I have confidence in our warriors, that they will win the day. Has our captain, Windlord SwiftSlayer had speech with you?'

'No, my captain, he has not.'

ThunderWing nodded, sighed, and considered as he looked out toward the mist-shrouded hills in the distance, from whence the enemy would probably come.

'I am but captain of the lesser band, so I cannot gainsay his word. But if he does not say otherwise, let the better part of your guards be concealed, that the enemy does not know your full strength. If the foe strikes with overwhelming numbers, send your messenger back through the trees at wary speed as soon as you see them. No, send your messenger whatever their strength. It is better that we return in numbers too great than too little. Wait until they are close before you counter their advance. Haply, the surprise of the hidden guards will give them pause.'

'It shall be as you say, my captain. May the Great Spirit-Wind give strength to your wings and hands.'

It wasn't until the following moon that the attack finally came. Many of the Windlord's band, taking the tone of their captain, had begun to doubt that the "…barbarians would have the stomach to fight," and became complacent and lazy, neglecting their exercises.

ThunderWing still felt that the thunderstorm was about to burst, and kept his troops vigilant. He slept lightly and rose early.

One morning, he paused in the act of drilling his troops to visit his beloved. He tried to convince her to hide in the inner caves in case the battle was carried as far as the *eyri*es.

'No, my lord,' she answered firmly. 'In most things I will submit to you, but I must be close at hand if you return wounded or…'

She looked away.

'…..Or if you do not return. Nor will I abandon my egg-children to the wrath of the enemy.'

Before he could respond or console her, the messenger of the Watchers suddenly burst through the bushes above, breathless, and with a few feathers missing.

'My captains! My captains! The enemy is come upon us! …In numbers greater than any mouse-plagues that I have seen!'

ThunderWing swung into action immediately. He summoned the Crier of the *eyri*es to announce the call to war.

'Come!' he said to the exhausted messenger. 'Drink from my stream and rest a moment, for I will need you to guide us in stealth to where the enemy attacks us.'

He sent a warrior hotwing to rouse the Windlord in his *eyrie*. Turning back to his nest-mate, he saw her cowering over her eggs, her whole body shaking, her eyes filled with fear.

'Fear not, my love. We will triumph. We are warriors of *Mawha*. If we are worsted at the mountain walls, we shall fall back to guard the *eyries*.'

She looked at him pathetically, beak open and panting.

'It is for you that I fear!' she said in a small and frightened voice. 'I know you, ThunderWing, son of HighSoarer! You shall be in the forefront of the battle, and may be the first to fall!'

He held his head against hers and nibbled her beak tenderly.

'That is folly! A wise captain must keep his warriors with him when the enemy comes in greater numbers. I will return. Sing your songs to the Great Spirit-Wind that he brings us the winds of victory. Farewell!'

His troops, with his lieutenant above them, were already airborne and hovering nearby in formation when he and the messenger joined them.

There was confusion below among the *eyries* as members of the other Warband washed the sleep out of their eyes, grabbed a quick bite to eat, said hasty goodbyes to their kinfolk and joined their comrades in the air. Windlord SwiftSlayer fumed and fretted above them all, furious that the *Hrah'eyri* had chosen such a barbaric time in the morning to attack, and that his Warband was so unprepared. He looked over at the disciplined Warband under ThunderWing with contempt and scarcely-veiled jealousy.

'Go, hide among the trees if you lack the stomach for battle, son of HighSoarer!' he bellowed, looking terribly like his disgraced son. 'I shall grind the rabble of savages to the dust—alone if need be! Onward, the *Mawh'eyri!*'

Leaving the latecomers to follow when they could, he sped off eastward, where distant battle-cries and screams could be heard from the bordering mountains, his troops following in ragged lines.

ThunderWing and his troops, still in disciplined order, followed the messenger into the trees.

Along the way, he questioned the messenger about the initial attack, the tactics, and the number of the enemy.

'They almost took us unaware, my captain,' she said, her eyes wide with fear. 'They emerged silently from the mist in the valley and immediately set upon the guards who showed themselves. Those who were concealed at your command, saw them and attacked when they engaged the others. The first attack was repelled when my master sent me to you, but I could see waves of them flying over the mist. Perhaps there are more, still concealed. I had thought the *Hrah'eyri* of the East were all smaller of stature than those of the West, but there are giants among them! Our guards held their own, but they were hard-pressed. We came only just in time, but in lesser numbers than they. The Watcher-Captain himself is wounded, but fights on.'

ThunderWing looked grim.

'Then it may mean war has fully come upon us! We will have need of more warriors. I can hear the sounds of battle yonder, so I will guide my troop from here. If you have the strength for it, return to our *eyries* and summon three strong and fleet *eyreirë* in my name. Send them to the *eyries* of the Middle Mountains for another Warband to come to our aid—and in urgency. I believe there is at least one in readiness under Windlord StormRider.'

'I go, my captain!'

She swerved outward from the following army and disappeared among the foliage. ThunderWing halted his troop on branches just inside the forest edge, where they could look out over the plains below and the rocky ledge of the cliff-tops nearby.

They saw an appalling sight.

SwiftSlayer's warriors had engaged, giving the guards some relief, but the *Mawh'eyri* were grossly outnumbered. They fought valiantly, slaying two Wild Eagles to every one of their own that fell, but there were large *Hrahe* captains among them, some even greater in size than the *Mawhe* warriors. Fighting and screaming birds filled the air above them and below the cliff edge. The rocky ledge was filled with wounded. Some lay still among them. Beyond the battle in the air, he could see yet another wave of Wild Eagles descending upon them.

He silently summoned StormFighter and spoke his orders in a low voice.

'Take now your own band as I spake earlier, and circle the battlefield through the trees. We shall engage this new wave of the enemy that are coming. When we do so, come forth and engage as I have shown you. May the Great Spirit-Wind give you strength and speed.'

'I go, my captain!'

ThunderWing turned to his brother-in-law.

'I have promised your sister that I would stay with my bodyguard. But one must lead for others to follow. Can you and your kin stay with me, my kinsman and comrade?'

'Unto the death, my captain!'

The final wave of foes came crashing down upon the *Mawh'eyri*. ThunderWing raised his wings, ready to advance—then froze.

He could see where SwiftSlayer was battling at the top of the melee, his own bodyguard, his kinsmen, keeping him safe from any massed attack upon him.

Suddenly, from the middle of the mass of painted warriors descending from the skies, one large warrior shot out and advanced ahead of them, shrieking a name that ThunderWing had heard before.

Rather than engage the bodyguard of the *Mawha* captain, the large *Hrahe* dropped like a stone from above, skillfully weaving around the protective but undisciplined body of warriors to crash headlong into Windlord SwiftSlayer himself.

They both fell to the earth, pecking and scratching viciously, the dismayed bodyguard in hot pursuit.

Attacker and attacked smashed into the sharp rocks below, the large warrior on top. SwiftSlayer went limp, and his slayer let out a cry of bitter victory. He was immediately set upon by his enemies, and would have been torn to shreds if they had not also been set upon in their turn.

A shudder shot through the ranks of the fighting *Mawh'eyri*. Their leader was apparently dead, and what was meant to be an easy victory for him appeared to be a crushing defeat. They were leaderless. The *Hrah'eyri* yelled a song of victory.

But only momentarily.

With a roar, ThunderWing and his company rose from the tops of the trees and descended upon the *Hrah'eyri* in what appeared to be endless waves. No sooner had the invaders recovered from that first shock, but StormFighter and his warriors came pouring in from the other direction, crying, 'The armies of the *Mawh'eyri* are upon you!'

The effect devastated the morale of the invaders, and many fled back toward their hills. It was just as well, for another cloud of raiders appeared to be coming. These hesitated as the fugitives fled through their ranks toward the hills, crying: 'Flee! Flee! They are too many! They are too strong!'

Yet the newcomers to the battlefield were not actually warriors, but mostly female camp followers.

There were also the Vultures. They were outcast eagles who lived on the edges of the barbaric tribes' habitations, expecting to get easy pickings from the Eastern *Eyries* and maybe beyond as well.

Some of them were also vultures in the true sense—degenerate, cannibalistic eagles that would feed on the flesh of the fallen, no matter who they were.

They all expected an easy victory because of their superior numbers, and were dismayed to see the battle still raging. Some fled back to the hills, but others remained, hovering to see the outcome.

Even with the number of their foes greatly reduced, ThunderWing could see they were still outnumbered two to one by those that fought on defiantly. A dark mood or hidden force seemed to drive them. The captains and chieftains among them rallied them time and again

ThunderWing gave orders to target the largest enemy warriors, who were clearly the captains and sources of inspiration for their forces. Soon the superior fighting skills of the *Mawh'eyri* began to tell, as one by one the great captains fell before them.

The cost was high. For the smaller *Hrahe* warriors, even with their chieftains fallen, fought savagely, driven more by hate than fear. They still had confidence in their huge numbers and gave no quarter. Some remaining captains took note of ThunderWing's strategy. They gathered many followers around them as bodyguards, forming a phalanx, and descended upon the greatest of the *Mawh'eyri* warriors they could find and trap. In dismay, ThunderWing saw FastFlyer, son of StrongFoot, Champion Perpetual, brought down by a dozen enemy warriors. He fell to swamps below and breathed his last, taking all his slayers with him. Never again would he return to his *eyrie* in the West. He had promptly responded when ThunderWing first called him.

Open warfare was useless now.

'To the caves!' ThunderWing called to his lieutenant.

He would now employ a last stand strategy in which he had trained his own troops—though he had clung to the hope that he would not need to resort to it.

The cliffs above and below the edge were dotted with many caves and tunnels that connected them. From their youth, warriors of the Eastern Marches explored these caves and tunnels extensively, so they were thoroughly familiar with them. The *Mawh'eyri* used them to full advantage, especially those of ThunderWing's own troops; trapping, swooping, and then retreating. With the stone at their backs and with their dual training as hunters and warriors, they were able to repel attack after fierce attack. Occasionally, ThunderWing led some out on counterattacks, but only to bring down remaining chieftains if they were left unguarded.

The day wore on, and the *Mawh'eyri* grimly held on.

Then, finally, they heard the sound they had longed to hear: the great battle-cry of the Middle Mountains. It was Windlord StormRider who led the final charge.

At last, the remaining enemy began to capitulate—but not all.

ThunderWing was engaged in a personal hand-to-hand fight with a huge chieftain. They circled each other, swooping, lashing out with beak and talon. ThunderWing was lesser in size but greater in maneuverability, and so landed the more telling blows. But he was exhausted. He would have to retreat to the caves again if help did not come soon.

Suddenly, unlooked for, two warriors from Middle Mountain swept past him and sent his giant eagle foe spinning to the rocks far below. The remaining enemy screamed in fear and frustration before retreating in complete disorder.

Relieved and thankful though he was, there was something that bothered him: Beneath the war paint, many of the giant chieftains looked very much like *Mawh'eyri* warriors.

He was in for another shock.

He was able to call off his own troops so they could rescue their wounded from among the dead, while StormRider pursued the fleeing foe.

The first casualty ThunderWing looked to was his erstwhile captain. Even with their mutual dislike, the old warrior Windlord had fought heroically, so he deserved an honourable burial with the traditional cairn of rocks.

Finding the body of the great *Hrahe* warrior still lying upon him, he heaved the body off, only to find the enemy warrior was still breathing, though faintly. He looked into the enemy's face, the face of SwiftSlayer's bane.

It was *Kharòn* the Dispossessed.

'Son of SwiftSoarer! What devilry is this? Have all the Wild Eagles from West to East joined forces?'

The rebel's eyes opened slowly and widened when he recognized the captain above him.

'Son of HighSoarer?' he said with a croaking, husky voice. 'Slay me if you wish, but I no longer count you my enemy.'

The habitual expression of bitterness had totally gone from his face, revealing it as it might have been in happier times—noble and tranquil. He was finally at peace with the world, even though it was doubtful that he had much time to live in it. His body was shattered and bloodied beyond healing.

'Let us speak no more of enmity, son of SwiftSoarer,' said ThunderWing, moving him to a more comfortable position. 'I would rather count you my friend.'

'Not, maybe, if you have heard what I have done. My own folk of the West held me in lesser esteem for our defeat at your hands. So once again, I was dispossessed and journeyed far from the *eyrie* of my mother's kin. I aligned myself with the barbaric *Hraherekhi* in the Eastern Hills beyond, and they took me as a chieftain's lieutenant, for I was greater in stature. But my goal was not to raid your *eyrie*s. I would even have stood guard over yours, though I doubt not you will not believe me. But surely you know what, or whom, I was seeking.'

The face in the dream came vividly back to ThunderWing's mind.

'I believe you in all this, for so it was foretold unto me in night visitation.'

Kharòn nodded and closed his eyes for a moment. Hearing activity nearby, he opened them again.

'I have avenged myself and the blood of WindSinger the Fair. Now I have paid in my own blood, and somehow it seems all in vain. But there is one thing more to speak of, son of HighSoarer, before I return to Mother *Eyrie* Earth.'

'If you have the strength, I would allow you to return to your folk in the Eastern Hills beyond the mountains.'

'It is too late, for I have lost too much blood, my friend, but you have my thanks. But hear me, Captain ThunderWing, Windlord-to-be. Do you know from whence our greater warriors come? Those whom we name as chieftains? They have the blood of the *Mawh'eyri* in their veins.'

ThunderWing gasped.

'How can this be? Are they traitors?'

'So some would say among your folk. But they are the sons of many *eyrierë* that have fled the tyranny of your traditions, and fled from bitter servitude of nest-mates that would have treated them cruelly.'

His breathing became more laboured and he closed his eyes in pain. Opening them again, he grasped ThunderWing's talon firmly and spoke clearly and urgently.

'There is a dark force I do not understand that has driven many of our wild tribes to this madness of hatred—a hatred that goes beyond vengeance for our past wrongs. This war is not won yet, son of High-Soarer, and never shall be while the Tears-of-the-Sun are lost. But that alone would not drive us to such a dark bitterness as this. Nevertheless, I know you shall conquer. I can see with the eyes of death that you are destined to soar to greater heights yet. If you do so, give thought to all those that suffer injustice among all the *Eyri* winged peoples, both yours and mine. Then perhaps my life—and my death—will have not been totally in vain. Farewell, my friend. May the Great Spirit-Wind … lift you to … still … greater heights.'

His eyes remained open, but the strength in his grip gradually loosened and he fell back upon the ground.

'Farewell, son of SwiftSoarer!' said ThunderWing, a lump in his throat. 'If ever I do become great, I shall remember your words and do what I can.'

He gently closed the rebel's eyes.

'My captain! Son of HighSoarer! Champion Perpetual!'

It was one of SwiftSlayer's lieutenants. Now that his own captain was dead, ThunderWing was in command of all.

'Speak, son of FoeCrusher.'

'My captain, we have found a small band of the accursed enemy trapped in a cave below the Tears of the Eastern Marches. They wish to surrender, and would speak with you—for they named you by name— or would die fighting to the last *eyrion*. Shall we attack them? Their position is strong and many of our warriors may die before they are rooted out.'

'I will come and speak with them. Meanwhile, I wish to see a cairn raised for your captain here, but also for this *Hrahe* champion that lies near him.'

The lieutenant was astonished.

'My captain! Should he not be rather thrown down into the swamplands for the carrion-beasts to feast upon?'

Wrath flashed in ThunderWing's tired eyes.

'Do as you are bid! He has more honour than many of our own warriors.'

The lieutenant looked dismayed and bowed low.

'So be it, my captain.'

ThunderWing hovered near the cliff face, near where the waterfall dropped to the green, wet depths. There was a tinge of red in the foam. Fallen warriors floated in the shallow waters.

He approached the half-hidden cave, surrounded by warriors of *Mawha*. Before him, he could just make out the defiant faces of the darker and smaller enemy, with one large, but dark chieftain before them all.

'I am ThunderWing, son of HighSoarer, captain of the Eastern armies of the *Mawh'eyri!* You have no hope of escaping alive, for we surround you in overwhelming numbers! Do you surrender? Are you willing to parley?'

The chieftain turned his fierce painted face toward him and spoke in the strange, slurred accent of the Eastern Hills.

'I am *Khahama*, son of *Khahomono*, chieftain of the *Hrahmarha* wingfolk. If you are indeed ThunderWing the Merciful, we will surrender. But if this is a trick, we shall die fighting and take some of your warriors with you!'

The rest of his nearly-hidden band growled their agreement. The captain of their enemies was unperterbed, however.

'And how do you know me as ThunderWing the Merciful, son of *Khahomono?*'

'I have heard tell from one *Kharòn* the Fatherless, who came from the western tribes. He won honour amongst us for his prowess in battle. I fought by his side and he became a champion among us, perhaps chieftain of my tribe, if I ever fell in battle. He spoke of you and your brother as worthy of our protection, if we prevailed. You spared him in the Battle of the West. If you spare us also, we swear by our gods that my tribe will not again attack your borders for as long as I live.'

ThunderWing thought for a moment before replying. He drew near and perched precariously on a rock near the entrance so he could speak with the enemy out of earshot of his own troops. The chieftain came closer, revealing a wild but noble face, showing he probably did have *Mawh'eyri* blood in him, as *Kharòn* had said.

'We of the *Mawh'eyri* will not spill any more blood than is needful, son of *Khahomono*. You have invoked the name of *Kharòn* the Dispossessed, who has suffered great injustice at our hands. My father, Windlord HighSoarer spoke for his part, and held him in high honour. It was the last wish of the Dispossessed that there should be peace between our winged peoples. This, therefore, I will swear to you, by the wings of the sun: If you will call upon your wingfolk to live in peace with ours, I will speak to Windlord Council to send embassage to put away our differences if we can. Return to this cave at one turn of the seasons from this sunflight, son of *Khahomono*. I will look for you to talk peace between us and perhaps even cohabitation. Go in peace, and fear no reprisals while

I live. Go through the mists below, for our other Warband flies above in pursuit of your army.'

The face of the chieftain softened somewhat.

'It seems that my comrade-at-arms was right. There *is* some honour among your wingfolk. I swear by all the gods of the hills and rocks, even by the great Spirit-Wind also, whom we serve, that I shall do all in my power to heal the hatred between our winged peoples. I have seen your prowess in battle, outnumbered though you were. Now I have seen your mercy. I shall return to this place one turn of the seasons from this time.'

He looked ThunderWing squarely in the face.

'Sadly, while the Tears-of-the-Sun are lost to us, our winged peoples will not talk of peace, I think. But, by the wings of the sun, if they are ever found and returned, I would call ThunderWing, son of HighSoarer my High King! Farewell, and our thanks.'

Ordered to stand clear and let the enemy go, the warriors of *Mawha* grumbled a little, longing to avenge the deaths of comrades. But they all stood in awe of their captain who, once again, worked miracles against impossible odds.

'The Tears-of-the-Sun.' ThunderWing muttered to himself. 'Will they be ever found?'

Windlord StormRider returned from pursuing the fleeing host. He had wisely refrained from attempting a punitive raid upon the *eyries* of the *Hrah'eyri*, rebuking his warriors who urged him to do so.

He alighted next to ThunderWing, lying exhausted but still vigilant.

'They have fled indeed, and are hiding in the caves of their hills. They shall not return speedily, I think.'

'May it be so indeed.'

The Windlord looked at the carnage all around the cliff's edge.

'Once again, you have stayed disaster from our *eyries*, son of High-Soarer! This was an host of war, not a raid merely. How you withstood such an onslaught I know not, and greatly do I wonder at it! Go now and rest. Our troops from the Middle Mountains shall keep watch until the watchposts can be filled and all is restored again.'

Nodding his thanks, ThunderWing dismissed the Warbands as the healers and hunters came to treat the wounded and bury the dead. There were masses of dead enemies lying everywhere, and the best that the hunters could do was to sweep them over the cliff to the misty marshes below. A dishonourable funeral for brave warriors, but they would have been prey to carrion crows if left overnight. Hopefully, the waters below would hide them while they slowly returned to mother earth.

More cairns were raised for the remaining fallen warriors of *Mawha*. ThunderWing noted with weary eyes how the rocky outcrops and ledges were stained with blood. He could not get the smell of blood out of his nostrils

A light spring rain began to fall, partly washing the rocks clean, but they would retain a red stain for many moons' rains before the Eastern Mountains would forget that day's battle. The river and waterfall nearby were stained red, and the waters were undrinkable.

The once-lovely "Tears of the Eastern Marches" now wept tears of blood.

Washing the worst of the blood-stains from his feathers, Thunder-Wing wearily flew off toward his own *eyrie*, only to be met half-way by his nest-mate, flying with the last wave of healers and hunters.

She wept for joy as they clasped talons. He brought her down to a small hill, too tired to talk in mid-air.

'O, my lord!' she wept, releasing all her pent-up anxiety. 'The messenger told me that you carried the battle alone, and that the Windlord Captain had fallen. Are you wounded? I see blood-stains upon you.'

'No, my love,' he replied with the rasping voice of a dry, hoarse throat from constant shouting. 'I am wounded but lightly and miss feathers but a few. Our kinfolk stayed with me as you wished. SwiftWing our cousin is fallen. Our captain is slain as are many others, but all is well. I wish only for a drink from our stream and a warm nest-bed. I will eat no flesh this sunrest. I have no stomach for more blood!'

'Then come! There is a sombre mood amongst the returning warriors, and they are few indeed among those of the first Warband. We shall speak of the battle on the morrow's sunflight. Come!'

CHAPTER 9

THE SONGS OF THE GREAT SPIRIT-WIND

The lament of the widows continued well into the next day following the battle. It would take many seasons before they could appreciate what such a costly victory truly meant to them.

All the Windlords came and looked over the battlefield with deep grief. They called for GoldSinger, daughter of StrongFeather, to come and sing a few dirges over the cairns that dotted the battlefield. Her voice, though as pure as ever, held a forlorn and desolate tone, for her choirs forsook her. The singing birds, along with the rest of the creatures of the Eastern Walls, had fled in terror at the coming of the hordes of Wild Eagles. It was not until many moons had passed, and the waters of the river ran clean again, that they returned.

She stood by each cairn of stones and sang:

As swift as the winds of the Narrows he came
Neither foe nor his prey before him could flee.
SwiftSlayer the Windlord was true to his name
But he fell as he battled the wild Hrah'eyri.

FoeHunter, a champion, went forth undismayed.
Though foes overwhelming they fiercely surround him,
His hands never wearied, his bite never stayed.
'Neath piles of his foes he had slain here we found him.

A champion of laughter was GladWind the Brave.
With laughter he loved us, and laughing, made war.
And laughing he fell and his life gladly gave
That the East Mountain eyries are safe evermore.

The song of StrongSinger, oft heard in these lands,
It rang forth defiant, as fought he alone.
It lifted our hearts and it strengthened our hands.
Now still is his voice as he lies under stone.

And so she sang until tears choked her voice. Some of the warriors that had fallen she had known well, from youth.

After showing their respects to the cairns of the dead, the Windlords were called to Council in the Great Cave in the Eastern Mountains, normally reserved for feasts. The loss of warriors had been so great that no-one in the Eastern *Eyries* had the heart to celebrate their victory in any case. ThunderWing was also summoned.

After the preliminary ceremonies, StrongFeather, as eldest Windlord, lifted his head and spoke in grave tones.

'Brother Windlords, I need not say that it has been a season of grief for us all. We have been beset both from within and without our borders. But this battle we have last endured on our Eastern Marches is of great significance. I call upon ThunderWing, son of HighSoarer, Champion Perpetual and Captain of the Eastern Warband, that he gives us report of the deeds and occurrences of that dark day.'

ThunderWing stepped forward. Speaking with a heavy heart, he simply reported the facts as he saw them, although he refrained from mentioning his last speech with the Dispossessed.

There was silence for many beats of the heart. The enormity of the attack had taken everyone, even ThunderWing, completely by surprise.

StrongFeather was about to invite Windlord StormRider to give his views, but the energetic warrior-Windlord forestalled him. There was much he wanted to say. He stepped forward and stood by Thunder-Wing's side.

'Windlords all! I have seen many a strange thing in this battle. This was not a barbarians' raid only. This was full war. By the overwhelming host that they loosed upon us, I think that their intent was to occupy the whole of the Eastern Mountains and to fortify them—perhaps even to carry the fight to the Middle Mountains. Who knows? They did not expect us to be in such a state of readiness, nor that our Warbands would be so skilled and so valiant. We would have faced disaster had it not been for the foresight and captaincy of the Champion Perpetual before us...'

'....And for the valour of the fallen Windlord' interposed Wing-Smiter in a subdued voice.

'I do not doubt the valour of the fallen great one, Windlord,' returned StormRider with a touch of impatience. 'He has found an honourable death as is meet for such a warrior. But I have questioned some of his Warband—and there are but few that remain—and those of the other Warband. If the fallen Windlord had heeded the counsel of our captain here, it may be he would still live. Many more would have survived and the battle would have been shortened. So say all that returned from the battle.'

WingSmiter was silenced.

StormRider glanced toward ThunderWing, whose head was bowed in both grief and embarrassment, and continued his oration.

'Do we understand the meaning of this victory? Our captain before us showed the value of the hunter's skills and the warrior's, both. He prepared and skilled his troops as a strong wall of stone to withstand the force of a host of war three times the size of ours, and stood his ground for many watches of the sun before my Warband and I could relieve him. At this I marvel! Had he not done so, I dare to say that the Eastern *Eyries* would be lost to us and would have fallen to the Wild Ones, and I would have assailed them in vain. Our kin, our children, our nest-mates would have been slain or enslaved. Nothing less than all Warbands gathered from all our *eyries* would have sufficed to drive them out, and at great cost. Not all of the barbaric tribes were united in this, but if they did, now that we are of lesser strength than before, could we prevail? Would our *eyries* survive? Do we wish for this?'

There was deep silence once again.

He walked around the ring and looked piercingly into the eyes of each one present as he drew to his conclusion.

'And so, my brother Windlords, I see no other flight-path but to train our warriors in the ways of the hunt, and in tactics of war, as displayed most remarkably by the sons of HighSoarer. It was Windlord HighSoarer, their father, that I served under as a young warrior in the wars of the past. Now I would gladly serve under his sons, many seasons their elder though I am.'

'I also fought at his side in those days,' said StrongFeather solemnly, stepping forward to join him. 'I see the spirit of my friend in his sons. Yet less skill he had than what his sons have shown. We lost many good warriors in that war long past. Some of our *eyries* were destroyed that could have been saved. As we have seen, the enemy becomes more cunning and more determined with every attack. I have never known the wild tribes so united as this. The time is come to seek a leader who will train all our Warbands, strengthen all our defenses—yet also will hear the voice of the Great Spirit-Wind who protects us. If we were not warned, we would have faced terrible defeat and devastation. It is fortunate that we took heed to the warning.'

With a hint of a glare, he looked at the Windlords who had been skeptical of the warning of the night visitation. Their eyes fell before his, sheepishly.

StrongFeather drew himself up to his full height as he came to his climax.

'Hear me, then, brother Windlords: Who will oppose my counsel, that we call upon ThunderWing, son of HighSoarer, Champion Perpetual, Victor of the battles both of the West and the East, that we name him high-captain of the whole war host of the *Mawh'eyri*?'

Most of the members of the Council clapped their wings together and stamped in enthusiastic endorsement. Even ThunderWing's former detractors were forced to see the wisdom in the promotion, and nodded their heads.

Without the late SwiftSlayer's influence, there was less opposition to change.

But one who did not agree was the new High-Captain himself. His heart sank as his dream of living out the rest of his days in peace in his own *eyrie* faded away. As the noise of the Council's affirmation faded away, all eyes were upon ThunderWing, awaiting his response.

'O Father-of-Many, Windlords all, I thank you for such an honour, well beyond my desserts.' he began with a low voice and bowed head. 'But I confess that I am weary still. I have but lately become a father, and had hoped for rest and moments with my lady. I feel also that I have much to learn of the ways of the wind-song, for in them is our strength. The night visitation was the best that I could do. Many of the *eyreirë* in the Northern Mountains could do better, little though they were listened to.'

"*I feel also that I have much to learn of the ways of the wind-song, for in them is our strength.*"

He lifted his head and spoke more confidently.

'Consider also, my Windlords, the captains of the Warbands. Will they stomach a young warrior that would usurp their authority?'

A mild ripple of amusement spread through the gathering.

Windlord WindChaser of the Northern *Eyrie*s came and bowed before him.

'We of the North are at your service, son of HighSoarer and of the lady LightWind. Your mother is held in great honour among us indeed, and the fame of your deeds goes before you. As captain of the Northern Warband, I will gladly submit to your high-captaincy. It is many generations since the Wild Ones of the far north have raided us, so there could be many more than we know of at this time, awaiting their chance. We will have need of your counsel in this.'

ThunderWing responded with slightly-dazed courtesy. It occurred to him that he would like to see his mother in the Northern Mountains. He would need her wisdom more than ever.

There was no representative from the Southern Marches, and the *eyrie*s were few and far between. The hills of the *Mawh'ree* were nothing to the ramparts of the North, East and Western cliffs and mountains. Nonetheless, they still provided a very adequate military presence there with the large population of warriors and spectators at the *Mawh'ree* tournaments.

'Fear not, my son,' StrongFeather assured him quietly. 'My own son, the captain of the Western Band holds you also in high honour, little though he would show it. He has it in mind to seek your counsel on matters of war already. My *eyrie* folk miss your presence and that of your lady.'

'Do they, O my father?' replied ThunderWing, feeling cheered. 'Then we will see them at the hunting......'

He broke off, realizing that he may not be able to hunt anymore, nor visit the ordinary *eyrie* folk. His heart sank again.

'Again, have no fear, my son,' said his father-in-law, with his hissing chuckle. 'Your new duties shall not burden you from sun-arise to sun-rest. There shall be much time for you to hunt and gather as you wish. Only in time of war shall it become your first duty. Go now and rest with your nest-mate for this change of the moon. Yet you are master of your times now, unless battle calls you. We shall summon you only for councils of war. But you may also come and go to our Council when you wish. Such is now your right. I know your mind and your wishes in this matter. Alas! You cannot escape your destiny now, my son. I also would shed my honours if I were permitted. There is a cost to greatness, I fear.'

"There is a cost to greatness, I fear."

'So my mother has sometime said, O Father-of-Many. Yet there is another matter I wish to speak of, but for your private ear only.'

While serving *eyrierë* came with refreshments, the Windlord took his son-in-law into a quiet cave, out of earshot from his peers, who were busy celebrating.

'"Father-of-Many" they call me, my son,' he said jovially. 'Yet I still rejoice to hear that I will see my children's children and soon. Do you wish for a Windlord's blessing upon them and a seer's naming also?'

ThunderWing's weary and set face relaxed as he looked up gratefully at the kindly old Windlord.

'SilverSong, our loved one would rejoice at that, my father, as do I. But...'

His face became sad again. He was not sure how to begin.

'That is not the concern I speak of. Do you recall one WindChaser, the son of SwiftSoarer?'

'I remember him well. He was unjustly banished, although most within the Council would not see it so. He could have become a mighty warrior, even a champion. It is said that he loved a fair young *eyreira*, chosen by the fallen Windlord whom-we-shall-not-name. She fled to the Wild Eagles because she would not submit to the nest-match.'

'She fled indeed, father, but failed to find her freedom. She was pursued and slain by him-whom-we-shall-not-name. WindChaser sought vengeance on the Windlord, but fell at the hands of him and his warrior-kin......'

Shocked and horrified, StrongFeather listened as ThunderWing unfolded the tragic history of *Kharòn* the Dispossessed. He sat silent for a while when the story was done.

'Such is the justice of the *Mawh'eyri*. Justice! It has been done upon him-whom-we-name-not! I knew SwiftHand and his daughter Wind-Singer the Fair. It was noised abroad from the Eastern *Eyries* that she had fled in pursuit of the banished one. How the fallen Windlord who desired her could live with the memory of her blood upon his hands, I know not. He would not speak of her, and would become enraged if any should ask. It is all of a piece.'

'....And her tale is not the only one of its kind,' ThunderWing added grimly.

'True, alas! Much is to be done in the hearts of our *eyrion* before the mountains of *Mawha* are fully filled with songs of joy again. What were the dying words of *Kharòn* the Dispossessed? Did he die in bitterness?'

'No, father. He died in peace, the hand of friendship within mine. It was his dying wish, rather, that I seek to find peace among all *Eyri* folk.'

StrongFeather considered this.

'It is a tale that moves the heart. Nevertheless, his wish is as a mountain greater for us to conquer than the peak of *Mawharikhan*. Perhaps one day we may send embassage to the tribes of the West, but such is the hatred between us, it will not be a simple task. This last war has enflamed hatred toward the barbarians of the East among us, and talk of peace would be spurned among the *eyries* of the East for many a season yet. I counsel you to keep your thoughts on this to those whom you would trust with your life. It is a worthy goal, but it will be a rough flight to find it.'

'Such is my thought also, father. There are many matters of war that we must attend to first. When we are shown to be strong and our borders impregnable, maybe the Wild Eagles shall be willing to talk of peace. Meanwhile, my beloved demands my speedy return. I fear her wrath more than many hordes of the *Hrah'eyri*. I shall take my leave, if I may. Farewell.'

He was sent on his way with the Council's blessing, but he wondered how his beloved would take the news of his promotion.

As he alighted, she could tell by his sheepish and hesitant demeanour that he had something uncomfortable to tell her.

'Speak, my lord! You have been at Council for many sun-watches. What have they said?'

He told her in detail all that had transpired, carefully building towards the climax of the Council's decision. When he finally came to the announcement of his new rank, she squealed with delight and embraced him, dancing around him, singing:

'Hail, ThunderWing, High-Captain of the war hosts of *Mawha!* He is *my eyrion!*'

Then she stopped and a stricken look dawned in the expressive eyes that turned toward him.

'What does this mean for us, my love? Shall I see you but little, now that you consort with the great ones? What of your children? What of your poor little nest-mate?'

He hastily reassured her, repeating her own father's words. She looked relieved, but in spite of his reassurance, he knew that there was much to do in his new role.

He began by visiting the wounded in the Caves of Healing. None wished to share the same cave as NightFlyer, still slowly and ungraciously recovering from his near-fatal attempt upon the Great Summit, so ThunderWing had an excuse to avoid meeting with him again.

The first he visited was StormFighter, his lieutenant. He had insisted on being in the forefront of the battle, with few bodyguards, and suffered for it. It would take a few moons before he was ready to return, but he was happy. His eyes shone with gratification at the visit. Upon inquiry, he was dismissive of his wounds.

'They are but scratches, my captain. And I bear them as trophies, won in such a glorious battle, fought at your side.'

ThunderWing nodded, not sharing his enthusiasm. The younger warrior noticed this.

'Are you not overjoyed at your victory, my captain?'

'It is *our* victory, my friend. But it cost us very dearly. Have you not heard the lament of widows in the Eastern *Eyries*? Many eaglets are deprived of their father. No, I do not greatly rejoice. But it could have been worse. I will now speak with the wounded of the Eastern Warbands to glean news and give succour where I can.'

Most of the other wounded were from the Eastern *Eyries*, members of the fallen Windlord's band. They freely acknowledged that they had underestimated the strength and determination of the Wild Eagles, and they wished their captain had listened to his second-in-command. They had nothing but praise for ThunderWing's band, who carried most of the battle alone, yet had suffered so few casualties.

ThunderWing returned to his lieutenant before he left the Caves of Healing.

'I will ask the Council that your own valour be rewarded, my friend. Is there anything I might do for you? For truly, by the wings of the sun, I deem that I would be languishing within these caves—or even slain—if not for your valour!'

'My captain, you honour me above my desserts. But if a reward you would give me, grant me this boon: that I may serve you and your *eyrie* as captain of your bodyguard, while I have breath.'

Deeply moved, his captain stared at him for a moment.

'How can I refuse so courteous a request? How is it that I and my *eyrie* have inspired such devotion?'

The wounded warrior's eyes fell.

'All *Eyri* of worth do love you and your lady, my captain. If I fall in the service of your *eyrie*, I would ask nothing more of life.'

He rose painfully to his feet, spread his broken wings, and bowed.

'By the wings of the Great Spirit-Wind do I swear my fealty!'

He staggered, and ThunderWing stepped forward to support him to a resting position again.

'Gladly do I accept it, but you are still a fellow-warrior in my eyes, not a servant, my friend.'

Just at that moment, a gust of wind swept past the cave's mouth, distracting ThunderWing's attention. His budding sensitivity to the Great Voice stirred. It was as though he heard long, drawn out, hissing words.

'Eeeeeeviiil issss heeeeeere!'

The dust and mists of that wind passed by, and he had a clear view of NightFlyer's cave across the valley. The entrance looked as dark and brooding as its occupant.

'Is this a warning of some mischief that my rival is hatching, I wonder?' he muttered half to himself.

StormFighter pulled himself together from his momentary weakness.

'Truly, my captain, there have been strange doings of late in that cave yonder. It seemed to me as though a dark cloud hovered over the mouth of it soon after I was carried here. They say that NightFlyer broods in dark thought, and will not stir during the day. He speaks not a word, even to those that feed him, although he hungers for news of the world.'

ThunderWing considered this for a while.

'Surely he cannot have recovered enough to do mischief, for he was still greatly shattered when I spoke with him last. Nevertheless, if you will serve me while you grow in strength, StormFighter, captain of my bodyguard, I ask this of you: Keep watch over yonder cave. If the one within comes forth for any purpose other than to stretch his wings, then send me word via the hunters that feed you. I must go, for many tasks call me.'

'I hear and obey, my captain. May the Great Wind bear you upward to greater heights still! Farewell!'

The hunting season had passed its zenith.

There was no apparent danger from the Wild Eagles. It seemed they were completely shattered after their attempted full-scale war. It was rumoured their seers had prophesied it would be an unqualified success. Yet they had been defeated, and at great cost, by a force one third their size.

Now that the threat to the borders seemed remote, ThunderWing turned his attention to the potentially greater danger of the *Khriki* spirits, the Raven-Winds that dwelt on the Great Mountain.

It was reported that they sometimes haunted the Middle Mountain *eyrie*s at night, sweeping around the mountains with their mocking, croaking wail. Their main weapon was fear, and it was said that they could even dive in and out of the substance of the mountains themselves. The *eyrie* folk trembled and hid behind their stone walls. On the eve of the battle at the Eastern Mountains, they had ventured even as far as the southern *eyrie*s of the Middle Mountains, where Windlord StormRider and his warriors awaited the call to battle from the Eastern Marches. It was noted that the wind-demons did all they could to demoralize them, but he and his well-disciplined troops held their nerve.

Where would the Raven-Winds strike next?

ThunderWing was perplexed.

'But what can we do?' he fretted to his mother. 'The White Warrior-Storm may sweep through the mountains as before, but the demon-winds will merely hide at his coming. I unwittingly lured out the Black Storm, and by chance the White Warrior caught him. But who can do the same against so many, and know the right moment of opportunity when the White Warrior comes? It is beyond *my* strength and skill.'

'It is a task beyond any but the Great Wind himself. You have learned your lessons well, my son, for you heard his voice in night visitation and at the Caves of Healing. Perhaps we can hear him again. Come with me and WeatherWing the Seer, to the Northern Mountains. There we shall find caves away from the noises that distract us. In quiet and solitude we shall sing the Windsongs, listen in silence for the counsel of the Great Spirit Wind, and perhaps learn more of the Trance of Prophecy.'

SilverSong was disinclined to let him go without a fight.

'You will be called to deeds of daring, I know well!' she complained. 'Can I not have you to myself for but one more season? Will your children awake and hatch to find you gone forever? There is a price for any poor *eyreira* to pay, who joins with a great warrior as nest-mate!"

'We only seek counsel, my love!' he replied, harassed, trying to placate her anger and fear. 'It is for the sake of our wingfolk.'

She was not convinced. Angry tears welled up in her eyes.

'No! I can feel it in the wind! You willingly go forth to great peril and may never return to see your hatchlings! I shall grieve until my last flight into everlasting sleep!'

The more he said the more bitter she became.

Finally, his heart heavy, he just nibbled her averted cheek lovingly and took wing to join his mother in the Northern Mountains.

The Valley of Peace, set in a sheltered part of the Northern Mountains, was a paradise. It was hallowed ground and no hunting was permitted, save for the fruits and herbage. Consequently, it abounded with all kinds of living creatures that found it a sanctuary from predators.

Streams meandered among lakes, bordered by fragrant green and flowering shrubs, mid-season's blooms, and fruit-laden trees. It had been set aside especially for the Windlords, or any others of high rank, to meditate or merely refresh their spirits.

ThunderWing could not appreciate the beauty that surrounded him, however. He sat before his mother in the sunlit Cave of Meditation with his head down, his spirits very much in need of refreshment.

'Do not be downcast, my son. She cannot yet see your duty as you see it. Yet her heart is as the gold of her feathers. Give her time and she will fly the same path with you. Am I not myself an *eyreira*? I feared for my own lord's life when he went off to war. But I knew in my heart that I must let him go.'

'Am I going to war, mother?'

'If I hear the voice of the Great Spirit-Wind aright. But you will not always be alone.'

At that moment, Windlords StrongFeather and WeatherWing the Seer alighted at the entrance to the cave and exchanged greetings and polite inquiries. Having three of the folk present that he respected the most was a considerable consolation and relief to ThunderWing.

'I am here to observe proceedings only,' explained StrongFeather. 'I am not skilled in these matters.'

'Your time will come, brother Windlord, for you are needed here. You have other gifts that I lack,' said WeatherWing, settling himself into a comfortable meditative position, and fixing his eyes on the youngest one amongst them. 'But we come now to seek counsel of the Great Spirit-Wind. This, I believe, is a summons for us all, and you not the least, O son of HighSoarer, Champion Perpetual. Your father endeavoured to hear the voice of the Great Wind, but it also drew the wrath of *Mawharikhừn*, who also could hear the voice of the Great Spirit-Wind, but fears him and hates all who call upon him. You have avenged your father, but now it is your calling to help us defeat the new evil that dwells upon the heights of *Mawharikhan*. Are you with us?'

'I am.'

The older ones exchanged nods.

'Then there is hope for the *Mawh'eyri*,' remarked StrongFeather. 'The Raven-Winds grow bolder and more insolent of late, as though driven by a new and evil wind of intent. It is certain that they wish to drive out the *Mawh'eyri* from their *eyries* in the Middle Mountains, perhaps even beyond. Who knows? Some Windlords murmur that had *Mawharikhừn* stayed upon the mountain, they would have been safer. They forget that the Black Demon-Storm would have destroyed us also, for at times he came forth to spread terror among the *eyries*. So let us address our present enemy and silence the gain-sayers. But these are enemies beyond our own strength. To cast them forth, we need to seek the wisdom and power of the Greatest Wind of All. ThunderWing, my son, he has called you to be part of this war—perhaps to lead us in it. Let us now seek the heart of the Great Wind without delay.'

Beginning with LightWind, one by one, they began to sway and hum, sometimes in unison, sometimes in harmony.

ThunderWing was more familiar now with the usage of the Wind-songs, but had never experienced it like he did at that moment. He could feel the love of the two Windlords and the lady for each other, for their wingfolk, for the Great Spirit-Wind. He sensed that they were calling for someone beyond their own world, not only with their voices, but with their hearts and minds. He felt himself being blown along with them into this strange otherworld.

His mother, with an expression of ecstasy and peace upon her face as she swayed to and fro, began to sing in an ancient tongue that came from the first ancestors of the *Mawh'eyri*. He recognized the occasional word, but much of it was as mystifying as it was picturesque. The song seemed to take him and gently rise up with him upon its wings. Then WeatherWing began to sing the same in intertwining harmony, totally lost in his trance-like state.

As time went on, ThunderWing slowly relaxed and let go of all his cares and plans for the future, becoming lost in the same sense of otherworldliness. A warm breeze seemed to blow around the cave, without ruffling any of their feathers. The beauty of the moment brought tears to his eyes. He knew he was in the presence of the Great Spirit-Wind himself. He spread his wings to be wafted along with the breeze, but they were actually the wings of his heart.

The cave appeared to gradually moult and blow away. Instead, he was standing in a stony valley at the base of the Western Mountains, with trees overhead. Before him was the dying hunter, with dying words on his lips: '*You are destined for great things, my captain. With dying eyes...I can see beyond the sight of those whose eyes are whole. Do not forget the lessons you have learned among the hunters, for these shall aid you in your greatest hunt yet.*'

The vision faded away, only to be replaced by the face of the rebel *Kharòn* the Dispossessed as he saw him last.

'*I can see with the eyes of death that you are destined to soar to greater heights yet, son of HighSoarer. If you do so, give thought to all those that suffer injustice among all the Eyri winged peoples, both yours and mine. Then perhaps my life will have not been totally in vain.*'

Then he found himself floating in a strange land, on a white and fluffy sea with white islands dotted all around him. He was chilled to the bone. His breath came in short gasps. It seemed as though he was falling into darkness.

Suddenly, the darkness cleared and once again he found himself in midair—air that was thick, warmer, and breathable, with dark clouds gathering above him. He heard the harsh but haunting sound of a raven's call and looked up to see one of the Raven-Winds flying straight in his direction, a dark and misty beak open to devour him. He waited defiantly until the last split-second, then dropped, just as he had when the Demon-Storm attacked him, many seasons ago. The Raven-Wind passed over him, with a thwarted croaking cry.

The scene changed to a powerful, windy storm and he was caught in the middle of it, desperately trying to keep himself steady. He bore a mysterious burden in his clenched talon. Then his wings felt heavy and burdensome and he lost consciousness, falling into darkness again.

He awoke from his trance, the blood coursing strongly in his veins. It was nearly dusk. The sun was very low, shining red through the opening of the cave. There was such a stillness and peace around him, he wondered if he had merely dreamed all the tumultuous visions he had seen.

He knew in his heart he had a new calling. But was it now? Weather-Wing had hinted at it in the previous season.

The others had emerged from their trance, and were waiting patiently for him.

'Speak, my son. What did you see? For it lies heavily upon you.'

He described his visions as best as he could, and then his mother spoke.

'I also saw these white islands, my son. The great one was none but *Mawharikhan* himself. I was able to look upon the very peak of him. The sea of white is the clouds in which his head floats. Upon his peak I saw a flat table-like rock and upon it, a rough-hewn rock placed there by an ancient race, long before the coming of the *Mawh'eyri*. It was fashioned as an eagle that guards its *eyrie*, weathered though it was. Around the rock I saw a half-ring of stones that shone as golden and as bright as the sun.'

'It is many years gone by that I saw those rocks, Lady LightWind.' said WeatherWing, 'It was when I conquered the mountain's peak as a proud young warrior and earned the title of Windlord. But the Rock of the Eagle is all I saw clearly. I could only dimly see a glimpse of gold near it, for my head was light and I thought only of the Resting Caves and safety, I confess.'

StrongFeather nodded his head.

'This also I saw from afar when I flew over it, Windlord, and had not the strength to endure those heights any longer. Yet the ancients have passed down a tradition that says whoever shall find one of the *Khanirhidhi,* the ancient Stones-of-the-Sun, it shall adorn his neck at his crowning as King of Eagles, and his word will be law for as long as he lives. Can it be that this ring of sun-stones is the same, of which they speak?'

'So I believe. I might have been Windlord-King for life had I taken the chance offered me, but I had not the strength. I doubt that any warrior has such strength, unless the Great Spirit-Wind give it him.'

'It is so, Windlords,' said LightWind.

ThunderWing opened his eyes wide in astonishment. He would have spoken his mind then, remembering the words of the Wild Eagles of the east, and the fallen Dispossessed. But there were more urgent tasks at hand, so he fell silent.

His mother's face face clouded over.

'I also saw another vision. One that troubles me greatly. It seems that the Great Black Storm has arisen again, and hides within the Wailing Hills of the West!'

The others were stricken to dismayed silence. She sighed deeply.

'He will not venture to reclaim his throne upon the great mountain as yet, for he fears the messengers, the White Warriors of the Great Spirit-Wind, and those of us that have learned to summon them. Yet he has sent his own messengers to espy our strength and go before him. I saw even the Raven-Winds bow before him also before they departed their former *eyrie* within the Wailing Hills. Their faces were set toward the Great Summit *Mawharikhan.*'

'The more reason that they be destroyed!' her son exclaimed. 'I, too, saw the Demon Storm in night visitation, and heard his threatenings. These are sent by him indeed! Are they his only servants?'

'Not all, for I also saw a vampire-like shadow arise at his bidding. It was none other than *Zhakha* the sorcerer. He spread wing and flew toward our mountains, bearing his potions and wielding a feather-cloak of darkness. None can see him when he flies in the shadows wearing this cloak.'

'Is there no end to these invasions?' groaned ThunderWing. 'I know nothing of this new foe!'

'Yet he is but a messenger of evil, and is of little strength,' answered StrongFeather reassuringly. 'He abides near the Wailing Hills. His skill lies only in the furtive shadows of darkness and cannot bear the light of day as can his master. Before courage and goodwill he will flee. Your father and I pursued him to the borders in the wars of old. Yet he could do mischief yet again if he could find soil for his dark seeds.'

ThunderWing remembered the happenings at the Healing Caves, and related what his wounded bodyguard had seen. The others looked at one another, concerned.

'It would be wise if I look to this, my son, for I could see that Night-Flyer's heart may well be soil for such dark seeds. Much malice can summon much greater evil.'

"Much malice can summon much greater evil."

'Take the hunter-warriors with you, mother. Seek StrongHand and his band, for they are now skilled in war as in the hunt also. He will guard you well, and his hunters need not sight alone to find their prey. Not the darkest bats have escaped their vigilance yet.'

His mother smiled proudly upon him.

'You speak as a wise captain indeed, my son. I shall do as you bid me, so your mind is at peace and your main task before you shall be the lighter.'

She turned toward the Windlords.

'And you, Windlord WeatherWing the Seer? What did you see?'

The great seer scratched his crest-feathers with one talon and looked a little puzzled.

'All I could see was my friend and fellow Windlord StormRider. As the youngest and strongest of us all of the Council, he will still dare the wild winds when the fit seizes him, returning to us almost unscathed. I saw him in vision, riding the White Warrior-Storm once again, but in pursuit of our Champion Perpetual here. But that is all. I saw no more.'

They all digested this for a moment and waited for someone to speak.

With a deep sigh, ThunderWing arose and shook all his plumage ruefully.

'I see my duty clear, Windlords, mother. I will do what I must do, but I fear more the wrath of my nest-mate than a multitude of storms.'

'I shall speak with her when I can, my son. I have felt that this is your destiny for many a moon. But the time and moment to face the enemy is a matter of great skill. You have done so in your battles of the past, and done it well. This battle shall call upon all those skills and more, for it requires strength of body, of mind *and* of spirit. May the Great Spirit-Wind guide you and give you strength in what you must do.'

For a moment, her parental feelings shook her habitual majestic calm and priestly authority. Tears filled her eyes and her voice quivered. 'Our Windsongs shall…go with you, my dear son.'

'Hail, brother Windlord!' cried StrongFeather, as he and his son-in-law ascended onto the ledge of *Eyrie* StormRider, which overlooked the southern central plains and valleys. 'I bring you one who would learn your skills in the Storm-Dances.'

The youngest and most active of all the Windlords was sunning himself on the ledge, one of his favourite pastimes; when he wasn't flying to and fro between the Southern Hills and the Middle Mountains—or riding the high winds. He rose to meet his guests with great affability.

'You are ever welcome, Father-of-Many. Welcome also, son of High-Soarer, Champion Perpetual. Why do you wish to ride the storms? Have you not yet had enough adventure to satisfy even your intrepid spirit?'

StrongFeather told him of their experiences in the Cave of Meditation, and the messages they received while under the Trance of Prophecy. StormRider opened his eyes at the news.

'So. The Great Wind-Spirit speaks, and the time is ripe. That is welcome news indeed! The accursed "Crow-Spirits," as I call them, have been haunting our *eyries* at night—even as far south as ours. Some of our folk have left their *eyries* out of fear of them.'

He examined the young captain-champion before him.

'Now it seems that once again you are destined to be the bait that shall lure out the predators. Then the trap shall be sprung. But will you, the bait, survive it? Who can tell when the trap shall be sprung? They are strong, and are as cunning as the Demon-Storm you trapped three seasons gone. It nearly cost you your life, as it did your father.'

'So says my mother, Windlord' bowed ThunderWing, speaking soberly. 'I understand the perils of this venture, which shall call upon all that I have learnt—skills of body, mind, and of spirit. But to survive the onslaught of the evil winds, I must learn the ways of the winds as you alone can teach me. Are you willing to make a storm-rider out of a mere hunter?'

The Windlord's eyes brightened at the prospect of sharing his delight in battling the elements with a proved and skilled warrior.

'Not many have the strength and skill to do it. But by the sun's wings, I think you have it! Come! Let us go up to the nearby peak of *Mawhanokha,* the Windswept Mountain. It is nothing to the great peak of *Mawharikhan,* of course, but there you will get some good sport and learn some of the Storm-Dances. The winds are wild and blustery there.'

StrongFeather chuckled, watching the look of eager anticipation spread over ThunderWing's face. He was still a young warrior in many ways, in spite of his brilliant victories.

'You both make me feel as the eldest grey-feather of all, for this is all beyond my strength. But the season's end draws near, and we must be ready for the right time and moment to strike. I shall away to see my daughter while you dance among the mountains, my son. Farewell!'

CHAPTER 10

THE SERVANT OF *MAWHARIKHÙN*

SilverSong sat hunched over her precious eggs, looking the picture of desolation and despair. She watched as her father's retreating figure disappeared around the mountainside, flying toward the Central Mountains to join her *eyrion* in battle with an overwhelmingly strong enemy.

She had been sulky and ungracious toward him, even when he had spoken kindly and comfortingly to her, urging her to be reasonable.

But how could she be reasonable when the great champion she adored put the needs of the all *Mawh'eyri* wingfolk before his own nest-mate, his *eyrie*, his egglings! Now it seemed that her father was just as bad.

Eyrionis!

They were all the same. All they thought about were battles and war and glory. They took no thought for their poor struggling *eyrierë*, who raised their hatchlings often without any help. Now those she loved the most had forsaken her, bent on the most perilous venture one could imagine—so few against hopeless odds. They might never return.

The hours passed, and she felt a few small movements in one of the eggs beneath her. It would not be long before they hatched—maybe even that same day. Would they ever see their father?

Even when a passing gust of wind stirred her feathers, she did not move. She knew the nature of that wind, of course, for she was well trained in the Windsongs, and could hear a voice in it. In times past, this was a call to supplication song, but she refused to respond.

'I have lost the will to sing,' she replied in passive defiance. 'Will the Great Spirit-Wind make me yet another widow? I live only for my egglings now.'

Finally, she rose wearily to get a drink, and stared moodily into the mirror-pool nearby. It was a small basin ThunderWing had carved out of the rock and it was filled by a small trickle diverted from their mountain stream that flowed past the *eyrie*.

The surface cleared to reveal a lovely *eyreira* face with sad, liquid eyes. She noticed a small greyish-white featherlet among the gold and bronze of her plumage, so she ripped it out impatiently. Was she growing old prematurely? But what good were her looks now if her *eyrion* wasn't there to admire them?

'Your beauty has not faded, as your pool-image will tell you,' said a vaguely familiar voice above her.

It came from the small crag above the cave entrance. She glanced up, surprised, expecting to see a relative or neighbour paying her a visit. Normally, visitors announced their arrival, according to the customs and protocol of the Mountain Eagles.

When her eyes got used to the glare, the form of her visitor became clearer. She gasped.

'NightFlyer!'

True enough, there he sat in all his former magnificence, fully plumed and without a feather out of place, looking very pleased with himself. It seemed as if the seasons had rolled back and he was as he had always been before he attempted the Great Mountain, except that his manner appeared more self-assured than ever. The only real difference she could see was a fearsome kind of dark ring around his eyes. It made him look both powerful and menacing. One thing had not changed: his arrogance.

'Yes, it is I, NightFlyer the Great, the Renewed, the Reborn. Night-Flyer the Fairest, free of his father (who fell into folly, it is said. Little loss to the world is he). But hail SilverSong the Fair! Yes! Beautiful and desirable as ever, but your wisdom has lost much of its lustre, if accounts I have heard are true. No matter. That will be amended. Is this your *eyrie*, indeed? With only a faded device and dimmed markings to display your lineage?'

He had also lost none of the sneering tone of the serpent's tongue.

SilverSong, rallying at the mockery in his voice, recovered from her stupefaction.

'How is this, that you have passed our sentries unchallenged? Were you not lying in the Caves of Healing, still shattered from your fall?'

He did not like to be reminded of his failure.

'Fallen I may have been,' he snapped, 'but from an enemy's blow far greater than any warrior has suffered, and lived to tell the tale.'

He flew to a rock overlooking the pool, stretching his wings and turning this way and that to admire his restored plumage. She backed away toward her nest, her old fears rising again. Where was her nest-mate now when she most needed him? Where were the watchers?

But the apparition above hardly noticed this. He fixed his darkened eyes upon her.

'Hear me now, SilverSong the Fair, my nest-mate-to-be! All that folly of conquering the mountain's height is now past. I have now arisen to greater heights than ever my weakling rival shall ever achieve. Yes! And greater than that again. I have now a power and strength beyond those of any of these little eaglets who call themselves warriors. A strength and skill even beyond those of our boastful Windlords in their youth, now cowering in their caves. Not for nothing did they fear the dark power that reigned in the Great Summit for many generations of *eyries*. He has arisen again, greater than before! And I am his servant!'

SilverSong was aghast.

'You have aligned yourself with *Mawharikhùn*, the accursed??'

'And why not? Curse it if you must, but darkness will always swallow the day in the end. So shall the reign of the *Mawh'eyri* cease, and the reign of *Khanmarohunu,* the Great Dark-Storm shall begin. No longer a prisoner. *Mawharikhùn* no longer. He shall reign from his throne on the Great Mountain. I sing his songs from henceforth, and thus did I call upon his true name, the name taught me by the Raven-Winds his servants. And he answered me from beyond the Eastern Hills! He sent his bat-messenger, *Zhakha,* sorcerer of sorcerers, to me, yes I, Night-Flyer, the Father-Free, to offer me great strength and power to execute his will. It was written and sealed with my blood upon the Covenant

Stone. Strong potions were given me that restored my strength and beauty....'

He paused, a little discomposed.

'... But mark you, this is in the seal of secrecy, or the bargain shall be undone. At least you will not betray me when we fly from this place.... on pain of death!'

SilverSong felt as though she was living her worst nightmare.

'Fly...from this place?'

'Yes! Yes!' he cried exultantly, taking to wing and cruising slowly around the cavern ceiling. 'Away from this accursed place. Away from this guarded prison in which your kin have kept you! Away from the choking bonds of *Mawh'eyri* tradition! Away from the trammels of *eyrie* duties! To greater heights...to reign over all...to live in luxury! But you must forswear the service of this so-called Great Spirit-Wind, my dear. For *Khanmarohunu* is lord of all! *He*...shall be worshipped as Lord of Winds, and all these little Windlords and their Wind-singers shall be banished, or perish. *He*...has given me back my youth. *He*...has given me the secret cloak that makes me fly unseen through the shadows.'

He landed nearby in a patch of light, making his golden feathers shine. He stared compellingly at her again.

'And *he* has chosen *me* to be his regent.'

SilverSong blinked in bewilderment.

'Fly...unseen?'

In answer, he spread his wings downward and closed his eyes. A barely perceptible shadow in the shape of grey wings emerged from his back. They rapidly spread in size and engulfed his entire body, casting his form into a thin shadow. Then he spread his own shadowy wings again and glided toward the shade of the cave.

The moment his shadowy form entered the shade, he vanished completely from her sight.

She cried out in fear, backing closer toward her nest.

'Where have you gone? What devilment is this?'

A moment later, he exploded back to visibility—right next to her. She screamed with fright, but he just laughed. A look of gloating triumph was in his darkened eyes as the shadowy cloak folded like wings under his feathers. His voice took on a wheedling, silky tone.

'Do not fear me, my lovely one. Can you not see the power that the Dark Storm gives us? Thus did I avoid your foolish sentry-watchers and removed the most vigilant of them from my way. Come! There is no need to scream for help. *I* am your protector now. Have I not desired you for many a season? Confess! Have you not truly desired me?'

She shrank away from him in horror.

'You…slew our watchers??'

He dismissed this with a sweep of his wing.

'Lesser creatures must give way to the greater. That is why you must now forsake this feeble *eyrion* of yours. That is why you must forsake his nameless *eyrie*. Fury as I have seldom known came upon me when I heard the news. In my anger, I swore to the skies that he shall fall by any means, fair or foul. Hence the summons came from me and the dark messenger found me in the Cave of Healing. This illegitimate son of HighSoarer! It was the depth of folly that you should be deceived by such an imposter, my dear. But I am gracious, for I have forgiven you, and your beauty still haunts my darkest dreams. What can this nest-mate offer you? He lacks beauty and cunning, except in deceiving all his following. Has he won a few little battles with the Wild Eagles? Champion Perpetual they call him for that?

He laughed hysterically.

'What dotards are these Windlords! How easily a *Mawha* warrior's honour is won then! No matter. With myself as their captain, their master, those worthless Wild Ones shall prevail over these once-mighty *Mawh'eyri* in the end.'

He raised his beak and his voice to the skies.

'ThunderWing, the fallen weakling shall bow before me and own me as the greatest king of all the tribes and races of the *Eyrië!*'

He bent his head down in a kind of gracious condescension toward her, in the manner of a father offering a little girl a treat.

'And you? *You*…shall be my queen.'

SilverSong felt disgust and anger rising in her breast. Her fear of him and her recent resentful thoughts toward her nest-mate were all forgotten, swept away by a wind of fury aroused at such overweening conceit, and the gross disparagement of her own beloved *eyrion*. The contrast between the rivals became so marked as to seem ludicrous to her.

'*You*?? The greatest king of all *Eyrïe*?'

She bent her head back in loud, ironic laughter. She confronted him, beak to beak, her own exquisite eyes flaming fiercely.

'You live in a world far removed from the clear light of day, Night-Flyer, night-dreamer, wind-cave, boastful blowfish! You are but a black and treacherous vulture that hides in wings of darkness to drink *Eyri* blood. You think that by sorcery and treachery you can conquer the spirit of my wingfolk? You are nothing but a dangling feather upheld by the cruel talon of *Mawharikhìn*, who would drop you when your usefulness is done. And you call this greatness? My lord, my *eyrion*, has fought and laboured long for his wingfolk. He has earned his greatness, unlike you! His *eyrie* shall remain and rise to greatness that will endure long after you have fallen into dishonour and darkness! How I became besotted with you in those seasons gone by is a folly I will never understand. Begone! Or my screams will awaken all the *eyries* of the Eastern Mountains against you! And if my lord returns, he will execute *Mawharagh* in judgment upon you for your treason, your crimes against our wingfolk!'

NightFlyer stepped back, bewilderment and wrath battling for supremacy in his face.

'You...you...refuse my offer of sharing my greatness? You...dare... insult the most supreme ...the king of all *Eyrïe*? Are you so truly sun-smitten? I cannot believe you mean those lying words!'

Suddenly, it seemed as though all his feathers stood out from his body, and he gave a great howl of fury and frustration. The blackness of his eyes deepened as though to obscure them completely. A few of his feathers fell out.

'You have rejected me!' he snarled, panting hard. All his beauty seemed to have disappeared, revealing the raging predator within.

'You have chosen slavery or death instead of a throne. So be it! Your precious little *eyrie* shall perish first. Then you shall come with me, willing or not.'

With a whoosh, he swung his shadowy cloak over himself and disappeared from view. SilverSong screamed, long and loud, knowing his intent. She jumped back toward her nest only to find him sitting upon it, leering, holding one of her eggs high above the other with his talon.

'So shall all my enemies fall and break!' he cried, a fiendish light in his eye. He lifted the egg higher as SilverSong screamed again and sobbed. She hid her eyes, expecting to hear the dreaded crack.

But it did not come.

Instead, a thunderous burst of wings brushed past her with the cry, "For *Eyrie* ThunderWing!" This was followed by a shout and the unmistakable clash of eagles colliding in battle. Gasping, she opened her eyes just in time to see a vaguely familiar warrior, ragged-looking and covered in wounds, with many of his feathers missing. He was locked in a fierce struggle to the death with a furious, astonished enemy. She also quickly noted that NightFlyer had let go of the egg in the surprise of the tackle, throwing it into the air.

Motherly instincts, together with her training as a hunter, immediately spurred her into action. She leapt in the air, and skillfully caught the egg with talons and feathers. She brought it down carefully and laid it gently next to its twin, noting with relief that neither were the least cracked. Exhausted with her emotions, she spread herself over her nest, looking fearfully at the deadly struggle at the end of the cave. Who was her rescuer? Would he prevail?

Dust, feathers, and curses flew in all directions and it was hard to separate the forms of the two combatants. She gave her shrill call for help once again, which she regretted, for it distracted her unknown champion momentarily. Taking advantage of this, NightFlyer broke away and flew into the air, followed closely by the wounded warrior. The latter was gasping with pain and his breathing became loud and labored, but SilverSong instantly recognized him. He had frequently been in her lord's company when his troops were in training.

'StormFighter! Have a care, for he is armed with....''

But it was too late. Free to wield his secret weapon, NightFlyer vanished from sight, leaving his assailant stunned and bewildered. He cast around, trying vainly to locate his invisible foe.

'He has the power of the unseen, O champion!' she cried urgently. 'He has taken a blood-pact with *Mawharikhùn!*'

Again it was too late. StormFighter crashed to the ground before her, smitten with unseen talon and beak. He had few feathers to fly with now. SilverSong's head sank to the sand and she sobbed hopelessly.

The cloak was swept aside and the panting form of the renegade eagle appeared, sitting triumphantly atop the twice broken body of the brave warrior.

'Victory!' the victor puffed out, spitting out feather and blood with a laugh. 'Fool that he presumed to assail the greatest *eyrion* of all. So shall all my enemies fall and break! Is your nest-mate so improvident that he keeps the wounded about him to guard you? Instead, he has gone to sing songs to the wind in the Northern Mountains, so it is said.' He laughed again.

SilverSong raised her head from the sand defiantly.

'By trickery and sorcery you have gained advantage. But you must slay me before you will destroy my egglings. And many more fine feathers you will lose if you attempt it, for I am hunter trained also. What will you do with your fine plumage then, O fair NightFlyer? And it seems that much has been lost already.'

To his dismay, NightFlyer glanced down on his plumage and saw that she had spoken the truth. Many of his magnificent gold-and-bronze feathers had taken on a decidedly greyish hue. A few more were missing.

'The covenant! *Mawharikhùn* has betrayed me!'

'Or rather you have betrayed him, just as you have betrayed your wingfolk,' she taunted him. 'May you moult and die, O greatest of all!'

He turned dark eyes, now filled with hatred, toward her.

'You have also declared yourself a bitter foe, have you not, O fair one? Very well. ThumpWing the Clumsy shall return to his *eyrie*, finding his nest-mate ravished and slain, and his eggs broken in pieces. I shall be away into the wild with the *Hrah'eyri* where I shall grow my own wings again, *without* aid from dark winds that change. Then I shall conquer the *Mawh'eyri* in my own right. With that, my dear, despair and die!'

He advanced toward her menacingly.

Somehow, she did not feel afraid, but began to sing one of her most powerful Songs of Supplication. It was answered almost immediately.

With the silent stealth of the experienced hunter he was, Strong-Hand seemed to appear from nowhere, swooped out of the air and fell upon the snarling renegade with all his weight.

Winded but cursing still, the hapless foe rolled over, moaning as StrongHand stepped back, covering any approach to the nest.

'Yield, you traitor!' commanded the hunter-chief. 'You must face the judgment of the Windlords for your crimes.'

'Beware his cloak! He can fly unseen,' warned SilverSong again.

'It shall not avail him, sister, hunters do not need sight only to stalk their prey. Are you safe?'

His prey did indeed disappear, but as soon as he moved, with the marks in the sand, and noises he made, other well-trained hunters who had arrived unobtrusively in their captain's train, swooped and pounced. They bound him with vines as easily as if he was fully visible to them. The captive squealed and cursed, regaining visibility briefly to reveal a face made hideous by hatred, driven to the point of madness. They dragged him away, struggling and howling, spitting curses upon the whole race of Mountain Eagles.

SilverSong sighed at last with relief.

'Safe at last! Never have I been so glad to see your brute strength, O my good brother!'

'We are of one *eyrie*, if not of one blood, my sister. My mother summoned us to go with speed to protect your *eyrie*. And none too soon I see! But who is this who lies close to death before you? He has fought many battles all at once, by all the look of him.'

'He is the most valiant of all our followers: StormFighter the Faithful,' she said with tears starting from her eyes.

She left her nest and with a sob, laid her head against the shattered and bloodied head of her now seemingly lifeless preserver.

'Our *eyrie* would have been destroyed, and I slain, were it not for him. My lord had made him captain of his bodyguard for his valour in the Eastern War, from whence his first wounds were inflicted. Still weak and wounded as he was, he must have followed the evil one here, and fell upon him. But he was no match for unseen malice in its full strength. Farewell, StormFighter the Faithful! We shall raise your cairn in the place you have fallen, forever watching over the *eyrie* you saved with your death.'

StrongHand was deeply impressed.

'If that is so, then I shall never scorn any warrior again, for as long as I live. But is he dead indeed? The throes of death are upon him, if I read the signs rightly. He lives, but death is surely close.'

At that, the eyes of the fallen warrior slowly opened, and a rasping whisper came from his beak.

'I am more than close to death, O chief of hunters. Farewell, lady of the greatest captain of all the *Mawh'eyri*. I am not the only one to die because of that traitor's madness. Three good *eyrion* sentries lie dead, slain cowardly by hidden beak and talon. It was only by following the path of slain sentries that I found the traitor's intentions in time.'

'This I know, good warrior-champion,' answered SilverSong brokenly, cradling his head in her wings. 'I and my egg-children owe you our lives, and I thank you. O that you had your own *eyrie* and nest-mate, and could live in honour and peace!'

'No lady, fairest of the fair. To lie forever within my captain's *eyrie* is an honour beyond all my hopes. I will find peace in my return to mother earth's *eyrie*. But with my dying breath I will confess it: Ever since you first appeared among us, the warriors of *Mawh'ree* in the Southern Hills, I have loved you, as have many other warriors. But it was never profane desire as had that traitor-coward. I was content to serve you from afar, and never grudged you to my beloved captain. Now that you are with me at the end, and having served you with the last of my strength, I shall die content.'

He closed his eyes, and never moved from his last post again.

SilverSong lifted up her voice and wailed.

'No! I am not worthy of such devotion! I, who caused the fall of good warriors because of my vanity. I, who berated my nest-mate when he went forth to do his greatest duty.'

She wept bitterly. All the other hunter-warriors present assumed the traditional grieving position. They remained so for many heart-beats until the flutter of approaching wings roused them. The first to appear was none other than LightWind.

The moment she saw her, SilverSong flew into her embrace with a gasping sob.

'O Mother! Mother of my beloved, there has been great evil and great grief in this place this sunflight! I have fought battles of my own, and they have been won, but at great cost!'

Comforting her daughter-in-law with both wings, LightWind calmly surveyed the scene, looking with troubled eyes upon the fallen champion before the nest.

'Be comforted, my child. I sensed that evil may indeed visit this place, and your lord sent me here with the hunter-warriors. But the full tale shall be told in due course. You are safe, I see, and I have heard your cry of repentance from afar, which allayed my own fears. There is one here with me who may bring consolation to you, and who seeks it also.'

SilverSong looked beyond the comforting wings and cried out delightedly as she saw a welcome sight.

NestMaker was also one of the large progeny of *Eyrie* StrongFeather. She was neither as beautiful, headstrong, nor as brave as her younger sister. Neither was she as skilled in song as her older sister. Nonetheless, she had the goodwill and kindness of heart that characterized most of her family. She had lost her own nest-mate, a valiant warrior, in the recent War of the Eastern Mountains, but her nobility of spirit led her to comfort many other widows, rather than dwell on her own grief.

The sisters embraced warmly, and SilverSong lost no time in pouring the whole story of NightFlyer's treachery and her ordeal into her sister's astonished ear. LightWind listened gravely, nodding her head occasionally as she saw pieces of the grand puzzle fall into place.

'The spirit of *Mawharikhùn* has been at work while we slept. It was his plotting and moving that united many of the tribes of the Wild Ones against us. His schemes were foiled by the valour and captaincy of my son, your beloved. But the treason of NightFlyer and his terrible pact with *Zhakha* the sorcerer, servant of the Black Storm, it has taken us all by surprise. Treason against their own has ever caused the fall of many great ones. Windlord WeatherWing, the hunters and I had gone to the Caves of Healing to seek answers, even from the traitor himself—but we were too late!'

'That is when we flew hotwing to this place when we found he had gone,' StrongHand continued. 'Windlord WeatherWing could sense the presence of evil there. Other wounded warriors in the caves saw which way the renegade went before he drew forth the fiendish feather-cloak of darkness. He wrapped himself in it and vanished. But it seems that StormFighter, still wounded as he was, was the only one with the courage to follow the traitor here.'

SilverSong wept again on her sister's shoulder. But at that moment, Windlord WeatherWing arrived with his attendant hunters and warriors.

He bowed and greeted them, surveying the scene with the same understanding as his fellow-seer. He bowed to her and laid before them all two strange and sinister cup-like vessels. They were large, black seed-pods—the kind often used for ceremonial occasions. These, however, had evil-looking symbols carved upon the sides, and the handles were twisted into ugly shapes. A faint, unpleasant reek pervaded the air, causing the hunter-warriors to shrink back from them in fear and disgust.

'Much is now made clear, lady of the fallen,' the seer said somberly. 'A brooding darkness hangs upon the mouth of the healing cave where the traitor dwelt. Also, I have found these vessels which had contained potions of great potency for evil purpose.'

He waved a talon toward the black vessels with distaste.

'I have heard of these rites of evil amongst the *Hrah'eyri* of the North and far Eastern Hills. Surely this was the bond that united the quarreling tribes and drove them onward in mad hatred against us in the War of the Eastern Mountains. *Zhakha,* the sorcerer-vampire brings a black stone that has been breathed upon by *Mawharikhùn* himself. The covenanters, high-chieftains of the *Hrah'eyri,* cut their talons and their blood drips together upon the stone, binding them in thralldom to the black Demon-Storm forever. Such a stone I found in the traitor's cave—in the midst of our own fair mountains! It must be brought out into the open on a warm season's sunflight and consigned to the purging tongues-and-feathers of the sun, that the black curse may be destroyed by the servants of the Great Spirit....'

'....Even as my son will attempt to do with the Raven Wind spirits,' sighed LightWind, her anxiety showing momentarily as WeatherWing bowed his head in deep thought. 'As servants of the Black Demon-Lord, they could do much harm to our wingfolk from within our midst if they cannot be exposed and defeated. Much I have learned as has my son, the high captain. He has become mighty in strength, in the power of the Great Wind and in wisdom, little though he regards the greatness that it brings. Since his fall, he has risen to greater heights than any other, both by his prowess and by the power that the Great Spirit-Wind has given him. He has lifted him to greater heights when the strength of wings alone grew weary.'

'"Strong winds need no wind!" Such were the words of my brother when he flew to attempt the heights of *Mawharikhan*,' StrongHand remarked with a reminiscent smile, but without his former derision. 'He has learnt much from his fall, and has grown indeed, greater even than our own father, I feel.'

At that moment there was the sound of distant thunder, and gusts of wind swept by as a storm approached. Windlord WeatherWing lifted his head suddenly as though he had awakened from a long sleep by a clarion-call. He spread his wings and his voice filled the cave with prophetic power and urgency.

'Take heed now *Mawh'eyri* folk! We are called to rise up now with strong wings, but they must henceforth be wings in the wind if we are to rise up to our greatest heights yet! Our captain has gone forth to do battle alone with the greatest servants of *Mawharikhùn*, but both with the skill of the warrior-hunter, and at the call and command of the Great Wind Spirit. None other is so gifted for this battle. But the Great Wind will only arise in His fullness if the will of the wingfolk fly with his will. Let our Songs of Supplication be heard! Let us join our captain in this battle, but from afar. For our fate now hangs as does the Balancing Stone of *Mawhala* upon the Hanging Crag of the Western Mountains.'

'Then I will go with haste to the Northern Mountains,' said Light-Wind decisively. 'I will raise the singers, skilled in the Songs of the Wind.'

'I will accompany you then, sister-seer,' said WeatherWing. 'For WindSinger, my nest-mate is there. She is mightiest in song when we are together.'

He turned toward SilverSong, still guilt-ridden from her past behaviour, grieving still at StormFighter's sacrifice and weary from her recent ordeal. The Windlord regarded her with austere pity.

'Hear me, Lady of *Eyrie* ThunderWing. It seems that you are also part of this battle, for your soul is intertwined with his. Most powerful of all is her song that follows her lover's flight, giving greater power to the wind under his wings. Yet you have fought a great battle already, it seems.'

'I must go to him!' she whimpered weakly. 'But my egglings! They are close to hatching. What shall I do?'

'You cannot go in your present state, my dear child,' interposed the lady LightWind, firmly. 'Whatever you decide, you must rest this sun's-rest, or you will faint whether you go or stay.'

'Also, consider, my sister,' added StrongHand, unfailingly practical, 'if our captain, my brother, must battle alone, he must not be distracted from stalking his prey, nor should the enemy sense any presence but his in this trap he must lay. I would guard you along the way should you decide to go at sun-arise, and your sister will guard the egglings. But I cannot risk coming too close, lest my clumsiness alert the foe. Nor would my brother wish to expose you to such risks. Can you not sing your songs in the safety of your *eyrie*?'

'That is wisdom also, my son,' agreed his mother, 'although the power of her songs may be lessened if she is not near. But whatever she decides must await the renewal of her own strength.'

She led the wilting *eyreira* to her nest, smiling at NestMaker, who had settled protectively over the eggs.

'Sleep now, my daughters, for so I shall call you. This is what your lord would wish. I and my fellow-seer must depart before the storm comes, however, and my son and his hunters shall keep watch over you. Farewell! May the Great Spirit's breeze sing you songs of sleep.'

SilverSong raised her weary head momentarily and sang softly:

'May my beloved have strong wings in the Wind...'

Then she settled down and went to sleep.

CHAPTER 11

THE RAVEN-WINDS

The leaves of the trees in the valleys were all but gone. The mountainside fir and pine-trees were laden with fresh cones as the three high-ranking *eyrionis* flew past them, onward and upward. Their sights were set grimly on the imposing mountain peak that dominated the landscape, completely ignorant of the drama unfolding in the Eastern Mountains.

'We must approach with caution,' said Windlord StormRider, lowering his voice. 'These are no mindless squalls we face. They are spirits with evil strength and purpose. One of them smote me with his wing when we fled from them once, but I hid myself and he passed. Somehow we must anticipate their movements and avoid them where we can, knowing they will return to seek us again. Be vigilant, and listen for their croaking wail.'

They all landed within view of Windlord's Crag, the great mountain towering above it, piercing the clouds. Apart from the occasional gusts among the rocks, everything seemed so still, yet there was a sense of expectancy in the air.

Even ThunderWing, with all his warrior training in mastering his fears, felt nervous. All of a sudden the whole task seemed too great—even impossible. He no longer felt the exhilaration he had experienced while learning the Wind-Dances just days before.

'O Great Wind-Spirit!' he sang softly to the air. 'How I long for my *eyrie*, and for my nest-mate, wrathful though she be. Why do we do this? For what purpose?'

A whispering gust of wind whistled through the rocks nearby and faded away with a sighing hiss. There was a voice in it.

Jusssticcce!

Another came up from below.

Peacccce!

Another brief, squally gust came around the side of the mountain where they stood.

For the Eeeyrieessss!

What had once sounded like the mere breath of mountain wind-sprites, now sounded very much like the reassuring whispers of his father as he remembered him in his childhood.

He felt confident once again.

Finally, gusts of winds came in all directions and united into one clear whisper.

Wings in the Wind!

Now he also knew what his strategy was meant to be, and what would come after.

He stretched his wings in anticipation, eager to begin the contest once again.

He looked to see if the two Windlords had heard it. StormRider was staring at the mountain and took no notice. He had not yet learned to hear the Voice.

StrongFeather, however, cocked his shaggy head to one side, then nodded knowingly at his son-in-law.

'Your mother has taught us well,' he commented.

ThunderWing was momentarily diverted, and chuckled.

'You have spent many a time with her indeed, Father-of-Many. I rejoice that she has such a champion to guard her.'

StrongFeather acknowledged the gentle gibe with a slight bow of the head.

'Well, such matters can await the more pressing matters before us now. If our hopes do not fail, I will speak to her, but let us fly a straight path while the wind so blows, or fail we shall.'

They cautiously approached the great mountain, using what remaining cover they could find among the thinning vegetation. The two

Windlords followed ThunderWing's lead, recognizing his hunter's skills. This brought them close to Windlord's Crag before the trees failed; and the last of the hardy windswept shrubs that barely clung to the thin, stony soil. The edge of the snow line shone dimly in the shadows of the lesser peak above them.

'Are we certain that the Middle Mountain *eyries* are safe if we rouse the wrath of the Raven-Winds?' whispered StormRider.

'Our folk there have been warned,' StrongFeather whispered reassuringly. 'But sadly, many have fled to the outer mountains. Few there are that will stay to defend if we fail.'

'And you, my friend, will you risk your own life in this venture? We are bred to peril, Captain ThunderWing and I. But should the eldest and most beloved of all Windlords imperil himself, when he is needed on the Council?'

'I may be a greyfeather, but I shall still be a warrior until my last fall!' retorted the old Windlord with a touch of defiance. 'But this shall be my last venture, my comrade, I grant you that. Fear not for me. I shall venture no further than what I can witness and report to Council, for I know that my strength is not equal to yours. Let us find an ambush watchpost where we can watch for the enemy. There I shall stay, for I will not imperil this venture with my old and clumsy wings.'

'You give strength to our resolve with your presence, O Father-of-Many, warrior of many seasons,' whispered ThunderWing, bowing briefly before him. 'Will you have a care for my hatchlings if I fail and fall?'

The old Windlord was touched.

'I will do so and gladly, my son. But you will not fail. Surely it is your destiny to defeat them if the visions you have seen are true.'

'I hope that is so, Father-of-Many. Was my lady still embittered against me when you spoke to her?

'She sat still upon her egglings with head down as I spake, so I know not her mind,' StrongFeather sighed. 'She was ever a headstrong *eyreira*, but her heart is as the sunstones, even as her mother's heart was. Your mother will visit her and maybe give better counsel and comfort than an old greyfeather can.'

ThunderWing stared at a small heart-shaped rock before him.

'I would have wished that my lady was here to sing to the Great Spirit-Wind for me, but my egglings are more of moment to her at this season. Besides, I would not expose her to the peril of these things.'

They furtively slipped through the rocks and crags, finding a cave with a better view of the great mountain, right on the edge of the winter snowline and near the long pass between *Mawharesha,* the lesser Consort Mountain, and *Mawharikhan* itself. They made a quick dash for it and took refuge behind some scattered rocks just inside it.

They did not have long to wait. Out of a dark opening high up on the mountain came a large and misty bird-like shape. When it hovered or sat, it became more crow-like. When it flew, much of its outline melted into a long dark trailing cloud, with only its burning eyes, forewing, and monstrous beak clearly seen. It was just as ThunderWing had seen it in his vision.

As it dove into the valley, another appeared around the side of the mountain and dived after it, giving out a cry that seemed to be a cross between a ghostly wail and the common croak of the raven. The reverberation of its eerie cry sent shivers down the spines of the three *Eyri* watching them.

'Who shall be the hunter and who the hunted, I wonder?' Thunder-Wing muttered. He turned to StormRider.

'How many are there in totality, by your reckoning, Windlord?'

'It is difficult to tell, for most of us had fled at their coming. I saw four at most when they assailed the Windlord's Crag.'

'On what do they feed, being spirits?'

'Who can tell? But some have said they prey on fear and grief. It is then that they are satiated and return to their lairs, so it is said.'

'Such is often the way of the spirits of evil,' commented Strong-Feather, staring grimly out on the gyrations of the wraithlike beings before them. 'Yet lately they seem to be moved by a dark spirit of hatred and destruction, as ever black *Mawharikhòn* revealed in his wrath. Did not your mother foresee it? But now they meet a foe who has conquered his fears. What do you now, my son? Can you hear the Voice?'

'I have heard him speak, father, but in words of consolation only, such as you heard also. I shall watch and wait at present. The sun comes close to its rest. We must see what his rising brings.'

The morning broke to an overcast day with a layer of clouds crowning the peak before them. A southerly wind rose and fell intermittently, and it was cold—a sure sign of the coming of the season of storms.

The three stalking warriors woke from their fitful sleep and ate the last of the travel-morsels they carried on long journeys. If there were any more delays, they would have to abandon the watch and hunt for their meals, or go hungry.

'What is your plan of war, O high-captain?' asked StormRider. 'If you hear the Voice command you to go forth, what will you do?'

'Of that I cannot say for sure, Windlord, for I must know the strength and skill of the enemy before me. If I can, I will draw them away from the mountainside, lest they find refuge from the White Warrior-Storms in their caves. But out there I shall be most in peril. If my strength and skill fails, I am in their hands, unless a White Warrior comes for them first.'

'Then I shall come with you! We can divide the enemy between us. You have shown yourself an apt pupil in the Wind-Dances, but you should not bear the burden alone.'

The other two looked at StormRider in dismay.

'I cannot forbid you your choice, Windlord,' replied ThunderWing, 'but can you hear the Voice of the Great Spirit-Wind? In truth, we cannot prevail without it. Would it not be better that all the enemy should be gathered together against me, rather than divided and scattered, to hide where the Good Servant Winds may not catch them?'

The Windlord looked mulish at first, and then bowed as he saw the sense in the younger one's arguments, especially when it was endorsed by the elder Windlord.

'You are the high-captain, let it be as you say. But I shall watch and await my own chances, if you fail. I cannot let such valour and skill be destroyed if you are smitten by them and fall.'

'I thank you, good Windlord. You encourage me.'

It wasn't until the sun was high that anything happened. Strong-Feather even dozed a little. The Raven-winds in the distance came and went, serenely confident that none dared to trespass on their domain. Gusts of wind and a brief shower came and went. ThunderWing continued to quietly hum the Windsongs he had learned from his spouse.

Suddenly, he sat up, fully alert. The clouds parted and sunlight streamed in upon the high valley-lands. Some of the wind-sprites blew past their cave. One swept in and was gone. He felt the same, strange stirrings he had experienced four seasons earlier, but this time he understood them. In the distance, there were six of the Raven-Spirits gathered together, forming a dark, smoky spiral as they flew up and down.

'It is time!' he announced, stretching his muscles to make ready for flight. 'The messengers of the Servant Warrior Wind have come! They tell me that he is at hand. I now commit myself to the call of the Great Spirit-Wind. Farewell! Sing the Windsongs for me.'

'May the Wind-Spirit give strength and cunning to your wings, my son! Farewell!' whispered the old Windlord, looking anxious.

'And I shall watch for you and follow you from afar!' added Storm-Rider. 'Farewell!'

Quiet stealth and concealment were no longer needed now. ThunderWing spread his wings and launched himself from the mouth of the cave, his war cry ringing throughout the mountains.

'*Highest heart! Highest height!* I come for you, accursed crow-spirits! I shall avenge all the fallen *eyri* you have smitten! Flee from my wrath!'

At the sound of his cry, the Raven-Spirits paused in their spiraling dance. They saw a solitary *eyri* warrior flying at great speed straight at them. They were so astonished and unprepared for such an assault, they scattered as he flew straight through the middle of them.

They recovered quickly. Some gave out a croaking laugh, while others snarled in rage at such temerity. They all followed, croaking and wailing in fury, determined to teach the insolent bird a final and fatal lesson.

ThunderWing glanced over his shoulder. They were gaining on him. Speed alone was not enough. He dove down toward the mountainside and hid behind a large rock.

With yells of triumph, the spirits descended on the rock, preventing any escape. But when they looked, he was not there!

ThunderWing exploded from a rock fissure above them, flying through the middle of them with a roar. He had learnt that trick both in hunting and at his last battle.

The spirits scattered in dismay again. They did indeed feed on fear, and they had never yet encountered fearlessness and courage. It shook their nerve.

But the largest of them rose up in fury once again, a fury born of fear. They knew, as ThunderWing was also aware, that they must destroy this new threat if they were to survive. ThunderWing soared up toward the peak and sat upon another rock, crying his war cry defiantly.

As the large Raven-Spirit approached, ThunderWing also took to wing and flew straight at him. The large, ghostly beak was opened wide as though to devour him in one gulp as they drew nearer. ThunderWing could see the vision he had experienced in real life now. The spirit's eyes blazed with anger, but also alarm. The eagle flying toward him did not waver, but seemed to gather speed, fixing his eyes on those of his formidable enemy.

At the last split second, ThunderWing dipped just below him, using his superior maneuverability. The spirit screamed in fear. Frustrated at being thwarted, he lost control of his flight-path, and disappeared into the mountainside at full-speed.

A spirit may move through the substance of the earth, but cannot see through it. It would take some time before he could stumble blindly back toward the surface again.

There were now five to deal with, for the moment. They had watched the strategy with amazement, but they knew as well as ThunderWing that he could not win in the end. He had to be exterminated.

Meanwhile, he kept up the aggressive policy, flying into the very face of the enemy. He swerved and dipped and soared as they tried to batter him with their misty wings or grab him with their fleshless talons. He hid in rock fissures and emerged from behind them. He circled around them, making them spin dizzily.

Finally, the largest Raven-Spirit emerged from the mountainside, thoroughly enraged.

This was what ThunderWing had been waiting for.

Following an inner prompting, he turned and dodged around them once more, then headed away from the mountainside into the open air. The Spirits roared after him, confident that he could not escape them now. There were no rocks to hide behind, and soon he would run out of energy and run out of strategies to fool them with. Their full focus was his total destruction. They were gaining on him. But they were unaware of the change in the air.

It took them all by surprise.

As ThunderWing soared upward towards a pass between the mountains and into full sunlight, there was a flash of lightning beyond their sight, but it lit up the clouds above. The thunder that followed seemed to scatter the loose rocks upon the pass.

Billowing cloud upon billowing cloud, a storm rose higher and higher as it came over the pass. The size of it was so huge, it filled their whole vision. The leading thundercloud was in the shape of a monstrous eagle's head. Terrible sun-like eyes fastened on his prey. Lightning crowned his crest. He himself was a spirit, sent as a servant and champion of the Great Wind-Spirit himself. The *Mawh'eyri* called him *Eyrinarhipi*, the Champion Eagle-Storm.

He came upon them all swiftly, huge cloudy talons extended. Flickering lightning, like glowing bones swept through his great arms and flashed out at the tips of their talons, ready to grasp the evil ones. They were all flying straight into his path. The trap was sprung.

StormRider watched the drama from beyond the pass, at a safe distance so that the Raven-Winds could not see him. At the coming of the Great Storm, he flew into the air, dancing and shouting for joy.

'He has trapped them! He has outwitted them! Wonder of wonders! This shall be a matter of song for many generations! The evil is destroyed!'

Then he landed, watching anxiously to see the small speck representing the heroic little *eyrion*. He could just make him out as brief sunlight flashed upon his wings, still speeding toward the billowing storm.

'Now, my champion, dive into the storm and ride it! Ride it as I have shown you, my son!'

But to his consternation, instead of disappearing amongst the tumult, he suddenly soared upward just as the billowing clouds were about to envelope him. He lost all interest in the dying moments of the terrified Raven-Winds, fluttering in vain, trying to stop their momentum and turn. They screamed above the roar of the storm as, one by one, they were crushed in the cloudy grip of the mighty Warrior Storm. He thundered in triumph and swept around the mountains in search of other foes, his long train of dark and grey tumultuous clouds depositing rain in his wake.

'The updraft!' cried StormRider frantically. 'It is the updraft that precedes the storm that has caught him! He cannot ride the wildest upper clouds, weary as he must be! I must seek him and aid him if I can!'

He flew off rapidly in the direction of the swirling masses of clouds.

The great updraft before the storm had truly caught the young champion. But instead of fighting it, he caught it in his wings and soared high—higher than ever before—*over* the storm. It felt as though mighty cloudy wings had taken hold of him and swept him upwards. Upwards and ever upwards he went, faster than his own wings could ever carry him. The rocks swiftly changed to snow as he swept by them. There was little time to feel exhilaration, he just kept climbing and climbing on the natural force that propelled him skyward. He was merely following the prompting within.

'Wings in the Wind!' he cried, his voice drowning in the tumult around him.

"'Wings in the Wind!' he cried..."

At the crucial moment, he snapped his wings against his body and let the momentum carry him. He shot like an arrow above the highest clouds that crowned the great mountains. As momentum slowed, he spread his wings, gasping for breath, and beat them hard. An eerie stillness surrounded him as he saw an ice-covered flat rock, bathed in a misty cloud, pass beneath him. There were no other rocks or crags within sight that rivaled its height. He was hovering over a white mountain amongst a cloudy sea of islands with a brilliant sun overhead, just as he saw it in the vision.

He looked up and saw a passing flock of wild geese in formation coming towards him. The wild geese panicked at the unexpected and unnerving sight of a natural enemy in their flight-path. Eagles were not designed to fly at this height. They almost broke their formation and scattered.

But ThunderWing was not interested in hunting prey outside his domain, especially at this moment. Panting for air in the thin atmosphere, he dipped and turned toward the peak which he had failed to reach so many seasons before. He knew that he had won a double victory, both over his foes as well as the Great Mountain peak. But he could not feel any sense of elation, conscious only of the torment his thundering heart and gasping lungs were suffering.

He dipped and turned toward the great peak again, preparing to descend. Then he paused, in spite of his body's suffering, and dropped to the peak to rest a moment and alighted on a flat rock suspended by four stones like a table. The high winds had cleared the snow.

Perched in the middle of it was a strange rock roughly hewn to the shape of an eagle, though its features were blurred by years of harsh conditions. It was surrounded by what seemed to be a golden glittering circle of stones.

Then it finally dawned on him: He was not only sitting on the Great Summit of *Mawharikhan*, he had found the legendary Stones-of-the-Sun! He could hardly believe it.

But would any others believe it at all? There was no sign of any Windlords to witness his success. He was thoroughly exhausted. It was deathly cold.

Yet his eyes were again drawn to the golden Stones-of-the-Sun, neatly arranged around the Eagle Rock, almost like an ancient ritual.

His breathing became even more laboured and a thundering sounded in his head. What use was his victory if he did not return alive to his nest-mate and children? She would raise their eaglets alone and in bitterness of spirit, thinking he sought his own glory rather than their welfare. What of all the change he meant to bring about for the good of his wingfolk?

Quickly, he leaped from the peak and zoomed around the mountain, his beak pointing in the general direction of Resting Cave. Saving his flagging energy, he half-soared, half-dropped, allowing for the lesser buoyancy in the thinner air. He fought hard to keep consciousness, and finally dove into warmer, thicker, more turbulent air. Breathing deeply, his strength returned somewhat and he added wingbeat to his descent.

He needed all his remaining strength and skill, for the train of the White Warrior Wind was not yet spent through the peaks. But he remembered the instructions from Windlord StormRider, and rode with, not against, the strong winds, even when it took him from his main course at times. Then he gradually tacked and turned back toward the cave entrance.

With his eagle's sight, he spotted it from a distance. Two birds watched from the cave's entrance, but they dove inside to avoid a gust of wind before he could see who they were. Then a sudden band of writhing grey cloud hid it all from his sight. He was swept away again.

He tried desperately to battle his way back to the right direction, but all his strength had deserted him, even to tack sideways across the wind.

'O Great Wind!' he sang between gasps. 'Watch over .... my ...*eyrie* .... my ....lady .... my .... children........ if .....I fall!'

Suddenly, out of a layer of dark grey billowing cloud below him burst StormRider.

'ThunderWing! My captain!' he called and winged strongly up to meet him.

'You are about to fall, if all the signs upon you do not lie!' he shouted urgently over the howl of the storm. 'Quickly! Windlord's Crag is below us. Drop through the cloud and save your strength.'

'Windlord!' panted ThunderWing. 'Please .... take it ... from my ..... hand ... before I ..... fall! It ... must not ..... be lost!'

'Take? What is this?'

ThunderWing held his right talon up as the Windlord flew close. The talon reluctantly opened to reveal a glowing golden stone. It could only mean one thing.

'A Stone-of-the-Sun!' StormRider cried out in amazement. 'What wonder is this? You have conquered all and brought back the greatest prize of all! Hail ThunderWing, Ruling King of the *Mawh'eyri!'*

But ThunderWing's strength finally gave out and the stone dropped from his talon as he plummeted through the clouds, unconscious.

He came back to consciousness to find himself out of the wind, snugly wrapped in feathers and leaves. He slowly remembered the last few moments before his fall and groaned.

'I have lost the stone!'

'No you have not!'

It was the voice he wanted to hear above all others at that moment.

'SilverSong! My love! I thought I would never see you again! Have you forgiven me?'

'It is I who must ask *your* forgiveness, my lord,' she replied, her voice quavering. 'I repented of my unjust rage and followed you here later. We, my father, Windlord StormRider and I, followed you from below when we saw your last flight. I was awaiting you with my father at the Crag, and my Windsongs followed you over the peak, as I prophesied many moons gone. The Windlords both broke your fall and bore you here to Resting Cave. I saw and caught the stone the way you showed me in the days of our youth.'

'You are the champion of all the *eyreirë*, my love!'

She placed the glowing stone carefully and reverently before him, then bowed down, her face in the dust.

'Hail, Ruling Windlord…!'

'Come, my fair one!' he protested. 'Do not mire your fair face before your nest-mate. I command that you look at me, that I may look upon my lovely chosen one. You would be my choice even now were you unjoined.'

She raised her face again as he commanded, but it was both tear-stained and rather dusty. She smiled gratefully but briefly.

'For many seasons I had sensed that it was your destiny to conquer all, even the Raven-Winds and the Great Peak within one sunflight. But I feared that you may fail of your destiny and fall, for to me it was the most impossible of all tasks that were asked of you. I thought it was your ambition that would destroy you, and I denied the truth to myself. But I have fought a foe beyond my strength also and seen our most faithful and valiant one die for our cause, before I saw where my duty lay. Yet it was not until your good mother spoke to me of your trueness of heart, the steadfastness of your resolve to save your wingfolk, and the visions you have seen that my eyes were finally opened. I will never doubt you again. Forgive me.'

Her voice betrayed the strain of the trauma she had experienced since she saw him last.

She sniffed loudly.

'You are now a Ruling Windlord. You are even King of all the *Eyrië,* possessor of a Stone-of-the-Sun. It must be woven into the *Khanir* for you to wear for the rest of your days.'

'No, my beloved. It shall be returned to the *Hrah'eyri,* as a token of the ancient confederation of peace among all *eyri* wingfolk.'

'As you wish, my lord. But surely they will elect you as High King. Your children will hatch to see the greatest *eyrion* that ever lived.'

She dipped her head into the earth again.

'Do not treat me as a god, my love. I do not desire what is due to the Great Spirit-Wind. It was by his power that all this was possible. But speak! What was this battle you speak of? Who was this valiant one? How are our egglings? Do they move?

She was at his side again, snuggling up to him the way he preferred it.

'Yes, my dearest. I heard a knocking sound again on one this very sun-arise. Much has occurred while you were away on your quest, both of joy and of grief. But the tale can await until you are strengthened.'

He started to struggle painfully to his feet.

'But we must away this moment! We must be there for the hatching!'

'No we shall not!' she commanded him, putting up her wing to make him sit again. 'I have my sister, NestMaker, sitting guard upon them, and if they hatch without my presence there, so be it. They are safe with her. My place is at your side until you come back to full strength. You are worth more than a multitude of hatchlings to me now. You must rest.'

'As you wish, my love,' the ruling Windlord of all *Mawha* meekly replied, and sank into a half-doze.

Moments later, a dozen Windlords arrived, led by ThunderWing's proud father-in-law and StormRider, both looking a little battered from their part of the adventure.

They all immediately bowed down before him, their faces in the dust.

'Hail ThunderWing, Reigning Windlord, Champion Perpetual, Seer of Visions, Victor in Many Battles, Rider of the Tempest and Bearer of the Stone-of-the-Sun! You shall be called the Greatest King of all the *Eyrië*!'

'I thank you, Windlords all,' ThunderWing responded graciously but sternly, shaking off his weariness momentarily. He had a momentous announcement to make.

'But let it be known to all that I shall call the Council together when I am recovered. We must seek to retrieve all the stones from the great summit, now it is free from our real enemies. The stones shall henceforth be renamed the Tears-of-the-Sun, and shall be returned to the ancient Federation of Peace among all wingfolk. The *Mawh'eyri* shall be sole custodians no more. I have spoken!' He lay down next to his beloved, exhausted.

Last to arrive was the lady LightWind, glowing with pride, with StrongHand in attendance. She had just overheard the new king's first decree and smiled at the resulting expressions of astonishment on the faces of the Windlords.

She and her oldest son both bowed low, faces in the dust. She took her place next to Windlord StrongFeather, placed her talon in his and proclaimed, loud and clear:

'Now begins a new age, in which the reign of the *Mawh'eyri* truly begins, for all the winged peoples will not withhold the high king-ship from our king at such a gesture. Now is the truth and the will of the great Spirit-Wind revealed. When our fathers withheld the Tears-of-the-Sun, we suffered generations of war. Because of the evil of our pride, the scourge of the Central Mountains came. But the Spirit-Wind in his mercy raised up our greatest champion to restore that which must be restored. The chastisement upon our winged people for our ancient sin is now forever removed. Peace shall reign amongst all *eyri* tribes once more.'

She turned her head toward the old *eyrion* at her side and smiled again. 'The season of my vigilance is passed. I shall retire to the *eyrie* of my own chosen warrior, knowing the fate of my wingfolk is secure.'

She bowed again to her exalted son.

'What are your commands, O Ruling Windlord, O great High King of all the *eyri*?'

'I desire three things in my new office,' responded the new monarch, rather wearily. 'First, a little food and drink…'

StrongHand, smiling, immediately bowed and left.

'… Second, a little peace while I rest. I must away soon to oversee my egglings.'

His courtiers bowed very low and began to disperse, but paused, astonished when he testily delivered his third decree.

'… And third, I shall abolish this foolish custom of abasement before me, with faces slavishly in the dust!'

"….. They that wait upon the Lord
shall renew their strength;
They shall mount up with
wings as eagles ….."

AUTHOR'S BIOGRAPHY

Born David A. Butler in Melbourne, Victoria.

Arthur lives with his wife and two cats in the Dandenong Ranges. His interest in writing began in early childhood, influenced by his mother. She was also a writer, providing scripts for ABC radio in the 1950s and 60s under the penname Russel Bavinton.

Arthur had been writing poetry, short stories, skits and articles for pleasure since his early days. He took to serious writing when he joined FaithWriters.com, an international writing community. There he won a number of awards, finally attaining to the level of Master Writer. These works may be viewed at: http://www.faithwriters.com/member-profile.php?id=26565

His first serious publication was a historical fiction work called "The Poor Preachers: The Adventures of the First Lollards." This is available at most online retailers, or at WestBow Press.